"I'm not the enemy."

Sam's voice was soft. "Marla, please, it's not just my duty to the tribe that keeps me here. Just this once, will you listen to your feelings and do what they tell you?"

Marla's resistance faded like the setting sun as Sam gathered her into his arms. All her bravado had vanished.

"Listen, Marla, just listen," he whispered, as his breath caressed her lips.

The simmering in her blood turned to fire. Instinct guiding her, she touched his face gently, tracing his jaw, then his lips. Her mouth parted, his tongue coming forward to touch her fingertips.

She knew she wouldn't be able to stop if she gave in now, if she faced her destiny with this man. But just then a flash of movement near the site set her heart hammering for a different reason. What she saw made her blood turn to ice. An unearthly glow emanated from a spectral warrior and from the ornate flint armor covering his torso. His eyes were visible behind a mask of evil—and they were leering straight at her....

ABOUT THE AUTHOR

Aimée Thurlo says that *Spirit Warrior* was inspired by her husband David's memories of people and places on the Navajo reservation where he grew up.

Aimée and David live and work in a small New Mexico town beside the Rio Grande with their horses, dogs and pet rodents.

Books by Aimée Thurlo

HARLEQUIN INTRIGUE

109—EXPIRATION DATE
131—BLACK MESA
141—SUITABLE FOR FRAMING
162—STRANGERS WHO LINGER
200—BREACH OF FAITH
217—SHADOW OF THE WOLF

Spirit Warrior

Aimée Thurlo

Harlequin Books

TORONTO • NEW YORK • LONDON
AMSTERDAM • PARIS • SYDNEY • HAMBURG
STOCKHOLM • ATHENS • TOKYO • MILAN
MADRID • WARSAW • BUDAPEST • AUCKLAND

To Mary Ellen O'Neill, Pied Piper extraordinaire to a mouse named Miles and a music critic named Clousseau.

Durango College is a fictional composite of the fine colleges in the Four Corners area.

Out of respect for the Navajo people, certain details of their religious practices and beliefs have been omitted or altered.

—Aimée Thurlo

Harlequin Intrigue edition published October 1993

ISBN 0-373-22246-7

SPIRIT WARRIOR

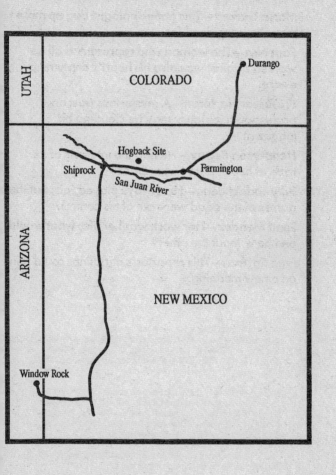

CAST OF CHARACTERS

Marla Garrett—This anthropologist dug up more than she bargained for.

Sam Nez—The woman who represented all he worked against was also his heart's consuming desire.

Professor Hartman—A mysterious past and professional jealousy may be clouding his judgment.

Henderson Begay—He had the interests of the tribe at heart, but at what price?

Billy Todacheene—He always played fair, but the games of the dead were out of his control.

Lena Mendez—Her work was her life; what would one be without the other?

Fred Saffron—This reporter's deadlines could take on a new meaning.

Prologue

Winter, 1972

Thirteen-year-old Sam Nez walked along the west side of the long, snakelike ridge the *bilagáanas,* the Anglos, called the Hogback. The icy wind slammed against him, filtering through the folds of his denim jacket. The sun wouldn't set over Shiprock for another hour; the winter skies overhead were still orange and red like flames from a sacred fire. That was plenty of time, so there was no reason for him to have to hurry home.

He shuffled along, every once in a while jabbing at an attacking bear or wolf with the makeshift willow spear he'd fashioned. He'd had a good day. Visiting his grandmother was always fun. She'd fix mutton stew and homemade bread, and tell him stories of the Anasazi who'd lived all over the Diné Tah, Navajo country. The ancient ones became real and alive somehow when she talked about them.

Grandmother came from a very special line of storytellers. Before the Navajo language could be written, it was people like her who'd kept the tribe's history. Grandmother was very old now, but people still came from as far away as Tuba City to hear her stories. He felt special just being related to her.

Sam glanced across the dry arroyo, tempted to take a shortcut over the low hills that led up to the Hogback itself. That route would save him twenty minutes and give him time to shoot baskets with his friend before doing homework. Tomorrow was Monday, so he couldn't really put off studying much longer.

Sam considered his options. He'd heard stories about *chindi* said to be around the ridge and the little hills beside it. They took the form of bright lights in the darkness, or animals that came from nowhere and left no tracks. That wasn't something to mess around with.

At the beginning of the school year, one of the Anglo kids, Danny from Chicago, had made fun of everyone. He'd gone around saying that the *chindi* were just make-believe and Navajos were dumb to believe in ghosts. But Danny was an idiot. The *chindi* weren't ghosts at all. After a person died, the good in him merged with universal harmony. But the evil in that person remained earthbound. And that's what the *chindi* was—everything bad looking for ways to cause harm.

The Hogback was a place where the *chindi* hung out, so it was a scary place to go, like a graveyard at midnight.

As he stared at the fading red-and-purple glow over Ute Mountain, he realized he'd been moving too slowly. He had to get home fast, or his parents would worry. He took a deep breath. *Chindi* had nothing to do with him. He'd jog straight home, staying away from the caves where they'd been seen.

Gathering his courage, he angled his way toward the Hogback. The ground was rocky and filled with brush that made jogging slow and difficult. Still, he struggled to keep up the pace, knowing that unless he did, it wouldn't turn out to be much of a shortcut at all.

He finally slowed down to catch his breath at the top of a hill. With his hands on his knees, he gulped in large lungfuls of air. Suddenly he heard the steady rhythmic chanting of a ceremonial somewhere close by. His skin prickled with dread as the sounds swirled around him like the wind from the north. He stood very still for a moment, trying to determine the direction it was coming from.

As a blast of cold air penetrated his open collar, he shook himself free of his fear. Those voices were human. But what would men from his tribe be doing out here for a sing? Maybe it was Navajo witches, or Skinwalkers. They had to hide from normal people because their ceremonies were always intended to create trouble. The purpose of the sacred rites was to bring good to everyone, but Skinwalkers twisted the rituals so they were the only ones who came out ahead.

Sam wanted to get out of there fast, but his feet remained glued to the ground. He wouldn't run. He owed it to the tribe to find out who these people were. Even if you didn't believe in their power, Navajo witches were dangerous. Anyone who acted as weird as they did, and went out of their way to try to hurt other people was dangerous, no matter how strong their magic was.

He stayed low to the ground, moving on his hands and knees. Ducking behind a boulder at the very edge of the hillside, he looked down. In the depression below, he saw four warriors wearing leggings, shirts and jeweled boots sitting around a small fire. Both their song and dress were odd, not ones he recognized.

More curious than ever, he peered intently through the gathering darkness, trying to make out their faces. Using his elbows, he hugged the ground and inched forward. Suddenly he felt something tugging at his pants, trapping him in place. Propping himself up on one elbow, he turned his head and saw a protruding root poking through his belt loop.

Of all the dumb things to happen now! He reached down and tried to break the wood off with his hand, but it wouldn't give. Remembering his pocket knife, he reached into his pocket. As he hauled it out, his house keys fell with a loud jingle. He froze, his heart in his throat as he realized the singing had abruptly stopped.

After flipping open the pocketknife, he cut his belt loop and freed himself fast. Sam scrambled to his feet, grabbed his keys, and as fear pumped through him, raced down the opposite side of the hill at breakneck speed. He could hear someone following him, but as he glanced back, all he could make out was a large black shadow on the hilltop.

Sam concentrated on running, shutting everything else out. Then suddenly the loud wail of a coyote erupted from somewhere in front of him. He slid to a halt and saw another figure rounding the hill to head him off. Sam whirled around, and with energy that came from pure terror, hurtled the narrow arroyo and ran down the other side. Forget the shortcut! He didn't need this much trouble.

As he raced along the rim, one of the warriors abruptly rose from out of the deep wash. He was so close Sam could see his face clearly. He looked familiar, except for the eyes. They were glowing, like a cat's eyes caught in the glare of a headlight.

Sheer panic overwhelmed him, and Sam Nez ran faster than he had in his life.

Chapter One

Professor Marla Garrett brushed her shoulder-length auburn hair away from her face and refastened her gray baseball cap. The summer wind blowing across the site was dusty and dry, sapping her strength and energy.

Her graduate students were all gone at the moment—lunchtime. The absolute silence of the desert was disturbed only by the whisper-soft breeze that rustled the tumbleweeds. It felt good to have some time alone. Crouching by the cave entrance, she ran her fingers gently through the top layer of sand. Her heartbeat quickened as an object beneath the surface caught her eye.

Making sure she switched on the video camera to document the find, she exposed the very tip of a dart still attached to a wooden shaft. From the way the stone was shaped, and from the markings on the spear handle, she was certain it was of Navajo origin.

She stared at the weapon, her mind racing. If this turned out to be the breakthrough discovery she suspected, it could lead to long-term funding for the scholarship program. It would guarantee that other hardworking students, like the financially disabled ones in her handpicked group, would have the help they needed to stay in college.

Marla rushed downhill to her tent and retrieved the cellular phone. Glancing at the number taped to the back of a notebook, she dialed quickly.

"Tribal Chairman's office," a woman's voice answered.

"I'm Professor Marla Garrett, project director for the new archaeological site by the Hogback. I have some information for Chairman Todacheene."

"Thank you, Professor Garrett. Please hold a moment."

Marla glanced idly around the small camp, then toward the cave where most of their work was currently focused. If this was what she hoped it was, the scene was about to change.

Just then she heard a deep voice. "Professor Garrett, I'm Todacheene. What's going on over there that we need to know about?"

Blunt and straight to the point, she noted. "Mr. Chairman, my college agreed to contact your office whenever our work uncovered artifacts or physical evidence of your ancestors."

"Yes, so that the Navajo Nation can send one of our people to supervise your digging," Todacheene added.

"Actually, the agreement was for an *observer* to record and photograph our work—in a spirit of cooperation," Marla clarified pleasantly.

"Whatever," Todacheene grumbled. "So, what have you found?"

"Although we've uncovered some pottery sherds and projectile points in the immediate area, nothing has shown a clear link to your tribe. But a few minutes ago, by the entrance to the cave I discovered a dart and shaft that I believe is of Navajo origin."

"What have you done with that and the other objects you found?" Todacheene asked pointedly.

Marla found his tone annoying. She fought the urge to say something outrageous—like she'd driven the truck over them. "They're all safe. Some of the pieces discovered earlier are in our lab. The rest are still in the ground, partially buried. We follow extensive protocols before actually excavating any artifact." She congratulated herself for being diplomatic for once. "I called because I thought

you'd want the opportunity to send over an observer now—
before we proceed any further."

"Yes, definitely. You'll be hearing from Sam Nez, our
representative, very soon. Please don't work the site until
then," Todacheene ended.

"We'll honor the agreement," Marla assured, then the
tribal chairman hung up without speaking again.

Knowing this was only the first step, Marla pulled a
folding chair and a textbook into the shade of the canvas
awning and waited for her graduate students. They arrived
a short time later.

Marla quickly recounted what she'd discovered and
watched their eyes sparkle with excitement. The group
consisted of four women and two men, ranging in age from
twenty-two to thirty-four. She'd never worked with a more
enthusiastic crew.

"Let's get to work, then," said Lena, thirty-four, who
was the senior member of the student team. She'd recently
returned to school after a divorce, and despite the hard-
ships, she was always eager to tackle the work.

Marla shook her head. "Not yet," she said. "I'm bound
by an agreement the college made with the Navajo Nation
a long time ago. If any artifacts or sites related to Navajo
culture are found, our department is to notify the tribe.
They have the right to have a tribal representative present
to monitor our work."

"But this isn't part of the reservation," Dulce, the
youngest member of the team, protested.

"Yes, but because we're only a few hundred feet from it,
I think I'd create more trouble than I'd prevent if I took a
stand on that point. Let's just be patient. It shouldn't be
much longer before I hear from them."

Time passed slowly as they sat around in the shade of the
awning, trying to stay cool. Marla made two more phone
calls, one to the department chairman, and another to the
coal company that was funding their project. She was
hoping they'd use their influence to speed up the process.
After several hours there was still no word.

Frustrated, Marla watched the day fade away while the students read, studied, or wandered about restlessly. For once, the concept of Indian time and their predilection not to hurry began to wear at her nerves.

THE FOLLOWING AFTERNOON Sam Nez sat across from the Tribal Council chairman's desk. "If it isn't on tribal land, no matter how close, we're on shaky legal ground."

"We'd still like you to go there as soon as possible. Will that present a problem?"

"I could be there first thing in the morning."

The elderly Navajo, Billy Todacheene, shook his head. "No, today. One day has passed since I received the call, and the archaeologists are getting anxious. I'm afraid they just might continue their work without our presence. They'd already uncovered a few minor things on the site, but yesterday the professor found an ancient Navajo weapon by the entrance to a cave there. That worries me a great deal."

"Old hunting kills and raiding sites are uncovered all the time. They've always existed between our Sacred Mountains. What's so special about this one?"

"I haven't told you where it is yet," Billy answered slowly. He paused for a long time.

Sam waited patiently, but with each passing second his disquiet grew. There was something wrong here. Billy would get around to telling him what it was, but he already sensed he wasn't going to like this at all.

"You know the ridge called Hogback—to the Dineh it's the earth's diaphragm, its 'breathing means.' It seems long ago there was a landslide along its side, and a cave was covered up. That's where they're digging now." He paused. "You know as well as I do that entire area has always been rumored to be a place of *chindi*. I wouldn't be able to send anyone there without some misgivings, but I must make a choice."

Sam felt his heart begin to hammer against his ribs. He'd sworn once he'd never go back there. But he was the tribal attorney now, not a thirteen-year-old boy. "I understand your position, Uncle," he said, using the term to denote respect, not kinship.

Billy looked at him pensively. "I knew you would go if I asked, but when I see your face, I'm not sure you should be the one sent," he observed. "Do you have some experience with that place?"

Sam shrugged. "I grew up near the Hogback. My grandmother's home was just a few miles from there."

"And?"

"It was just a place I was forced to pass frequently." He leaned back in the chair and tried to appear relaxed.

The elderly man's eyes were eagle sharp. "Your familiarity with it should make things easier for you then."

Sam felt his skin grow cold, but at least that was one reaction Todacheene wouldn't be able to see. "I'll go wherever the tribe needs me to be."

Billy stared at the bear hunting fetish on his desk. "I really wish the *bilagáanas* would just leave it alone. My grandfather, a *hataalii*, used to say that the shadows in that area guarded knowledge best left untouched."

Sam considered the situation, his eyes on the curtains that billowed at the side of the air conditioner. "Any archaeological find, even a minor one, will bring trouble. Thefts and desecration go hand in hand with those sites, and they always have."

"True enough, but for now, all we can do is protect our people's rights. If the artifacts found are of Navajo origin, they belong with the Dineh, not in the Anglo museums," Billy continued. "I've learned that the Anglo woman in charge is held in high regard, and is very careful with her research. If she says that the artifacts appear to be Navajo, chances are she's right. I'd like to see you get them to abandon the dig. Claim that a site so close to our land, where Navajo artifacts are found, should by rights be under our control."

"That's not going to work from a legal standpoint. Unless we can prove without any doubt that the artifacts are Navajo, this could drag out in court for months."

"There are a few things in our favor," Todacheene said obliquely. "I've done a little background search on this woman professor. It seems this Hogback project is being funded by a private grant. I also hear she's being considered for the top position in her department. It's very likely that she won't want the bad publicity of a court battle with the tribe."

"Then I might be able to deal with her." Sam consoled himself with that thought. Maybe they'd be able to reach a quick agreement and he could finish this business in one visit.

"It won't be simple," Billy answered as if reading his mind. "There's no telling what secrets that cave holds. I'm afraid there may be things in there that will attract *bilagáanas* by the hundreds. The problem is that none of them have any idea what they're trifling with." Billy stared out the window thoughtfully. "It's going to be dark in a few hours, the time when the *chindi* are strong. You may want to wait until tomorrow, now that I think about it."

Sam shook his head. "The *bilagáana* in charge will be impatient. They always are. I'll go and take a look around. If there's anything of value to the tribe at that site, I'll make sure we reclaim it."

Billy walked Sam to the front entrance of the building as he gave him directions to the site. "I'll never understand the *bilagáanas'* desire to dig up these things. To study history, yes, from that you can learn. But to take what belonged to the dead—" he shuddered "—I'll never understand *that*."

"If you accused them of grave robbing, they'd be horrified," Sam agreed. "They can't see that to us, that's precisely what it is."

Moments later, Sam walked to his Chevy pickup and eased himself behind the wheel. As he pulled onto the highway and drove past the massive red sandstone arch that gave Window Rock its name, his mind drifted back to that winter day so long ago.

Over the years, he'd tried to blame what he'd seen on a boy's overactive imagination. He might have been able to convince himself of that, too, if not for the one image which remained clear in his mind. The face he'd seen looking back at him from the arroyo that evening was the same as the one he now met each morning in the mirror. The figure had worn Sam's *own* face.

He reached deep into himself, striving for logic. Had that memory shifted and adapted itself into unerring accuracy throughout the years? It had been so long ago, and fear could alter one's perspective.

Sam continued the familiar trek north from the Navajo capital to Shiprock, where he turned east and drove along Highway 550. Eventually locating the turn that led to the site, Sam slowed down and pulled off the highway. He focused on the gravel road that corkscrewed to the south and led to an old abandoned sheep pen. His grandmother had used that place often during sheep shearing, but it was too run-down now to hold any livestock.

Taking a deep breath, he glanced up at the Hogback. The large geologic formation had been looming on the horizon for miles, but he'd avoided looking at it. Now, the realization of exactly where he was finally hit home, and it locked the air from his lungs.

He slowed the pickup to a stop beside several other vehicles, not far from a small campsite. Two young women approached. Almost automatically, he flashed them his most charming smile. "Hello. I'm the Navajo tribe's representative and one of their attorneys. Who's in charge?"

Nervous smiles beamed back at him. "Professor Garrett's been waiting for you for a long time," Liz, a petite brunette in tan shorts, said.

"You folks are always so impatient," Sam teased the woman.

"Well, we're all eager to continue with our work," Lena protested with a gentle smile.

Sam saw an auburn-haired beauty walking toward them from the camp. The Anglo woman moved with grace and fluidity, her jeans and summer top revealing a strong, slender frame. There was a wholesomeness about her, down to the freckles on her nose, that suggested a Norman Rockwell Fourth of July painting.

"Hello. I'm Marla Garrett. I'm the project director."

Sam offered the professor his hand in deference to her customs, although to her credit she had tactfully *not* offered hers. Most Navajos held an instinctive dislike of touching strangers. But in this case the pleasure was his. Her grip was firm, and the strength indicated she worked hard physically, not just with her head.

"I'm Sam Nez, the tribal attorney. I was asked to pay you a visit. We appreciate your willingness to share your discoveries with the Navajo people." The cool, self-containment in the hazel eyes that met his gaze made a slash of heat cut across his belly. There was a subtle challenge in her scrutiny that spoke of strength—and a will that matched his own.

"I wanted your chairman to rest assured that we'll treat everything here with the utmost respect. And of course whatever knowledge we gain, we'll share with the Dineh."

Sam appraised her without making it apparent. She was saying all the right words, but there were few clues as to what she was thinking. Normally he could read people well, but this woman would have made an excellent poker player. He almost smiled, thinking that the same had been said about him in the courtroom.

"I'd like to see what you've found so far," Sam said, wishing he could just have taken her word for it. "It may turn out that my presence here won't be necessary, and you can continue with your work uninterrupted."

"We've only prepared the site and excavated a few centimeters below the surface, but let me show you my videotape. You'll see for yourself what I found and where."

Marla watched Sam out of the corner of her eye as he accompanied her to the van parked closest to their camp.

Sam Nez had an overwhelmingly masculine presence that was impossible to ignore. His body was lean, yet she could see the copper-skinned muscles undulate beneath his light blue shirt. Confidence marked his strides and the uncompromising set of his jaw and shoulders warned her that he wasn't the type someone could cross easily. He adjusted his bolo tie almost as if he'd felt her gaze upon him, but his eyes remained straight ahead.

Surprised by the turn her thoughts had taken, she stifled a smile. It was nice to know that years of concentrating solely on her career hadn't suppressed some feelings into oblivion.

"We keep our supplies here where there's some shade and the blowing dust can't damage them," she said at last, opening the side door and crawling inside. "I have a player and tape set up—" She stopped speaking abruptly as her gaze fell to an empty spot on the floor of the van. Marla glanced around quickly, her heart lodged in her throat. "My notebooks are gone, too!"

Sam looked in the van, but finding nothing unusual, studied the woman instead. "What's wrong?"

"Someone's been in here." She searched beneath the boxes of equipment. "My notebooks, my photographs, they were right there in the middle of the van floor."

Sam tried to keep his face impassive. It was already starting. When the *bilagáana* scientists arrived, trouble always followed. "The video equipment case is right there," he said, gesturing toward it.

She opened it up and looked inside at the camera and player, with its tiny monitor. "But the videocassette is gone!"

"This looks like a prank," he said quietly. "Somebody took the records but not the equipment. Maybe one of your crew moved the film and notes without telling you. Why don't you check?"

"Some joke," she muttered. "But you're right. Let me go talk to them."

After a few minutes of questions and accompanying shrugs or blank stares, she gave up. Marla trusted all of them implicitly, and they never would have kidded with each other like this. There had to be another answer. "Maybe it was mislaid after I showed you all the tape last night. We'll just retrace our steps. We've all been here round the clock."

"Well, most of us have," Lena said. "Each of us has been away at some point, hiking around, or going on short drives to make the waiting easier. But since the discovery yesterday, no one's been near the cave or alone here at the site for any length of time."

Sam shrugged. "Then the artifacts must still be in the cave. This may be an inconvenience, but that's all. Let's go check it out."

Sam followed Marla as she walked briskly up the trail to the site. He wasn't at all sure what to make of her now. She might know her archaeology, but she was losing things one after the other. What kind of care would she be able to give the artifacts they found?

Marla stopped at the mouth of the cave and lifted the tarp she'd used to cover the partially unearthed objects. As a deadly yet familiar sound alerted her to danger, she froze. On the ground before her was a coiled diamondback rattlesnake ready to strike.

Chapter Two

Marla took a deep breath, and stepped back slowly. The snake had startled her, but she was used to them by now from all her fieldwork. She glanced over at Dulce, the herpetologist-elect in the crew, who nodded and moved forward with her ever-present forked staff.

"Come on, you sneaky rascal," Dulce urged as she pushed the stick under the snake and lifted it off the ground. "I'll find you a new home somewhere where you won't get in the way." Balancing the reptile carefully, she walked off.

Marla paid little attention to the snake drama. It was nothing in comparison to learning that the artifacts had been taken from the ground. This was her worst nightmare come to life. In a career where credibility was paramount, an irregularity like this at a dig was fatal. She cleared her throat, choking back the fear that tore at her. "It was here. I don't know what's going on, but I intend to find out."

She turned and faced her students. "I asked about this back at camp, but I have to bring it up again. Someone must have gone into the van sometime during the night and taken the documentation, then come up here. It could have been one of us, or an intruder. Did you guys see anyone at all go near that vehicle, or walk up this way?" Silence and shaking heads were her only answers. "Someone must have seen or heard something," she insisted.

Sam cleared his throat after a moment. "Look, even if someone took some of the items you claimed to have seen here—"

"Correction—the items I *saw*," she interrupted, "and everyone else viewed on the tape." Marla knew that even with the dated display on the tape itself, such things could be faked. All she really had now was her word.

"All right," he conceded. "What I was trying to say was that if this site is for real, there'll be other items here for you to uncover. And that's what you've got to concentrate on now."

"But..."

"You can't do anything about what's already lost except call in the state police," Sam added.

Marla gave Lena a quick nod. "Take care of that right now, will you? We'll need a police report to present to the department chairman and the dean's office."

"I'm on my way."

As Lena went down toward the camp, Sam looked at Marla. "In the meantime, why don't you show me what else you've found? I have to report back to the tribe." What he really wanted to do was judge the legitimacy of Professor Garrett's claim. If they couldn't produce anything substantive at the site, then he'd gladly leave and let Professor Garrett continue to waste her students' time. He'd see her in court if she tried to hurt the tribe in any way.

"The potsherds and projectile points found initially are already at our college anthro lab. Some are Anasazi apparently, and others are early Navajo, though dating hasn't been established. But we might be uncovering more soon. Why don't you stick around? That way you can be present the moment we turn up anything."

"All right."

Marla faced her graduate students. "We'll continue our work as planned. Let's set up the lights first, then bring in our tools and get started."

It took less than an hour before Tony, one of the two male students, exposed portions of what appeared to be an extremely well-preserved hafted ax. From the floodlights fed by a small gasoline generator, Marla could see the artifact clearly as it lay half-exposed in loose sand.

"A man-size fighting or ceremonial ax, with flint points set in the wood. This is a type associated with Navajos." Marla paused, studying it thoughtfully. "But something about it just isn't right."

Sam reflected on the evidence the uncovered portion revealed. He had the same uneasy feeling now he usually got when a witness's testimony didn't ring true. "Isn't it in remarkably good shape for something supposed to be several hundred years old?"

Lena brushed back her hair. "Yeah, I was thinking the same thing."

Liz zipped up her Windbreaker and shifted. "The sand wasn't even packed around it."

Dulce shook her head. "What strikes me is that this find was almost *too* easy."

Marla remained quiet, unwilling to trust her voice. Someone was trying to discredit her. But why? In a career field where grants were paramount, she had plenty of competition from other professors, that was true, but no real enemies that she knew of. "I also have my doubts about this ax. It certainly doesn't appear to be very old," she said. "But the other artifacts..."

"You mean the objects on the tape?" Dulce added with a shrug. "I wouldn't dwell too much on those. I'd say they're gone for good."

"She's right," Lena said.

Sam studied Marla's expression, and saw the distrust and hurt mirrored in her eyes. "What you've shown me here raises more questions than it answers," he said gently. "The loss of the artifacts unfortunately tells us more about present-day humans than it does about my ancestors."

"We'll have to run tests on this ax before we can be absolutely sure of its age," she cautioned. "That's the only way to determine if it was left here sixty years ago, or six hundred."

"Or sometime last night," Dulce added.

Marla glanced at Dulce. "Yes, you're right. The site could have been salted. What I can't figure out is why anyone would try to discredit our finds." She avoided looking at Sam. His dark eyes were so intense it felt as if she was baring herself in front of a stranger.

Lena gave him a speculative look. "We do know the tribe isn't thrilled to have us find a site this close to the reservation, yet still out of their jurisdiction."

"True," Sam countered coolly. "But we don't have a Navajo dirty-tricks squad going around interfering with archaeology. Thefts are commonplace when valuable antiquities are involved, so don't try to shift the blame onto us. If we're going to fight you, we'll do it in court." Sam stared thoughtfully into the inky black interior of the cave. "There's also another point I want to make. The fence right next to this site marks Navajo property. I think there's a good chance part of this cave extends into tribal land. Until we can determine that, and also what's been happening here, I'd like you to stop excavating."

Marla hesitated for a fraction of a second, then answered. "No. As the tribe's representative, you're welcome to stay, but our work will continue. There are other artifacts buried around and within this cave, and it's our job to find them."

"If the artifacts are Navajo, then they belong to the tribe, not to New Mexico, the college, or to you," Sam insisted.

His voice was smooth, controlled and infinitely deep. She felt it weave past her defenses. No doubt this man could make a shambles of the opposition in court. She disciplined her thoughts quickly, countering his argument. "You have your doubts that this site is legitimate. Why should our work here worry you?" she challenged.

"The only thing I know for sure is that there's been trouble here already, and chances are there's more to come. I have a responsibility to safeguard any antiquities that may be part of our cultural heritage. That includes making sure they aren't desecrated or stolen from the tribe," he said, his voice firm.

"And removing me and my crew from the site is your way of doing that? I wish you'd remember that I was the one who called and notified the Navajo government. I've played by the rules and done my best to be fair." No matter how handsome, this man was her opponent. That was clear, and she had to keep it firmly in mind. His goals were in direct opposition to hers, and he'd do whatever was necessary to further them.

"Nothing good can come of your work here," he said in a reasonable tone. "If you doubt that, look what's happened so far."

"Why do I get the feeling that you'd close the site permanently if you could," she challenged.

"I would," he admitted, "but that's not my call to make."

His honesty disarmed her for a moment. Gathering her thoughts, she focused on what she was here to accomplish. This was more than the chance to establish the scholarship program or earn the respect of her peers. It was the opportunity to learn from those who'd come before, and record that knowledge for future generations. It was a trust all archaeologists accepted.

"I take my job very seriously," she explained slowly, determined to make him understand. "An archaeologist is a witness who can vouch for the existence of a world no modern man has ever seen."

"What you're excavating belongs to our ancestors, our relatives, perhaps. Who could possibly have a better claim to this place than us?" he insisted.

His rich voice penetrated her skin, touching her nerve endings, soothing and exciting all at the same time. Marla concentrated, freeing herself from his influence. She was acutely aware that all of her students were watching, waiting for her reaction. "The knowledge we gain here benefits everyone, and needs to be preserved, protected and studied. I'm not leaving, but I will change the process we normally follow. For a start, I'll have the artifact we just found authenticated immediately.''

"That's a good idea," Sam agreed.

Lena glanced at Sam. "Why don't you ride up to the college with me, and you can observe the transfer? That way, you'll see for yourself how careful we are with the artifacts. Every precaution is taken to preserve them."

"Can't you do the tests or whatever's required here? The last thing I want is to remove something from this area that may belong to the tribe," Sam replied flatly.

"We can't. We simply don't have the facilities or expertise on-site," Marla answered. "The artifacts need to be taken to our anthropology lab. Once any link to your tribe is clearly established, and our studies are completed, I guarantee everything will be returned. You'll also be given extensive documentation that'll add to your tribe's cultural and historical knowledge. Go with Lena. Learn about the process we follow," Marla encouraged. "It'll help set your mind at ease."

"And what will you be doing?" Sam asked Marla pointedly. The woman seemed sincere, but things were obviously going wrong around here. He'd made a commitment to protect the heritage of the Dineh. There was no way he could leave if they were going to keep digging.

"I have to make out a report detailing exactly what happened, and that means I'll probably be up all night. You're welcome to stay here or go with Lena, but I have to get to work, so I hope you'll excuse me." She glanced at Liz. "Would you mind helping me get some of the paperwork together? You're the fastest typist."

"No problem." Liz followed her over to the picnic table they used as a communal desk.

As Marla moved away, Lena gestured to Sam. "First thing the guys and I will do is pack everything up carefully. Come on. You can watch."

Assuring herself that Sam was being taken care of, Marla began detailing all that was missing while Liz typed on a laptop computer. Minutes later, hearing a vehicle coming

down the dirt road, Marla glanced toward the highway.
"Finally. Here comes the state police."

The officer dusted the van for fingerprints, though he
twice warned them not to get their hopes up. The prints he
found would probably end up belonging to someone at the
site. After taking quick samples of everyone's fingerprints
to rule out, he finally packed up his equipment. "I'll let you
know if I have any news," he said, slipping inside his vehicle. "In the meantime, all I can do is increase my patrols
here, and ask the San Juan County sheriff's deputies to do
the same." He glanced at Sam. "You might ask one of the
tribal cops to make an unofficial check around here every
once in a while. If he sees anything suspicious, have him call
me."

Sam nodded. "I'm authorized to make that request, but
legally this is out of their jurisdiction."

"Yeah, but we've been known to overlap our coverage
because the territory we patrol is so large and isolated.
Should I radio the tribal police station in Shiprock and re-
lay a message from you? That would speed things up."

Sam nodded. "Sure. Tell them I'm here under Billy
Todacheene's authority. That should cut away some of the
red tape."

Marla was despondent as she watched the officer drive
away. This was getting worse by the hour. The tribal representative undoubtedly thought she was either incompetent or perpetrating a hoax, and the police sure didn't have
many clues they could follow up on. What she needed was
some time to gather her thoughts and reestablish control of
the situation. As long as she was in charge, nothing like this
could *ever* be allowed to happen again.

Marla turned to Lena. "Get that new artifact up to the
lab, Lena. I'll need to know what we're dealing with here as
soon as possible."

"I'll leave right now. Sam, are you coming with me?"

Sam stared pensively at the mouth of the cave, trying to
decide if it would be better to go with the artifact already
uncovered, or remain where he was. Instinct said stay with

the source. "I'll hang around here until everyone quits for the night, then go on home. But thanks for the offer."

"Then I'd better get going," she said. "I'd like to get to Durango before evening classes let out."

Sam watched Lena ease down the washboard track to the highway, then accelerate away like Al Unser. He wondered if Lena and the artifact would make it as far as Durango.

Just then Dulce came up from the camp, holding two cans of cola. "Would you like something cold to drink? These are fresh from the cooler."

Sam grinned at the young woman, who immediately turned red. "Yes, and thanks." He opened the can and took a sip.

"Dulce, what's *your* opinion of what happened at the site? Do you think Professor Garrett might have overestimated the importance of the missing items?"

Dulce smiled. "You mean was that stuff she showed us on the video faked, and the thefts a cover-up to avoid having phony artifacts exposed?" She shook her head. "No way. What has happened could hurt her far more than help. She has to answer to the college and the grant provider for what happens here."

"What about tonight? Will all of you be staying here to do paperwork? The tents are kind of small, unless somebody sleeps out under the stars," Sam asked.

"Well, no, most of us don't sleep over. Liz goes to her folks in Farmington. And Carmen and I share an apartment in Durango. Tony and Hector work nights at a pizza place, so they usually leave even earlier than the rest of us. Dr. Garrett and Lena are the only ones who actually live at the site. Of course tonight, Lena will probably get back quite late, depending on things at the lab."

Sam shook his head slowly. He'd intended to leave when they all went to bed, then return in the morning. But until the value of the site was determined, he had an obligation to his tribe. He still wasn't at all convinced the white woman wasn't trying to pull a hoax, so leaving her to her own devices would be asking for trouble. Unfortunately, that left him with no other choice except to camp out at the forsaken place.

He took a deep breath and let it out again. What a laugh fate was having at his expense! Here he was being forced to spend the night with an incredibly appealing woman he legitimately needed to keep an eye on. But it was to be in a place where he'd never be able to relax long enough to enjoy the attraction. He cursed his luck for having been asked to come in the first place.

Dulce stood there silently for a few minutes, then excused herself as Carmen waved to get her attention. The rest of the students appeared, except for Liz, and piled into their vehicles. Within three minutes they were gone.

Feeling a cool breeze coming across the mesa, Sam zipped up his jacket. Only the stars and a lantern inside Marla's tent lit the landscape now, and the desert temperature was already plummeting. He started walking toward the camp, trying to figure out exactly what to say to the professor, when he saw her approaching in the dim light.

"I couldn't find my flashlight, it must be in the van. Is there something I can do for you...." she added hesitantly.

"No, nothing's wrong. But when your student told me that you'd be here alone, I thought I should remain and at least try to persuade you to make alternate arrangements." As Marla came close he saw the moonlight collect in her eyes. They shimmered like two luminous pools that drew him in invitingly. Tension sizzled down his body. This woman brought the warmth of life to an impossibly cold business.

"You don't trust me here by myself?" she asked quietly.

For a moment he was aware of how much hurt she concealed behind her mask of professionalism. He had no desire to add to whatever troubles she had, but he did have a job to do. "I think that if you stay here alone and anything else happens, you're going to be leaving yourself wide open to accusations. There's also the possible danger to you."

"I don't have a choice. I can't very well leave this site unguarded and depend on the police. This place is my responsibility."

"*And* the tribe's."

"So are you saying that you're going to stick around and help me keep watch tonight?" she asked, puzzled. "I would have thought you'd want to stay as far away from here as you could."

"Personal choice has nothing to do with it," he admitted. "We both have responsibilities." He moved close enough to gauge the expression in her eyes in the faint glow from the tent.

Marla felt the heat of his body. Like liquid lightning, that awareness washed over her senses with a powerful and elemental intensity that made her breath catch. She stepped back, trying to keep her thoughts under control.

He'd made it clear he was here on business, and she couldn't fault him for trying to uphold a trust; it was the same thing she was doing. She met his gaze, and instantly regretted it. The intensity she saw mirrored in the obsidian eyes that focused solely on hers blanked her mind momentarily.

She cleared her throat and tried to gather her wits before he discovered the lapse. "Our lodgings here are primitive, just two tents and no amenities. Sleeping out here takes some getting used to, even with a sleeping bag."

"My tribe has slept on this ground for centuries, often with no blanket at all. I've also spent many nights out in the desert learning to make the land home. Don't worry about me, woman."

Marla understood why he hadn't used her name. To those of his tribe, names contained power. Using them diminished their strength and robbed another of a personal asset. Although the newer generation didn't necessarily hold to the belief, the custom had not been lost.

Yet in the primitive setting that surrounded them, that simple way of referring to her, had left her tingling in all sorts of very inappropriate places. "I doubt we'll have any more trouble tonight. The thief surely wouldn't return so soon." Maybe she would convince him to go. He was too much of a distraction and that was the last thing she needed right now. She wanted to remain on the lookout for trouble, not add some extra.

"The way I see it, we're both obligated to stay. No sense in arguing about it. That's just the way things are." He glanced around at the place that had haunted all his childhood and adolescent nightmares. Maybe being here as an adult would force him to confront and vanquish his fears once and for all. "Where's your helper?"

Liz came out of the tent that contained the lantern. "I'm here, but if I don't get going soon, my family's going to worry."

"Go then." Marla watched the last of her students climb into the passenger van and drive away from the site. "Let me see about a sleeping bag for you," she said, turning to Sam. "We can take turns keeping watch." With a plan in mind she felt much better. What she had to do was concentrate on protecting the site.

Marla stepped inside Lena's tent, and came out holding a tightly rolled sleeping bag. "Here, set this up wherever you want. You can use the tent next to mine, or sleep outside. Lena can share my tent if she makes it back tonight." She tossed the lightweight bedding, and he caught it easily. "For now, do you have something to do to keep from getting bored?" She tried her best to sound casual. "I'll be glad to bring the lantern out here to the table and share it with you, since I have quite a few reports to fill out."

"I have some paperwork in a briefcase—" He stopped speaking abruptly as a strange sound came from behind the supply van. Seeing her about to say something, he held up one hand, signaling for her to remain quiet.

"I'll use the phone to call the police," she whispered after hearing the sound again. "It's in my tent."

"Turn off the lantern, too," he said, his voice barely audible. "Unless I miss my guess, someone just tripped in the dark. What we need to find out now is how many are out there." He set the bag down.

"No, don't go yet. Wait until I make the call, then we can go check things out together." She pursed her lips in annoyance as he shook his head and disappeared into the darkness.

Sam never glanced back. He knew what had to be done. He had no intention of being taken by surprise in this forsaken place. At least the sounds he'd heard were reassuring in their own way. According to tradition, specific things were attributed to the *chindi*: animal sounds, bright lights in the darkness and even certain animals. But he'd never heard of a *chindi* besieged by clumsiness.

He inched forward slowly, moving like a hunter stalking his prey. Sam stopped about fifty feet away from the vehicle and moved to high ground. Taking cover behind a large boulder, he waited. For several long moments he neither heard nor saw anything. Then as he rose to change positions, a sixth sense warned him of danger from behind. But before he could even turn his head, something hard crashed over his skull. Bright stars erupted before his eyes. He blinked, trying desperately to clear his vision, but instead he felt himself slipping into a dark void.

MARLA TRIED TO MAKE the call, but the phone wouldn't work. She suspected that someone had deactivated the base unit in the van. Frustrated, she waited near her tent, the lantern off. Minutes ticked by, but Sam Nez failed to appear. Something was wrong; she could feel it. As the crescent moon slipped behind the clouds, the black gloom became almost impenetrable.

She'd have to go take a look. She thought about using the lantern, but that would give away her exact position. Discarding the idea, she glanced around, searching for some kind of weapon before setting out. There were plenty of tools, including an ax for chopping wood, inside the small metal storage shed. Only she'd have to make it past the supply van to get it. A chill passed down her body. Had the intruder found it already?

In desperation, she finally grabbed a long piece of firewood. The light cottonwood branch, about three and a half feet long, would break if she smashed it against someone, but it was better than nothing. If she could get to the shed, the ax there would serve as a particularly nasty weapon.

Marla headed across the grounds, staying low. As she reached the storage unit, she caught a glimpse of an indistinct shadow about twenty feet ahead. She edged back deciding to avoid the shed for now, when she heard a soft groan come from inside the partially open door.

Chapter Three

Marla froze in her tracks and glanced inside. Sam Nez lay on the ground, scarcely moving. Her pulse began to race as fear clawed into her.

Forcing herself to stay still, Marla listened for danger. Walking into a trap was a real possibility now if she made the wrong move. She glanced around, firewood in hand, searching for his assailant, but only the soft chirping of the crickets interrupted the silence. Even the shadow she'd seen ahead did not look particularly threatening, anymore. It swayed rhythmically, making her suspect that it had only been the ghostly outline of the drought-stunted junipers cast by moonlight.

Reassured temporarily, she stepped inside the metal shed. As she saw Sam's face up close, her breath caught in her throat. There was an ugly bruise on the side of his head and blood trickled down his temple. But he was alive. She was crouching next to him when she heard running footsteps circling the shed. Marla jumped to her feet and lunged for the door a heartbeat too late. The door was slammed in her face, and the outside bolt slapped solidly into place.

In total darkness now, Marla pushed against the door with desperate strength. But she'd heard the padlock outside click, and knew her efforts would be futile. She'd selected the shed and padlock herself to keep the artifacts they'd planned to uncover safe until they were transported. Unwilling to give up, she pounded on the metal with her stick and yelled at the top of her lungs, but there was no one to help. Her ears hurting from the din she'd caused, she finally admitted defeat.

Marla moved away from the door as she heard Sam shift restlessly on the floor. Feeling along the single shelf of the shed, she managed to locate the battery-powered lantern they kept in there as a spare. As she slid the thumb switch forward, the narrow yellow beam cut through the gloom.

Marla knelt beside Sam and saw his eyes open slowly. "How do you feel?" she asked softly.

"Nothing looks right," he muttered, blinking slowly.

"You may have a concussion. You took quite a blow judging by that lump behind your ear." She tried to sound matter-of-fact, but she'd never been so afraid in her life. She was unable to gauge the extent of his injuries or even do much to help him if she could.

"Not *chindi*," he said firmly.

"Ghosts? No, not hardly." She could hear footsteps outside again, and the sounds of urgent whispers too far away to reveal anything intelligible.

"It's so cold." A shudder ran through his body.

Since Marla knew that it was no longer believed necessary to keep a person with a concussion awake, that actually rest and warmth were essential, she unzipped her jacket and sat down on the floor, leaning against the side of the shed. Supporting him carefully, she gently guided him toward her and hugged the folds around him.

"You're soft," he murmured, using her breasts as a pillow.

His head pressing intimately against her generated a different kind of warmth and she shifted, trying to find a less disturbing position. As she moved to one side, she felt his lips graze the skin above her breast where her summer top failed to cover. Every inch of feminine skin in her body flushed with heated pleasure. He felt so masculine against her. His body was all planes and hard muscles. No matter how she tried to deny it, the very air seemed to tremble and spark, alive with emotions as vital as the desert night.

His palm brushed her shoulders slowly as he pulled himself even closer to her, his head buried against her neck. She heard him mutter something halfway between a curse and a growl as he nuzzled her gently, trying to mold himself into her softness.

Had he been fully aware of his actions, neither of them would have been able to disregard the intimacy of that moment. As it was, she tried to force her pulse to stop racing. "Rest now," she whispered. She stroked his face in a gentle caress, soothing away the lines of pain. Finally, he drifted off to sleep.

She held on to him, praying the warmth of her body would protect him from the cold desert night. He looked so vulnerable at the moment, and totally harmless. But in truth, he was neither. His hand wrapped around her waist tightly as he snuggled against her. Maternal instincts mingled with heated, more passionate drives that left her confused and restless.

She didn't want to be this close to him; she couldn't breathe or think. She listened for the sounds of a police car, hoping someone would stop by to check on them, but only more running footsteps stirred the night.

An hour passed. The wind rose and fell outside, whistling through the tiny cracks around the metal door. Marla aimed the lantern around, taking inventory of the contents of the shed. The tools were gone, and she remembered they'd been left up by the site, along with the generator and floodlights. Boxes of paper plates and plastic utensils made up most of the remaining items.

Seeing nothing that could help them break out, Marla turned off the lantern to save the battery and listened. Maybe she'd hear something that would give her a clue. But the wind sweeping across the desert conspired against her. The whispers and footsteps remained elusive and indistinct.

It seemed like hours before Sam awoke. Marla flipped the lantern back on as he left her embrace and sat up slowly.

His hand went to the egg-size lump on the side of his head, and he winced. "That was a mistake."

"You sound like you're back to your old self," she said, searching his expression for confirmation. "How are you feeling?"

"I think I need an entire bottle of aspirin." His eyes narrowed and he blinked several times. "And everything's still spinning." He stiffened as they heard something being smashed outside. "What happened? All I remember is climbing up the hillside behind the storage shed."

"You were apparently attacked. I waited by the tents, but I couldn't even get a dial tone on the phone. I decided to come and see what was going on. I never saw anyone except you, then before I knew it, I was locked in here, too. Since then, all I can tell you is there are people whispering and running around out there. I'm not quite tall enough to peek out that space between the door and the roof, but you are. Would you like to try? I could support you," she suggested. "Maybe you'll be able to identify someone later when we get out."

"That's optimistic, but it's certainly better than giving up and doing nothing," Sam answered.

She turned off the lantern, and they waited for their eyes to adjust to the darkness again. "Okay. Let's take it slowly," she said at last, placing his arm around her shoulders.

He leaned heavily on her, hating the way the entire shed seemed to spin and tilt crazily from one side to the other. With staggering steps, Sam made his way across the small shed. His head throbbed all the way to the base of his neck. "Are you sure I'm not too much for you?"

"I'll manage." Marla struggled to keep her voice steady as his weight pressed down on her.

Finally he rose on the balls of his feet and looked outside through the narrow space above the roof-high door. In the dim moonlight, he could see a Navajo warrior wearing traditional leggings and a ceremonial mask made out of animal hide. The terror he'd felt as a boy invaded every fi-

ber of his being, challenging all the courage he possessed as
a man.

"Tell me what's going on out there," she whispered.

He rubbed his eyes, trying to get them to stay focused.
Then as he glanced up again, he saw the figure split and
become two separate entities. He almost groaned in frustration. "My blasted sight isn't working right." He closed
his eyes for a moment. By the time he looked again, there
was only darkness.

Sam forced himself to remain standing though everything was spinning violently now. "Help me down to the
ground. Maybe sitting will stop the floor from sinking," he
managed weakly.

"This was undoubtedly a mistake. We may have just
made things worse for you, sapping your strength like
that."

"I had to try," Sam answered as he sat down and leaned
against the side of the shed. "If the world would only stay
still, I'd feel a lot better," he joked halfheartedly.

Marla cringed, hearing the sound of something being
dragged across the ground. "What are they doing out
there?"

"I don't know," he said, feeling miserable. "I saw one
man...who turned into two...."

"Double vision. You probably do have a concussion. Do
you remember anything about the person?"

He started to answer, then stopped. What could he possibly tell her? That he'd seen a warrior wearing clothing that
no Navajo had worn in two hundred years? She'd think he
was crazy for sure.

"Do you remember anything about the person?" Marla
repeated.

"He was wearing trousers. I couldn't swear to anything
else, it was too dark."

Marla started to speak, then stopped abruptly. "Listen," she said. "There's a vehicle coming up." As a flash
of red worked its way through the small crack above the
door, she turned the lantern on again. "It's the police! They

must have come to check on me!" The red flashers continued in a pattern, illuminating the shed every few seconds.

Marla immediately began yelling and banging on the door with the stick. With each shout Sam winced, but as tempted as he was to help her, he remained seated where he was. The woman was doing well enough on her own. Even a *chindi* would have run from that much racket!

A moment later, they heard the lock being forced open. A Navajo tribal cop threw open the door, one hand on the butt of his pistol and the other holding a powerful flashlight.

The officer's tension was mirrored in the deep lines of his face. Wordlessly, he crouched next to Sam, assessing his injuries. "I'll radio for an ambulance," he said after a moment. "But it'll be awhile."

"Just take me to Shiprock in your car. I'll go to the hospital on my own."

"You'll have to ride in the back seat."

"Suits me."

As they helped Sam out the shed, a state police car came bouncing up the dirt track. The Navajo cop turned to Marla. "He's got the authority to have this place sealed off until tomorrow. I suggest you let him do that, and get out of here yourself."

"I can't go, but I'll accept whatever help I can get."

Sam stopped. "At least call and notify the college. See if one of the faculty will volunteer to come out and help you keep watch tonight."

"I'll do that."

The Navajo cop helped Sam to the squad car. "You're lucky all you got was a rap on the head," he said in a low voice. "I wouldn't spend the night around here on a bet."

As Sam and the Navajo officer drove away, Marla felt torn between the desire to go with Sam, and her duty to stay. It had been a long time since she'd felt anything compete with her devotion to her job and the emotion surprised her.

Marla shifted her attention to the state policeman and answered his questions as best she could. He was the same officer who'd been there earlier. Together they checked her cellular phone, and discovered someone had indeed turned it off.

Switching it back on, she made a quick telephone call. "I should be getting some help before too long," she said to the officer. "My department chairman is going to see if he can get someone to come and stay with me tonight. I'm sure one of the staff will volunteer when they hear what's happened."

"If you can't or won't leave, then getting others here is the only sensible option," he said, then continued to press her for answers.

For the next twenty minutes, Marla related what had happened, but she simply didn't have any answers to give him. The frustration on his face matched her own.

The officer inspected the camp, then went up to the site. "There're some recent footprints all around," he said, "but with the wind softening their contours it's difficult to tell much about them. You have no way of knowing what might have been taken from the site?" the patrolman insisted.

"I wish I did, believe me. All I know for sure right now is that our equipment seems to be here, including the expensive cameras, the video cassette player and the generator."

"You say something was smashed. What do you think it was?"

"I'm not sure. Maybe pottery or..." Before she completed the sentence, more headlight cones penetrated the camp. She saw the college pickup and another vehicle bouncing up the dirt track.

A moment later, the three women graduate students arrived. Liz was carrying two gasoline lanterns. "Professor Hartman called and told me what happened! I tried calling Lena and though she'd already been to the lab, she wasn't at home. So I contacted Carmen and Dulce. We didn't want you to be alone after what happened!''

Marla smiled with relief at the young women. She hadn't wanted to be alone tonight, either. ''But your families will be worried.''

''Not as long as we're in a group,'' Dulce answered.

The officer placed his notebook into the shirt pocket of his black-and-gray uniform. ''I've done all I can for now, but I'll be back periodically, Dr. Garrett. Don't hesitate to call if you even suspect there might be trouble. With the distances we have to cover, it's not wise to wait until the last minute.''

''Will Sam Nez be okay?'' Dulce asked Marla as the officer strode away.

''I think so, but the tribe is going to be very upset about this.''

''Well, it wasn't your fault someone clobbered him,'' Carmen said.

''Try not to word it that way around him, okay?'' Marla answered with a wry smile. ''A little diplomacy could go a long way about now.''

''We're going to need more than that to keep this dig going,'' Liz said, exhaling softly. ''Trouble of any kind makes Dr. Hartman extremely upset. He was determined to avoid any more problems by making sure we stayed here as a group until he could assess the situation himself. In fact, he even insisted I take the truck Lena left at the lab when I mentioned my pickup had given me trouble on the way home. He wanted to be sure we'd get here.''

''But what about Lena then?'' Marla asked. ''She won't have a way back.''

''I left a note for her. Dr. Hartman said he was coming here in the morning and she could catch a ride with him.''

Marla suppressed a groan. ''Then I think we all better hit the sack. At first light we'll look around again and find out if there's anything that'll need to be replaced.'' She ran a hand through her hair wearily. ''I have a feeling we're going to have a very long day tomorrow.''

A GENTLE, EARLY MORNING breeze drifted through the flaps of Marla's tent and allowed sunlight to stream inside. She woke up slowly, grateful to leave the nightmarish world she'd entered in her dreams. All her fears had paraded through her mind's eye in hideous succession, leaving her more tired now than when she'd gone to bed.

Marla rubbed her eyes, stretched mightily, and wiggled out of the sleeping bag. By the time she was dressed, the others, including Tony and Hector, were already sitting around the small propane cook stove, eating breakfast.

She greeted everyone, and poured some coffee from the pot. "I've got to make a phone call to the PHS hospital in Shiprock and check on Sam Nez. After I finish that, we'll start compiling a list of what was damaged or stolen."

Liz held up a small notebook. "We're ready when you are."

Marla heard a vehicle coming down the road as she spread some scrambled eggs on a tortilla. Glancing up and seeing a white carryall, she sighed. "I'll bet that's Dr. Hartman." She rolled up the tortilla and finished it in several quick bites. "People, why don't you work on that report for me while I talk to Dr. Hartman?"

"Shall I also call the hospital?" Carmen asked.

Marla considered it briefly. "No. I'll do that myself. Let me get Dr. Hartman squared away first." Calling Sam was not something she wanted to do in a rush, or delegate. She wanted to hear his voice and reassure herself that he really was okay.

Marla waited for the college vehicle by the side of the road, and moments later Lena and Dr. Hartman stepped out. It didn't surprise her that Lena had managed to catch a ride with Hartman. She was usually hanging around the anthropology building when she wasn't in class. Dr. Hartman had also shown a professional interest in Lena, one of the best students that had come through their department in years.

Hartman straightened his six-foot frame and strode toward her. His appearance was meticulously neat, despite his casual clothing. Even in jeans, he looked like an ad for an expensive men's clothing store. His salt-and-pepper hair had begun to show more salt since he'd turned fifty-five, but it enhanced his looks, giving him a touch of distinction.

"I heard from the head of the Tribal Council at 6:00 a.m. this morning. I hadn't even had coffee yet," Hartman complained. "He wasn't pleased that their representative ended up in the hospital." Hartman crossed his arms across his chest. "And in just a few minutes, there are going to be protesters gathering on the Navajo side of that fence. I saw them coming as we drove up the road. I shouldn't have to tell you that the college doesn't need the negative attention all this will bring."

"It would be a mistake to abandon our work here. Although I can't be positive, judging from what we've uncovered so far, this is no ordinary site. I don't know who's behind the problems we've been having, but it would be wrong to let pressure groups dictate what we do."

"There were no pressure groups until yesterday's events," he countered. "Whatever happened is your responsibility, and so far your control of the situation is less than stellar."

She heard shouts as the protesters gathered less than a hundred yards away. "I'm willing to accept the responsibility, Dr. Hartman, but as you know this is a pilot project. That means the funding I managed to get for this dig is very limited. Our expenses are being covered, and there are tuition waivers for the graduate students. If it wasn't for that, none of these people would still be in college. They'd have dropped out. Our equipment has been donated or loaned from our corporate sponsor, and I'm an unpaid volunteer. The actions of thieves and vandals are always hard to predict, but if the department would like to provide me with funds for security, I'll be glad to accept the help."

"For the moment, that's out of the question. If the artifact you sent back with Lena proves authentic that might change, but I'm very skeptical based on what I've seen."

"I hope you're not implying that either my crew or I have in any way corrupted this site. . . ." Her voice was hard. If Hartman or the college administration started to question her integrity, she'd fight with everything she had at her disposal. Without a solid reputation, her career would come to an abrupt standstill. No findings she made would ever be seriously considered if her honesty was questioned, and she'd never be given the chance to direct another dig.

Just then, the protesters began to shout in unison. Marla listened, then shook her head slowly. Their slogan was short and to the point. "Stop robbing our dead."

Hartman rolled his eyes. "You better hope they get bored really fast." He touched Lena lightly on the arm. "Let's get started now. You can give me that tour you promised while Dr. Garrett tries to establish some order here."

It took all her willpower not to tell him precisely what she thought of his attitude. She took a deep breath and decided that she wouldn't wait any longer to call the hospital. Hartman had descended like visiting royalty, demanding, but giving nothing in return. Sam, on the other hand, had shown a great deal of courage last night, and for his trouble had barely escaped a cracked skull. The least she could do was take the time to telephone and show him that she'd been thinking about him.

Of course despite everything that had happened, the truth was he'd been in her thoughts practically all the time. For a variety of reasons, some even having to do with business, Sam Nez wasn't a man she could easily put out of mind.

Walking toward her tent, she heard another vehicle approaching. The shouts of the protesters suddenly increased in volume, and the angry cries turned into cheers. Marla turned around, a sinking feeling in her stomach. With her luck, it would turn out to be the Navajo tribal chairman and a judge—carrying a court order that would close them down for good.

Chapter Four

To her surprise, she saw Sam step out of an old pickup, which quickly spun around and roared away in a cloud of dust. His injury couldn't have been too serious if he'd been released this quickly.

As he approached she saw the wide rectangular bandage just behind his left ear, but otherwise he looked okay. Actually, better than okay. His jeans fitted him snugly, tempting her imagination. His khaki shirt accentuated the copper color of his skin and the darkness of his eyes and hair. She watched him for a second, thinking he was a tempting blend of old and new. In many ways it was as if he'd stepped out of the pages of those history books she'd studied for years, and come to life.

"I'm glad you're all right," she blurted.

"Head like a brick," he said with a chuckle. "But I'll have a headache for a few days. I see you've drawn a crowd," he said glancing at the protesters. "What's the news around here?"

She averted her eyes. Whatever his jeans and knit shirt encased was none of her business. Still, she couldn't resist a furtive glance before swearing to herself she wouldn't do it again. "I haven't had a chance to look around the site today. My department chairman is here, and you've already noticed the others who aren't so pleased by our presence." She motioned toward the protesters, who'd taken up their chants again.

He nodded, watching the crowd. "I'd heard in Shiprock that Henderson Begay suggested the protesters demonstrate from the land he occupies. He's one of our politicians."

"Want to walk around with me while I check for vandalism?"

"Yeah, that sounds good." He could still vividly recall the figure in leggings and moccasins. He also remembered the spot where the warrior had stood, and he had every intention of seeing if he could find moccasin tracks. That would let him know if he'd been hallucinating or not.

"Do you mind if we look at the metal shed first?" he asked.

"Not at all." Marla walked alongside him, matching his pace. "Are you sure you're feeling okay?"

"Yeah, I'm fine," Sam said, smiling. "I'm just trying to make sense out of the confusing images I remember from last night."

"Speaking of your injuries, do you ever go to a tribal medicine man?" Marla hoped she wasn't being impertinent. Asking questions was a sure way to get most Navajos to clam up. But she was genuinely concerned.

Surprised at her question, Sam nevertheless responded. "Sometimes a *hataalii*, or healer is contacted, and a sing is requested. But not everyone feels comfortable doing that."

"How about you?" Marla added, telling herself this would be the last question. She didn't want to offend or alienate Sam.

"Sometimes I feel caught in the middle. Half my education is modern, half ancient. I certainly believe in my culture, and practice its rituals to some extent. Being Navajo isn't easy in today's world—not by any means."

Hearing the chanting of the protesters grow louder, he turned around. "But enough of my problems, let's take a look at yours. I probably shouldn't tell you this, but I'm the reason they're here." Seeing the puzzled look on her face, he continued. "The reservation is vast, but despite that, news travels quickly. Once I was admitted to the hospital, the word went out through the hospital staff and spread like wildfire.''

''I wish I could convince them that to understand the present, we have to look at the past. Archaeologists, by uncovering the remains of that past, study societies, how they worked, what made them who they were, and from that, we learn about people today. I know it sounds idealistic, but what we're really talking about is mankind's heritage.''

''Your motives may be good, but the problem is that we've seen too much of our history stolen,'' he answered. ''Every day more of our culture is hauled away in cardboard boxes to some museum. It's not only the rights of the dead that are being violated, but it's also the rights of the living—*their* rights.'' Sam turned and waved toward the protesters, who cheered loudly. Sam's eyes were alive with emotion.

''But it's the rights of *all* the living that have to be taken into account. A portion of your own history could come to light as the result of what we do here.'' She had to shout above the protesters. ''But only if I'm able to continue my work.''

As the chanting went on unabated, Sam grew silent once again. A few minutes later they reached the metal shed. Sam walked inside and closed the door almost shut. He peered out over the top, verified the location where he'd seen the warrior, and returned outside. Reaching the area next to a stunted juniper, he began searching the ground.

''If you tell me what you're looking for, I could help you.''

He glanced up at her, then back down at the sand. The only tracks he could find appeared to be from hard-soled shoes, like boots. ''I wanted to check the footprints of the guy I saw near the brush last night, but these don't look right.''

She felt a rush of sympathy. ''Well, if you also remember, you did mention he turned into two men.'' She paused, then continued in a gentle voice. "When you get struck hard on the head, a little confusion is to be expected."

He stared at the ground, shaking his head, and finally shrugged. "Do you see any tracks here that don't look right to you?"

She studied the ground with him. "No. These must have come from the three women in my team who returned and spent the night. See how small they are?" Marla waited patiently as he continued to examine the spot. At long last, she cleared her throat. "Let's go see if we can figure out if anything was taken from the cave."

As she started uphill, she noticed his reluctance. She could sense that he would rather have been anywhere but here, yet he was doing what he had to do. Her admiration for him grew. "Do you think it's possible a group of protesters would sabotage the site?"

He considered it, trying to remain objective. "I suppose it is, but I doubt it. Most Navajos wouldn't come here, particularly at night, for any reason whatsoever."

"You mean because of the *chindi* threat?" She crouched near a shallow excavated quadrant beside the entrance.

"To you, it might sound like superstitious nonsense, but to us, it's a part of our religious beliefs."

"I meant no disrespect. But do remember that what has happened here at the site has nothing to do with *chindi*. No spirits I've ever heard of come digging in a cave using shovels," she said, pointing to the marks on the sand, "or steal film and lock people inside places after smashing them over the head."

"You have a point." Still, he wasn't ready to explain away the man in the leggings to a hallucination. It was too pat and didn't feel like the truth, somehow. His gaze took in the entrance to the cave. "This is the resting place of a people that have as much right to their graves as anyone else. How can you divorce all morality from that, and look at it coldly as just a quest for knowledge?"

"The same way you handle your court cases. You look at the overall picture, and focus on what you're trying to accomplish," she replied. "An attorney's job is to present his client's case in the best possible light. Whether or not he believes his client is right or innocent doesn't really matter. His client, under our system, deserves a defense. The morality of that, particularly under certain circumstances, is questionable. It's not that different for me in my profession. I also have to suppress any sentimentality or preconceptions and look at things objectively. Why is that difficult for you to understand? As an attorney, you have to do almost the same thing."

"I don't agree at all. My job is to be a buffer between the courts and those who need someone to protect them from a very complex system. Our work, or even the concepts behind what we do, have nothing in common," he said tensely. "But then, to be honest, what you're doing involves and affects my personal beliefs, so it's possible my outlook isn't quite fair."

"I'm sorry you're in such a difficult position," she answered softly. Pensively, she brushed aside some sand, but found nothing else buried beneath. "Something used to be here. I can see part of an outline and the differences in sand texture, but they've taken it away. I wonder if that's what we heard being smashed down by the shed." She grimaced.

Seeing Hartman approaching from downhill, Marla stood up. The graduate students, including Hector and Tony, trailed a few feet behind him. It looked as though they were eager and ready to work.

Marla introduced Sam to Dr. Hartman and watched the two men size each other up. In deference to Navajo ways, Hartman didn't offer to shake hands, and Sam remained neutral and polite, showing nothing of his thoughts.

"I'm terribly sorry about the difficulties you encountered here at our site," Hartman said. "We're doing our best with marginal funds, mostly from private grants. And at this point, it's impossible to tell who might be responsible for the trouble." His gaze drifted casually toward the protesters on the other side of the fence.

Sam's expression hardened. "They have a legal right to demonstrate, just as you presently have the legal right to dig here. But if Navajo artifacts turn up, understand that the tribe will do whatever is necessary in order to reclaim them."

"We have no problem with that, believe me," Hartman assured. "Our college has always worked in complete co-operation with the Navajo people. In fact, you're welcome to join us as we continue the excavation."

Sam's gaze was as cold as a desert night. "I'm not here to cause a disturbance, but to watch over what's being done. The rights of Those Who Came Before also need protecting," he said, using the literal term for the Anasazi.

As they began to work, Sam stood back, silently watching. With any luck the robbers had taken everything of value and whatever was left wouldn't merit the *bilagáanas'* time. He'd regret not seeing Marla again, but it would be a relief not to have to return to this place. And he could always pay a visit to the college and find a way to ask her to lunch, and maybe even dinner. He found the thought pleasing, and entertained himself with it as the others continued to slowly remove centimeters of sand within their own staked-out quadrants of land. Each was working part of a larger grid which extended into the cave.

The archaeologists seemed to relish their work, uncovering each fragmented piece of pottery, bead or arrowhead as if they'd discovered diamonds or gold. He suppressed a shudder. These items used by Those Who Came Before represented lives of real people whose Wind Breath had become one with the harmonious universe. All that remained here was contaminated and unclean. He fingered the small piece of flint he always carried. Traditionally it was said that flint gave protection against *chindi*. Navajo religion taught that the sound and light of flint created a circle of protection against the evil-minded. He wasn't sure if he believed that, but he'd carried it for many years—since he was thirteen.

After what seemed an eternity, they finally reached the first chamber of the cavern. Surrounded by the hard-packed earthen and rock walls, his skin prickled with unease. It felt wrong in here. He wondered if it was due to the abrupt temperature difference. It was as if winter had suddenly descended with a vengeance.

Carmen shivered. "It shouldn't be this cold in here. We're still close to the mouth of the cave."

"There could be a spring back there someplace, or any of a dozen other reasons," Marla answered. "Button your jacket."

Hartman zipped up his Windbreaker, and with a smirk at Marla, jammed his hands into his pockets. "Looks like this site is not going to produce anything except minor sherds and a bunch of projectile points. I'm not sure our sponsors will continue to support this dig. The bad publicity here certainly isn't going to be offset by meager results like these."

Marla ran her hand across the earthen and rock walls. "We need more time. This cave hasn't seen daylight for hundreds of years, yet it once sheltered the Anasazi and perhaps the Navajos. The evidence is right here below us."

Liz brushed off another arrowhead she found just outside the entrance at a new, lower level she was examining. Then she took a very careful photograph of it in place before picking it up. "This one's different in type and material from the others we found. It's made out of flint, not obsidian."

The news took Sam by surprise. So if *chindi* were here, flint didn't do much against them. He wondered about the events that had tied the evil to this area.

Sam heard a breeze whistle through the cave. Concurrent with the high-pitched wail, and beyond the scraping and mutters of the humans working here, there was also a deeper undercurrent of sound. As each wail subsided, a more rhythmic cadence reverberated in the cavern like the baritone beat of drums. He glanced at the others, wondering if they could also hear it.

Hartman shivered, visibly uncomfortable. "Is that the wind, or noise from outside?"

"Maybe neither, or both." Sam turned his attention to Liz. "Would you hold that flint arrowhead up? I'd like to take a look at it."

"Step over here by the entrance and check it out in the sunlight. You'll see it better." Liz held it out to him.

Sam left the chamber and moved closer to the mouth of the cave, but only for a better look. He'd touch that thing the day after an Indian was elected president of the United States.

As he approached the young graduate student, Marla followed him out, eager to see this new find. Standing near the entrance with the warmth of the sun on his face, he felt more relaxed. It was even easier to breathe out here away from the interior of the cavern.

Sam glanced at the arrowhead in the woman's palm when suddenly the newly uncovered earth beneath his feet shifted. Reacting in a heartbeat, Marla reached out to him. Sam grasped her hand to steady himself, but the cave floor abruptly opened up and they plummeted together into the darkness.

Chapter Five

Marla landed on her side with a hard thump that knocked the wind out of her. Gasping for air, she turned toward Sam. "Are you okay?" she managed.

Sam sat up slowly. "Yeah, how about you?"

Marla groaned as she got to her knees. "I'll have some colorful bruises, but thank goodness for the sand."

Sam looked up at the faces that peered down at them through the opening. "We're in one piece," he assured and heard the murmur of relief.

His gaze drifted around the log and mud enclosure. All but one end of the old hogan was covered by tons of dirt and sand. But it was that one area that instantly captured his attention. Less than three feet in front of them, leaning against the crumbling side of the hogan, sat the skeleton of a tall man. The warrior was protected with ornate flint armor and reed-woven breastplate. A large, lethal-looking flint-edged club rested inside his bony grip. At his feet lay the skeletons of three smaller armed warriors. "Slayer," he whispered.

"It can't be...." she said in a stunned whisper. Hearing movement above her, she turned her head and saw Dr. Hartman climbing down a rope.

"What's going on?" As his gaze fastened on the figure, Hartman's eyes widened.

When Hartman started to go forward, Sam quickly blocked his way. "No, stand back. This site may be holy to the Navajos."

"That can't be the god Slayer," Marla said. "This site is old, but it can't predate history." She was well acquainted with the Navajo creation story in which Slayer had played a prominent role.

"Yes, but only another Navajo would know to impersonate him. And we don't know where that armor, or club, came from. According to our religious history, it's like the ones Slayer used. I can't let you desecrate this site." Sam stood firm.

"Slayer," Hartman repeated pensively. "He's one of the Hero Twins the war gods sent at the beginning of the world to make the land safe, right?"

"Yes. They were the Sun's children."

Hartman rubbed his jaw thoughtfully as he studied the skeletal remains. "Despite all that, this site may not be directly linked to the Navajos. Judging from the weapons and items the other warriors have around them, I'd say they are Anasazi," Dr. Hartman commented.

"Maybe, but the individual leaning against the mud wall is clearly a Slayer impersonator. That's a practice that's part of our rituals. The way I see it, the warrior in the ceremonial armor died defending this place." Sam squared his shoulders and refused to step aside. "That makes this site of special importance to the Dineh."

As the men argued, Marla studied the structure, carefully brushing sand away from the sides. "It seems to have three main support beams," she said, thinking out loud.

"Like the male Navajo hogans," Sam said flatly. "There's no doubt in my mind that this site belongs to the Navajo people."

"Wait a second," Hartman protested. "First of all, you can't assume the armor on that skeleton is linked to Slayer just because it matches the traditional description. And discovering this structure has three support beams doesn't prove it was built by your Navajo forefathers."

"But the questions those facts raise are important enough for me to insist that this site be abandoned by the college."

"Why? The data we've uncovered brings up some interesting speculations, but there's nothing conclusive about it."

"This is the earliest connection I know of to the Navajo creation story. That alone should merit your respect."

Marla could understand the point Sam was making. To a Navajo, the legends of old comprised more than religion. They were the history of their race. "Any artifact that we find here on public lands will be treated with respect. If you're in doubt, stay and watch over the process, or bring someone else. I'll even stop working at night, in deference to your tribe's belief of the *chindi*."

"But you won't stop," Sam concluded, his eyes stony and hard.

"No." Marla forced herself to meet his gaze. She didn't want to take a stand against him, but he offered her no other option. If only he would try to understand that knowledge belonged to all of civilization, and superseded the rights of the few. "I can't."

Liz and Lena lowered the small aluminum ladder they had brought for deep excavations, propping it against one side of the roof opening above. Liz leaned over the edge, and held out a camera so Marla could see it. "Right, Liz. We'll need photos and sketches of everything down here before we touch a thing."

"I would like to speak to you and Dr. Hartman outside," Sam said to Marla, then climbed up the ladder.

Hartman hurried down and pulled Marla aside. "This is a very important find. If we can get the right kind of press, funds will pour into the college and our department. We need to stall Nez and give ourselves the chance to call a press conference that'll sway people to our side," he whispered.

"Publicity is the last thing we need! It'll attract too many curiosity seekers and thieves."

"Not if you handle it right. Trust me. I've dealt with this type of thing before." He climbed up the ladder before she could answer.

Marla hurried after him, and caught up with Hartman outside. As her gaze fell over Sam, who stood below the cave waiting, she suppressed a shudder. His uncompromising stance, and his implacable expression left little doubt that he was prepared for a fight. She realized at that precise moment that she'd underestimated Sam Nez. There was a relentless, single-minded purpose about him that frightened her a little.

"You don't have adequate security here," Sam warned. "That should be painfully obvious. To continue bringing out items you can't possibly protect proves what little regard you have for what you're uncovering."

"Wait a second," Marla interrupted. "You know that we've made some changes here. From now on, this site will never be left unguarded. One or more of us will be here at all times."

"Why does that fail to impress me?" Sam countered.

"It's your job to see only one side of this," she retorted, keeping her temper in check.

Hartman glanced toward the protesters, then back at Marla. "I'm going to go back in and supervise the graduate students. You should be able to explain our position to Mr. Nez without me."

Marla watched Hartman return to the newly discovered hogan. She had no desire to relinquish control to him even for a short time, but for now it couldn't be helped.

"You two don't trust each other though you're supposed to be on the same side," Sam observed. "And *that*'s the situation I'm supposed to have confidence in on behalf of the tribe?"

The rebuff stung. "Dr. Hartman and I may have our professional differences, but our answer to you and the tribe is identical. We stand united on that."

"Think of what's already happened, and what may lie ahead. It worries me and it should worry you." He paused as he glanced at the protesters. Navajo tribal police were now standing by. "I can't allow you to continue this excavation. If you refuse to stop right now, I'll do everything in my power to have your permit rescinded until our tribe gets a court hearing."

"We'll both do what we have to," she said, a trace of sadness in her voice. "I wish you'd try to understand that no one here is an enemy of your tribe."

"I know that your heart is in the right place," he said quietly.

The gentleness in his voice, and the intensity in his eyes made an unsettling warmth spread through her. She could feel the strength that was behind each word drawing her with a power more enticing that any she could remember. Before she could unscramble her thinking, he continued. "I'll get a camera and take photos of my own, just in case anything else happens," he said, then headed back toward his vehicle.

Just then, Marla heard Hartman asking Liz for the film she'd just shot. Liz's voice was equally as firm. "I'm sorry, Doctor, but I'm not supposed to do that. We have certain procedures to follow."

That exchange quickly brought Marla's thoughts back into sharp focus. Before it could go any further, she approached Hartman. He stood near the opening, peering down.

"Liz is absolutely right, Dr. Hartman," Marla said. "That film needs to be logged into our records right away. Then one of us will sign for it and take it in for processing."

"Do whatever you have to do quickly, then hand it over. I'll take it to the lab myself."

She took the film from Liz, who had come up the ladder. "Please don't force the issue, Dr. Hartman. We'll go through established channels with all our documentation."

"Once your name is in the paper, and you realize how this is going to help both of us, you'll see what I'm doing in a different light. Believe me."

"Unless you want to turn the tribe completely against us, I strongly suggest you at least make any announcements you have planned in a joint press conference," she said, walking downhill with Hartman.

Hartman shook his head. "You know what your biggest weakness is? You try to play fair all the time. You can't do that in the real world. Give me that film."

Marla reached into her pocket and handed him a small film canister. "I want it to go on record that I opposed this."

"Duly noted." He made a fist around the film canister, and strode toward the camp.

Marla reached into her other pocket, and with a worried frown stared at a second film canister.

"What's going on?" Sam approached her from behind. He glanced at the film canister, but said nothing.

Marla tried to read his expression, wondering how much he'd overheard as she quickly slipped the film back into her pocket. "Did you take the photos you needed?" she asked, hoping to divert him.

"Yes. I'm on my way to meet with the tribal leaders."

"We're locked in a win-or-lose proposition, and it shouldn't have to be that way. There's got to be a way to compromise."

"Not on this," he answered. "If you truly understood anything about our people, you'd know the impossibility of that."

Sam walked to his vehicle, then drove away down the dirt track. The woman was dangerous to his thinking. Every time he saw himself reflected in her hazel eyes, he felt everything male in him respond. He wanted her and the comforts of her body.

It was useless to deny the way he felt around her. He was at a loss, though, to explain how he could possibly be attracted to someone in such a repulsive profession. He suppressed a shudder. It seemed a waste for a woman as vitally warm and alive as she was to be immersed in the way of death.

He brushed her from his mind. She was not his concern. Nothing to excess, that was the cornerstone of his belief, of walking in beauty. Billy Todacheene, Henderson Begay and other tribal leaders were waiting.

Almost ninety minutes later, he entered Billy's office inside the government building at Window Rock. Tension lit the air like sparks from burning cedar. Although in public the tribal leaders stood as one, behind closed doors it was quite a different story. There were two distinct factions: one headed by Billy Todacheene, the other by Henderson Begay. The source of their rift, though simple, went deep. Both were fiercely loyal to the tribe, but the methods they used to pursue the goals of the Dineh were completely different. Begay, unlike Todacheene, utilized any means at his disposal to make sure the tribe came out ahead. And that, at the moment, worried Sam a great deal.

Sam took a chair opposite Stephen Roanhorse, Thomas Tsosie, Herman Clah, and other senior members of the Tribal Council. He saw the stunned faces as he recounted what he'd seen, then placed the roll of film on Billy's desk.

"This armor...could it be a fake, like the ax discovered yesterday?" Roanhorse was the first to speak, but the tension in the room had increased to an almost tangible degree.

"I doubt it, considering how it was discovered," Sam answered. "Even the air in that hogan smelled hundreds of years old."

"What can be done?" Billy asked directly.

"I can try to get her permit rescinded, but that'll take time."

"We don't have time!" Begay said, leaning forward. "We need to take direct action *now*."

"What would you suggest?" Tsosie countered pointedly. "We can't have the tribal police go arrest them.

They're not on our land and they haven't committed any crime an Anglo judge would recognize."

"We need to hit them through the Anglo press. They're working out of state by being here in New Mexico, thanks to the *bilagáanas* who gave her the grant. The last thing they need is bad publicity. The college depends on private as well as Colorado funds. We need our attorney to prepare a statement that's impossible for them to argue against. We have right on our side. Those artifacts are of religious and historical importance to the Navajo people."

"We don't have right on our side legally, not yet," Sam countered. "Even if we get into the courts, it can go either way."

"We can't just sit around while they take everything to their labs, desecrating what belongs to us." Begay's voice rose slightly. "We need to engineer a public outcry, and that can be done using the press."

"Let's start by talking to the professor in charge of the excavation," Billy said thoughtfully, and glanced at Sam. "Invite the woman here. Perhaps we can make her see that our concerns are legitimate, and must be dealt with. Together, we might be able to persuade her to abandon the site."

"Since when do the *bilagáanas* respond to anything unless it affects their wallets?" Begay leaned over Todacheene's desk, his hands clenched into fists. "You have to confront the issues directly and put a stop to this, quickly and decisively."

Billy snorted derisively. "Right. Let's swoop down on horseback and take them captive. Then we can ransom them back to the college, and make some money in the process." He walked to the air conditioner and turned it up. "We're a civilized people. They have their rights, and we have ours. We'll try to reason with them first. Then if that doesn't work, we'll try other methods, including the courts."

Begay strode to the door, stopped, and turned around.

"You use tactics that are destined to fail. I won't stay and lend my support to your show of weakness."

An uncomfortable silence descended over the room as two others followed him out in a silent show of unity with Begay. "I don't trust them," Sam said at last. "They're acting like they want you out of a job."

"All the more reason to bring the woman here," Billy Todacheene repeated. "Today, if possible."

"I'll see what she's willing to do."

Billy grinned. "I have every confidence in you."

Sam heard the men around him chuckle, and knew what they were all thinking. Over the years, he'd acquired a reputation for being a ladies' man, though it was undeserved. He was a normal man with normal wants and needs, no different from anyone else. If he'd dated quite a bit, it was because he was still searching for the right mate. He wanted to spend his life with someone who'd share his love of Navajo ways, and also appreciate the world outside the reservation. More importantly, he needed a woman who could understand that his duty to the tribe meant that sometimes work took up all his waking hours for weeks at a time. It was a tall order, and maybe a little unfair.

Sam stood and motioned toward the door. "Keep an eye on our angry friend, Uncle," Sam urged, referring to Begay. "He's not going to wait to see what happens next."

"A premonition?" Billy asked somberly.

"I prefer to think of it as a gut feeling."

Chapter Six

Sam arrived at the site at around three in the afternoon. Though the temperature was over ninety, he could see two of the students working near the mouth of the cave. He would have found their enthusiasm admirable if they'd been anywhere else.

As he walked toward the cave, Marla emerged from the opening in the roof of the wrecked hogan. She brushed her hair away from her face, and held it in place with a gray baseball cap with a cartoon mouse on it. The image of the serious professor and the silliness of the cap made him smile.

Her expression remained guarded as he approached. "What did the tribal leaders say?"

"They haven't seen the photos yet, but they're all very concerned, naturally. I know it's an imposition, but it would really help ease matters if you'd come and meet with them. You could explain your plans for the artifacts directly to them."

She said nothing for a long moment. "Is that your idea, or theirs?"

"Theirs," he answered candidly.

They were hoping to dissuade her from pursuing the dig. "We won't abandon our work, you know." She met his eyes and found her throat closing around the words. They were both locked into a collision course neither could avoid.

"It's a request, nothing more. What do you have to lose?"

His words were smooth and glided over with the gentleness of a feather dancing in the wind. Surely that had to be something he'd perfected to mold others into doing whatever he wanted. She took a deep breath. Well, she'd never been easily influenced. She could hold her own in any meeting. "I'll meet with them. Maybe we can find a solution that'll be mutually acceptable. When do they want to schedule it?"

"This afternoon, if possible."

She glanced down at her dusty jeans and her shortsleeved chambray work shirt. "I'll need time to wash and change clothes. The bucket system we have here is primitive."

"My home is less than half an hour from here. You could use my shower and get dressed there." He paused, then grinned. "Or in lieu of that, I could hold the bucket for you."

The suggestion made her tingle everywhere. "I don't think so, thanks. I'll manage somehow. But I still won't have anything except jeans to wear."

"That's okay. That's what they'll be wearing. They prefer Garth Brooks to Brooks Brothers. What did you expect?" he said with a smile.

She chuckled. "I'm not sure."

"You're making the right decision by coming," he assured.

"Why? Because it's what you wanted me to do?"

He grinned. "Of course."

"Don't count on that always happening," she warned, stopping by her tent to get some clean clothes.

"Believe me, I don't," he said, suddenly serious.

She glanced at him. His expression was somber, but beyond the strong lines of his face was a gentleness that tempered the determination etched there. Her heart quickened and she shifted her gaze to an area just behind the tents.

"Wait for me here. We have our makeshift shower set up just behind that brush."

What they had was no more than a barrel filled with water they used for washing their hands and faces. But it would have to do. As she cleaned up, her thoughts kept returning to Sam. Imagining him holding the bucket in a makeshift shower and letting water cascade over her naked body left her nerves pulsing. She started to hum a country and western song, determined not to give in to her wildly misbehaving imagination.

Twenty minutes later, feeling refreshed but a bit nervous, she went to join Sam. He was leaning against his pickup, his gaze falling on her in a slow, leisurely manner as she approached. Marla felt the power of that look sear right through her clothing. Her skin prickled with awareness. "I won't exactly make the best-dressed list," she said, feeling terribly self-conscious.

Her pale gold, long-sleeved blouse was tucked neatly into her jeans, revealing slim hips and a small waist. "Believe me, you look fine." If anyone could have swayed the opinion of the tribal leaders on this matter, his bet would have been on her. Only that was as likely as getting the sun to set in the east.

As she seated herself inside the cab of his pickup, the clean, fresh smell of her seemed to fill the air. To distract himself, he switched on the radio to a local station. As a familiar voice rose from the speakers, Sam muttered a curse. "I knew it!"

She heard the last few words of a speech, then Henderson Begay began to respond to questions from reporters. "All I want is what is ours. That site is of great religious significance to the Navajo people. To have it systematically desecrated by those who know nothing about our ways is an act of sabotage in every sense of the word."

As Marla listened, she kept a watchful, if furtive eye, on Sam. It didn't take an empath to know he was angry. Then came the next question.

"Dr. Hartman, chairman of the Archaeology Department of Durango College, called a conference earlier, but he canceled abruptly less than an hour ago. Can you suggest any reason for his actions?"

Henderson Begay paused, as if weighing the question in his mind. "He obviously realized that there isn't an argument in the world that will justify what he's doing."

Sam's eyes narrowed as he glanced at Marla. "Or perhaps it has something to do with a cartridge of film?"

Marla felt her throat go dry. She had her loyalty to the college to consider, but she'd never been much for lying. "I probably gave him the wrong canister," she said, choosing her words carefully. "I had two in my pocket. A simple mistake, really. After all, they hadn't been labeled yet because he was unwilling to wait."

Sam laughed. "Okay, but just for the sake of argument, why were you against having him hold a press conference?"

"A site like this could easily turn into a circus with the press and curiosity seekers. That's not what my work is about."

"But just think of the money you could raise if you made your find a little more public. People would want to be associated with your success," he said, watching her reaction.

"There are other ways to raise funds. I'm hoping the tribe will help out."

Sam almost choked. "The who?"

"You heard me. If the Council is that interested in protecting the artifacts, then maybe they'll offer to fund some of the security arrangements. That's going to be part of my proposal."

He shook his head. "What they want you to do is *leave.*" Still, he had to admire her quick thinking, and she was gutsy. He found himself liking her even more.

"Why were you angry with Begay? You don't approve of what he did?"

"No, I don't. He's taken it upon himself to speak for the whole tribe. That's out of line."

As he lapsed into silence, Marla wondered how this would affect the reception she'd receive. Dissension within the tribe would make any negotiations twice as difficult.

Forty minutes later, Sam escorted her to Billy Todacheene's office. Tsosie and Roanhorse were already there, and watched her with wary curiosity as they introduced themselves.

Marla seated herself in the chair offered, uncomfortable in the ensuing silence. It was impossible to tell the ages of the men around her, but they wore their authority with undeniable confidence. Roanhorse's copper, leathery skin was etched with an intricate pattern of lines, and there was an unmistakable look of toughness in his eyes. Tsosie appeared more youthful, and at first glance as harmless as a pastry cook. He had a round face and barrel-shaped body that went well with the kindly eyes that regarded her thoughtfully. But Todacheene was the indisputable leader here. His gray hair was fastened in a bun, *chongo*-style, at the base of his neck, and he stood ramrod straight. His gaze was curiously penetrating and as sharp as an eagle's.

"You've heard that one of our tribal officials has held a news conference?" Seeing her nod, he continued. "His points were valid, though his timing was ill-advised."

"I understand everyone's concern, and I want to assure you that we'll treat what we find with respect."

Before she could say any more, Henderson Begay entered, leaving the door standing open behind him. Tall, with jet black hair and eyes that were even blacker, he cast an imposing figure. Begay noted her presence with contempt, then glanced at the others one by one. "The conference will be broadcast again at six o'clock. Channel Seven sent a reporter by helicopter to interview me. Many Indians and Anglos all over the Four Corners will support our rights to whatever the hogan and cave contain."

"No one is trying to *keep* the objects from their rightful heirs," she answered calmly, "whoever they may be."

"Then you'll leave and turn over the site to us immediately?" Begay challenged.

Marla shook her head slowly. "No, but we could work together. Your unfortunate press conference may result in the very situation you feared the most. If you want the site to be secure, then you've got to help me protect it. Our funds are desperately short...."

"You want financial help from us?" Begay's voice rose, and he burst out laughing. "Lady, you have a lot of nerve."

"The items of Navajo origin will eventually be returned to the tribe. You have a stake in this, too."

"What you suggest isn't possible," Billy Todacheene answered. "We can't fund what we believe to be desecration." He paused and added, "And dangerous to everyone as well."

"Then please don't talk to the press anymore unless we agree to a joint statement. The last thing either of us wants is a horde of pothunters digging on both sides of the reservation fence."

Billy glanced at the others, not bothering to look at Begay, then nodded. "That seems reasonable."

Begay's expression turned hard. "You would make agreements with the college that is working *against* us?"

Billy's expression turned stone-cold. "I remind you that to work against the decisions made in this room is to work against the tribe."

"You are giving the college a big advantage," Begay insisted. "If I go along with you on this, it will be only on one condition."

"You can't overrule what I decide," Todacheene said.

"No, but I can make things very difficult. Hear me out."

Todacheene nodded once. "Go ahead."

There was an aura of danger in the room—she could feel it. Whatever was transpiring between the two men transcended this current argument.

"One of us must remain at that site all the time," Begay said. "There's danger there that *bilagáanas* discount too easily. We'll also need someone we trust to record every item found for when the time comes for us to reclaim what's ours." He glanced at Marla. "We want to make sure nothing gets 'lost.'"

"Our records are meticulously kept, and we'll cooperate with you."

Tsosie exhaled loudly. "How will we choose who stays at that place? No Navajo is going to want that duty."

"I'll volunteer," Begay answered. "My house is next to the site."

Todacheene shook his head. "And at reelection time you'll stand in the back of your pickup and tell the crowd you protected the Dineh from the bad judgment of the Tribal Council. No. The person who stays there must be someone who has nothing to gain." He glanced at Sam. "You're the logical choice."

"What? Me? I have clients among our people who need me to represent them, Uncle," he protested, "and tribal business, as well. I can't stay there full-time."

"There are two other attorneys that can take over your legal duties while you're away. This won't last forever."

Sam glanced at Marla. "Would you excuse us for a moment?"

Marla nodded, and with her heart in her throat, stepped out into the hall, closing the door behind her. Sam at her side on a twenty-four-hour basis? It was incredibly difficult to stay focused on her work around him now! With everything else that was going on, this was the last thing she needed. Surely he'd be able to talk them out of it.

She held her breath as Sam stepped out of the office a few minutes later. It was impossible to read his expression. "So what's their decision?" Her heart hammered against her ribs.

"I'm to stay at the site unless my presence elsewhere is required. That means that I'll be there unless I'm working to stop you."

An enemy in the camp. And this one would be dangerous to her on every imaginable level. She felt her mouth go as dry as the desert air. "I said before that you're welcome to join us, but we don't dig on a twenty-four-hour basis. Surely there's no reason for you to be there *all* the time."

"I agree, but unfortunately they don't. Would you come with me? I need to stop by my office, then we'll go."

As she accompanied him down a series of short hallways, she felt a momentary sense of dislocation. Above the sounds of telephones ringing and people laughing, the Navajo language station could be heard coming over the radio. In the very midst of the familiar noises was a different culture that regarded her as an intruder, and a hostile and dangerous one at that.

They stepped inside his office a moment later, and Sam waved her to a comfortable chair. After taking out several folders from the file cabinet, he glanced back at her. "Can you wait here for me? I need to meet with the attorney who'll be taking over some cases for me."

"No problem."

She was staring out his window overlooking the red cliffs when she heard portions of a conversation outside.

"You wait," one man said as they walked past Sam's open door. "He'll have the *bilagáana* woman eating out of his hand before long. Why do you think Todacheene ordered him to stay there? Sam is *good* with the ladies."

The men laughed and the sound seemed to cut right through her. She'd thought she'd seen caring and gentleness in his gaze, but now she wasn't so sure. Maybe what she'd really seen was an act meant to manipulate her. She felt betrayed, but not so much by Sam as by her own desires. Maybe all she'd seen in his eyes was what she'd wanted to find mirrored there.

A few minutes later, Sam stepped back inside. "Are you ready? If you'd like, we could stop and have dinner on the way back. There's a café not too far from here that has terrific mutton stew."

"No, I'd rather go straight back," she said calmly.

He gave her a long, speculative look. "Is something wrong?"

She shook her head. "Not yet. But gossip is easy to get
started, and could harm both of us. We need to keep our
association on a business level."

His eyes were gentle. "Are you afraid the attraction between us could lead to problems?" His voice was soft, so
that only she could hear.

"Attraction? I think your fantasies are getting away from
you," she countered.

He walked with her to his pickup. "You shouldn't hide
the truth from yourself, woman," he answered, undeterred. "That can only create bigger problems."

The directness of his statement stopped Marla in her
tracks. She gave him her haughtiest look. "I'm impressed.
You bring new meaning to the word 'egomaniac.'"

His expression turned hard as if her evasion had done
nothing except try his patience. "Acknowledging what
happens when you and I are together doesn't mean that either one of us has to do anything about it," he said calmly.
"But denying it means we leave ourselves unguarded."

Her mind was reeling. So what was he saying? Was he as
attracted to her as she was to him, or was it only a well-
planned campaign? "We both have jobs to do. Let's concentrate on that, and stop trying to analyze things that have
no answers," she answered finally.

He nodded. "You may be right."

And that, she figured, was as close as they'd ever get to
agreeing on anything.

THE FOLLOWING MORNING, around midday, Marla and
Lena drove down the highway toward the site. Clusters of
boulders that had tumbled from the heights of the Hogback littered the landscape around their destination.

Marla slowed the heavy recreational vehicle to a crawl as
a pickup hauling firewood in front of them turned off onto
a side road. "This RV is just what we needed, Lena. We
had to have something more secure than tents to sleep in
after all the trouble we've had."

"Yeah, I'm glad you remembered this old thing. I'[ve]
forgotten all about it."

"It was donated to the science department several year[s]
ago to use for field studies. But it's been just sitting in [a]
parking lot since last winter."

As they drew near the site, Lena leaned forward. "That'[s]
the biggest crowd of protesters yet."

Marla's gaze strayed over the faces as they drew near.
"Begay must have received support from all over. I se[e]
quite a few Anglos there."

Some of the protesters moved to block the path leadin[g]
to the site, and Lena tried frantically to wave them aside.
"They want to keep us from going in!"

Marla groaned. "One of Begay's tricks, I'm sure. H[e]
might even have some reporters in the crowd." She tappe[d]
the horn lightly and slowed the vehicle to a crawl. "Get of[f]
the road," she yelled, leaning out the window.

Begay came to the front along with a dozen followers[,]
smiling benignly. "We're not moving."

Marla stopped the RV, put the vehicle in park, the[n]
opened the door. She stood on the running board, lookin[g]
down at Begay although she spoke loudly enough for ev[-]
eryone to hear. "If you continue to violate our rights, I'[ll]
call in the state police. Then you could all be jailed." Sh[e]
glanced at the others. "All, that is, except this politi[-]
cian—" she gestured toward Begay "—who has enoug[h]
powerful friends to make bail instantly."

Marla slipped back behind the wheel, noting that non[e]
of those blocking the road had moved. "I'm comin[g]
through now. Please step aside." She switched on the ig[-]
nition and started inching forward.

Lena suddenly bolted upright. "Stop!"

Marla slammed on the brakes, but not before she hear[d]
a loud thump and a scream.

Chapter Seven

Lena leaned forward, trying to look out the windshield. "He stepped out of nowhere! Then he hit the side and bounced back. Did you hear that horrible thump?"

"I've got to help him." Marla switched off the ignition and leaped out of the vehicle. Pushing her way through the noisy crowd, she saw the supine figure on the ground beside the fender. The man's face was contorted in pain, and his legs splayed out at an odd angle. The thought that he might be paralyzed made her tremble. People were giving him room, staring, but not offering any help.

Abruptly she heard a familiar voice boom out from behind her. "Harvey, get up. The game's over. Go home."

Marla turned and Sam walked closer, a disgusted look on his face.

"Come on, Harvey, enough."

Marla stared in horror as Sam prodded the injured Anglo man with his foot. Instead of helping the victim, Sam actually seemed on the verge of bursting out in laughter!

"Get up, you old trickster."

"Okay, okay," the man grumbled, rising easily to his feet and dusting himself off.

Marla gaped at him, dumbfounded. "What the—"

Harvey, a small man in his late fifties, rubbed his ribs with one hand. "I must be getting rusty. I don't do my rolls as smoothly as I used to." He glanced at Marla and shrugged. "So I made a miraculous recovery."

He disappeared around the side of the RV before she could say anything to him. "What the heck was that all about?" she asked Sam.

"Harvey is accident prone. He has a history of 'being struck' by cars driven by rich tourists. Then, just as soon as he gets money for medical care, he has the most miraculous recoveries."

For a moment her knees felt weak. Relief, then anger swelled inside her as her eyes swept the crowd. They'd quieted down considerably, watching to see what would happen next. She looked over at Sam. "I wouldn't have known if you hadn't been here. No one else would have told me," she added pointedly.

"That's probably true," he admitted, then shifted his attention to the others, mostly Navajo women and men. "I suggest that you all clear the road. This isn't going to accomplish anything, and some of you could get hurt for real." As he moved to help an elderly Navajo who had sat down on the road, he added, "I'm on your side, believe me. I just don't want any of the Dineh injured or in jail."

Begay met him near the fence line as the crowd began to thin out. "Too bad she heard that last part, Nephew," he said, avoiding the use of his name. "You lost a few points. But you still have a woman there who owes you a favor."

Sam headed back past Begay as if he scarcely merited his attention. As he noted Marla's hardened expression, the reason for her abrupt change of mood back at the tribal government center suddenly became clear. She must have heard gossip about him.

For a second he considered explaining, but then changed his mind. The way she felt about him made no difference. He couldn't see his future linked to a woman who inventoried graveyards as her profession. And as long as he kept that firmly in mind, he'd be just fine.

"I'll tell you what," he said to Marla. "I'll pull up ahead of you in my pickup. You can drive the RV on in behind me."

"Okay," Marla replied.

As he drove up, people stood silently on both sides of the road. Sam checked the rearview mirror more often than was necessary trying to assure himself that she was all right. Judging from the earlier pallor of her face, she'd been badly shaken.

As soon as they reached the site, however, she seemed to relax. Here she was as clearly in her element as he was out of his. Sam walked with Marla to the cave, and joined two of the students inside the partially caved-in hogan. The structure had been reinforced with a simple scaffold of steel tubing to prevent any further collapse.

With the strap of his camera slung over one shoulder, Sam felt like a tourist who had wandered into a dangerous part of town. Despite his uneasiness, though, he methodically recorded their progress as they uncovered the club and the flint knife at the feet of the Slayer impersonator. They used artist brushes and puffs of air from plastic squeeze bottles to clear away the sand. The dirt removed was lifted by bucket up out of the hogan, and sifted through wire screens by others in the crew working above.

As Marla sketched each object within the grid they had laid out, he reached into his jacket pocket, touching the small pollen bag he carried for personal safety.

"You're a very brave man," Carmen said, looking up from where she was working. "Your religion tells you that this place is dangerous, yet you stay because of your tribe."

"I'm just doing my best to safeguard everyone here."

"How?" Tony asked.

Marla turned around, feeling the power of Sam's voice and its effect on her. She didn't want to respond to him, but it was like trying to fight something that was meant to be. She shook herself free of the enchantment.

"Most people from my tribe have personal wards that offer protection. I'm carrying one now." He pulled out the small pouch. If they could learn more about The Way, maybe they would understand why a site like this deserved to be protected. "Inside is corn pollen and a rock crystal. The pollen is sacred to us. It symbolizes the continuity of life, peace and harmony. The rock crystal is linked to our creation. At the beginning, a crystal was put in the mouth of every person so that whatever he or she said would come true. So when you put them together in a bag, the pollen is there for well-being, the rock crystal to make the words of the prayer come true."

"That's beautiful," Carmen said.

"Our ways go back to antiquity. It's what defines us and holds us together as a people. Without that..." He shrugged and looked from one to the other. "Sites like these touch the heart of the Dineh. It's our past, but it also affects us now. You can't separate our beliefs from who we are."

Carmen glanced at Marla. "Isn't there something else we can be doing to prove that we do respect and value their customs?"

Marla saw the expressions on her students' faces. Sam's argument had touched all of them. "We're doing all we can, and will continue to do everything in our power to see that Navajo beliefs are taken into account. That's why he's here."

Sam started to say something, when soft, muted crying came from somewhere above. "Is there a child nearby?"

Marla stood up. "No. At least I didn't see one." She climbed to the top of the ladder, and caught Lena's eye. "The sound didn't come from inside the cave, did it?"

Lena glanced at the others working alongside her. "I think it was out here someplace. But it's hard to say exactly where it came from."

"We have to look around," Marla said firmly. "Caves are too dangerous for kids to mess around in."

Those in the hogan climbed out, and together with the students already at ground level made an extensive search of the area. A short time later, the teams met by the cave entrance. None had found any evidence of a child. Marla tried to hide her anxiety. "Maybe it was a trick of the wind," she said, then glanced at Sam. That explanation didn't really satisfy him, either. "Let's continue working, but keep listening. If we hear it again, try to pinpoint its location."

Sam watched Marla as she excavated her sectioned-off square of hogan floor. The students above and in the hogan had paired off and seemed to have an easy rapport working together. Marla remained alone. Even though her job required her to work with people, the woman seemed to be very much of a loner.

His mind was alive with speculations, when they all heard the sound again. He froze, scarcely breathing. It wasn't a crying sound, but faint words spoken in a high-pitched voice. The hairs on the back of his neck stood on end.

"It came from outside. I'm sure of it," Marla said, looking up toward the entrance hole. Those working above had gathered around the ladder, waiting for instructions on how to proceed.

"Let's go take another look," Sam suggested. "Split up and concentrate on an area, say, twenty yards from the entrance. If the sound had been any farther away, we wouldn't have heard it, not over the protesters outside."

She nodded. "One more thing." Suddenly cold, Marla zipped up her nylon Windbreaker. "This might be another trick, so keep your wits about you. And don't make the search obvious. It's better not to raise too many questions for the people watching."

Sam walked beside her as they emerged from the cave. "I don't think this is something the protesters cooked up. They've stayed away from the site itself."

"There were some Anglos in the crowd who would approach."

"True, but I don't believe the Navajos among them would allow it. They may not know exactly what's been found, but they don't want anyone messing around with things here."

"Then how else would you explain that cry? It sounded like a child and there are no children here."

"I don't think it was a child's voice." He paused, then ran a hand through his hair. "The sound was close, but we're still off the mark."

"In what way?"

"That's just it. I can't say exactly. But I know I'm right."

Ten minutes later, they gathered around the cave again. The others had drifted back casually, making it appear as if they'd all simply taken a break.

"Anyone have any theories?" Marla glanced at the puzzled faces. She had to admit it was unnerving, and not finding any explanation made it even more so.

"Maybe it *was* just the wind...." Liz said slowly.

Tony shook his head. "Don't think so."

Carmen frowned. "Okay, so we know it wasn't a kid. We would have found the child or some footprints. Let's give it a rest for now, and get back to work. Maybe an idea will come to us later."

The tension was high among them, but the only sounds they heard were the protesters, chanting in unison again. Marla studied her students' faces, realizing that no one had mentioned the possibility that had undoubtedly occurred to all of them. Maybe there was something to the Navajo belief in the *chindi*.

Marla stared at the ground, her thoughts troubled. She preferred to think that what they'd heard was some unexplained phenomenon created by air currents around the cave or hogan. Yet unsettling events like these just added strength to Sam's contention that the site would yield nothing but trouble. Fate, so far, seemed determined to prove him right.

MARLA HELPED THE OTHERS pack up the flint club and the most intact of the Anasazi warrior's weapons and personal items, including a quiver. They left where they were the Slayer impersonator's armor, which was wrapped around the skeleton, and the remnants of clothing from the warriors at Slayer's feet.

"What will you do with the bones and armor?"

"We'll pack up and transport them tomorrow. I don't want the remains disturbed until they are ready to be moved. Everything will receive less handling that way."

"What about that box with the club? Are you making a special trip to the lab with it today?"

"No," she admitted reluctantly. "This artifact will be making another stop. If I'm right, it'll make it possible for me to request additional funds for this excavation."

"What do you plan to do?" he asked suspiciously.

"There's an anthropology seminar tonight in Farmington, at their community college. There'll be professors from other colleges attending, and in fact, one of them is the expert who'll be correlating the dates for the wood from the hogan. But more significantly, two alumni from our college who are known for their generous donations will be there. I'm scheduled to give a lecture about this site. Since this flint club is easily transportable, and the best preserved artifact we have on hand, I plan to use it to illustrate how important our work here is."

"Then I'll have to go with you on behalf of the Dineh. Any part of the Slayer impersonator's armor or weapons is invaluable to my tribe."

"I hope you can understand why this is necessary. It's really the fastest way I have to get the funds needed to boost security here. Right now, all we have is one guard the college agreed to provide as a night watchman. To make things even more difficult, the only line of demarcation we have to this site is the sign that Liz placed at the start of the track leading up here. But that's not enough. I want fencing, and whatever else I can get."

Sam nodded. "I don't doubt your motives, but I still have to be there. To you it's a valuable artifact, but you really can't even begin to imagine all the religious ramifications connected to it."

She conceded the point. "Be ready to go at about seven-thirty."

Hector left shortly after four-thirty to get dinner for all of them, and returned thirty minutes later. Gathering around the picnic table beneath the canvas awning, the group made themselves comfortable.

Hector handed out paper bags containing fries and green chili cheeseburgers. "By the way, a reporter from one of the TV stations is hanging around with the protesters. She asked me a few questions when I turned off the highway."

Marla felt her stomach fall. This was the very last thing she needed now. "What kind of questions?"

"She asked how it felt to work on a site that had such a strong link to the supernatural, and whether we'd seen or heard anything out of the ordinary."

"The *chindi* again," she muttered.

Sam shifted, catching Marla's attention. "I would like to ask a favor of you all. In respect for my beliefs, would you refrain from saying that word? Our elders tell us we shouldn't disturb what should remain at rest. By referring to them, particularly using that Navajo word, we believe you are in essence, calling them to you."

Marla nodded. "Sorry about that. We'll watch that from now on."

One by one they finished dinner. "Dulce and I could stay here tonight if you'd like, Professor. We don't have anything that pressing," Carmen said. "I know you have that seminar tonight, and the guys have to get to their jobs."

"Thanks for the offer, but it's not necessary. We'll have a guard here shortly, and Lena will be in the RV with the phone. There's no need for you to alter your plans."

As the group dispersed, Marla began walking uphill to the dig, intending to take one last look around. Sam fell into step beside her. "Your work . . . does it get lonely? I know the students are here with you, but your relationship with them is strictly professional."

Marla nodded. "It has to be, but I don't mind, really. Fieldwork is the best part of my job. I get so absorbed in the work, nothing else seems quite as important. And that's exactly the way it should be."

Sam nodded his understanding. "But you need more than work, everyone does. Harmony depends on balance."

She stepped up to the mouth of the cave. "There's balance in my life, though it might not be readily apparent to others. I have my goals, my hobbies, and I'm content."

"Content isn't happy," he countered.

"Am I being cross-examined here, Counselor?" she said, smiling.

His attention suddenly shifted to a flicker of light flashing beside a clump of brush a hundred yards away. He narrowed his eyes trying hard to make out the object aimed at them. Recognition came an instant later. In a heartbeat, he grabbed Marla hard by the waist, and dived into the cave.

Chapter Eight

"Have you gone crazy?" Marla tried to push Sam away and get up, but his grip tightened.

"Stay down. Sniper!"

"What?" she uttered in stunned disbelief.

Sam waited for a volley of shots, but none came. "Don't move," he warned. Hugging the ground, he slipped over to the other side of the cave opening and peered out carefully. The person had shifted, and now he could see that what he'd taken to be the scope of a hunting rifle was in reality the telephoto lens and tripod support of a camera.

Marla crawled up next to him and groaned. "It's somebody taking photos, probably a reporter. I bet we just gave him some interesting shots."

"Yeah, well, hang on. It's our turn now. I'm going to circle around, and give him a thing or two to worry about."

"No, you'll only make this worse. He's free to take photos from outside the site."

"Not from where he's hiding. He's on reservation land, and that requires a permit from the tribe. Care to bet that he doesn't have one?" Sam smiled. "Let me play this out."

Sam casually walked out of the cave, then hurried around the camp. From what Marla could see, the photographer hadn't moved. A few minutes later, she saw Sam spring out from cover, haul the man to his feet, and grab his camera.

Marla came out of the cave and jogged down to meet them. She came as close as she could, but didn't cross the fence.

"That's my film, bozo," she heard the man with the camera protest. "I want it back."

"You have no permit, and that means you're breaking Navajo laws. Either relinquish it to me, or you can explain what you're doing to the tribal police. If I call them, your camera will be confiscated as evidence."

He cursed. "Okay, already. Take the film!" He glanced around and noticed Marla standing there. "Professor Garrett! What's been happening here? Police reports say there's been a lot of unexplained incidents in this area recently. Do you agree that supernatural forces are at work here?"

"Whoever's causing the problems is as human as..." She paused. "Never mind. Let's just say that the kind of trouble we've had isn't unusual for an archaeological site." She waited as the man jumped the fence and came toward her.

"I'm Fred Saffron, and I work for *Grapevine*," he said. "Our tabloid is first-rate. If you'll cooperate by granting me access to your work site, we could both come out of this winners. You'll have national publicity, and that'll get you extra funds—which I'm sure you can use. I'll get a story my editors and readers will love."

"This is just a dig like any other," Marla said with a shrug. "Boring to anyone who isn't interested in archaeology."

"I've spoken to some of the Navajos farther back along the fence. They insist that ghosts are defending their property, and that's what's causing your problems here. How do you explain hearing pottery being smashed, then finding no traces of it? And what about the strange, wailing voices?" When Marla didn't answer, he continued quickly. "Do you believe in the presence of evil?"

"You're here," she retorted.

Sam laughed. "Okay, let's go. I'm going to escort you back to the road."

"You're making a big mistake, Professor," Saffron insisted, drawing away from Sam. "If you don't cooperate, I'll still run my story, but you won't have any input into it. How does this headline grab you? 'Ghosts Declare War On College Professor'."

"I wouldn't worry about ghosts, Saffron," Sam answered, giving him a nudge toward the road. "I'm the only threat you should be concerned about."

Marla returned to the site, and saw that her students hadn't left. They all stood waiting with worried expressions. She smiled, trying to reassure them. "Everything's okay," she said, and explained about the tabloid reporter.

Lena gave her a quizzical look. "How did he know about the sounds? We certainly haven't told anyone." As Sam approached, Lena gave him a hard look. "Maybe someone's giving out information that's keeping those coyotes hungry out there."

"I missed the first part of this. Care to repeat?" Sam said, his voice low.

Marla saw anger flicker in his eyes. "Lena, this is not—"

"Let her speak," Sam said, his voice resonating with quiet intensity.

Lena's voice faltered, but only for a second. She repeated what she'd said. "Your sympathies are not with what we're trying to do. Why wouldn't you leak information meant to disrupt us? Perhaps you did it hoping to shut us down."

"If you really believe I'm capable of that, then you're not going to believe any answer from me. There's no sense in my standing here and arguing with you."

As he strode off, Marla turned to Lena. "He has to stay here according to the agreement made between the college and the tribe. Don't make things worse by venting your anger."

"Admit it, Professor. You know I made some very good points."

"Yes, but what have you accomplished by antagonizing him? Instead of catching him in what you thought he was doing, you've warned him. If he was guilty, then he'll be even more careful from now on."

Lena's shoulders slumped. "Okay, you're probably right. I have a tendency to blurt out whatever I'm thinking, particularly when I'm angry. I guess I blew it. But I still stand by the points I made. There's been a leak, and he's the logical choice."

IT WAS SHORTLY after six when Lena and Marla, declining Sam's help, placed the box containing the club into the van and locked it for safekeeping. Lena glanced at the gathering of protesters, her eyebrows furrowed. "Is it my imagination, or did that crowd suddenly get much larger?"

"There *are* more of them there," Marla said. "And it looks like some of them are going to pay us a visit." She saw several vehicles heading their way up the dirt track.

"Should I call the state police?" Lena asked.

"Do that right now," Marla said. "I'll go meet the vehicles."

"I'll go with you," Sam said. "I don't like the looks of this."

Marla met them fifty yards from the camp, stopping the vehicles by standing in the track and blocking their way. She shouted to the drivers. "I'm sorry, but this area is restricted. We have state permits that allow us to search here and control access to this site. The sign you passed clearly stated that. You'll have to leave."

The man and woman inside the first van got out and produced press IDs. "The public, including the Navajos in this community, have a right to know what's been happening here," the woman said.

"I'm sorry, but I can't let you remain here. We can't maintain the integrity of the site with crowds of people tramping around. Historical and religious artifacts are too easily damaged by increased activity, and we have to insure their safety. The Navajo tribe understands our reasons for restricting access, and supports it, by the way," she added.

"We have a job to do, too, and we're professionals. Let us in for fifteen minutes. We'll interview you and some of the others, shoot some footage, and leave."

Marla saw a cameraman come up from the second van, and begin to film the activity. She motioned them back. "You'll have to leave. For the time being this site is restricted to college personnel and the tribe's representative."

As they argued, Sam saw Fred Saffron disappear behind one of the television station's vehicles. Realizing he was trying to outflank them, Sam headed him off, blocking his way. "Going someplace?"

"Look, man, you've got to allow the press in there to get the story. That's the only way to stop these confrontations. If you don't, we'll be back every morning. We have a responsibility to the public."

"And I have a responsibility to my tribe. They expect me to protect their interests, and that's exactly what I'm here to do. Now get out of the restricted area."

Marla saw Sam escorting Saffron back as she continued to confront the woman reporter. "As soon as we decide to allow the press in, I'll let you know. Until then, you're just wasting your time."

"You can't keep us in the dark forever," the woman argued. "Sooner or later we'll find a way in there."

"She has other eyes watching." Sam gestured toward the protesters. "They'll prevent you from going where you don't belong. The Navajo people might have been legally forced to accept the college's presence for now, but the same doesn't hold for you. I would advise you not to incite them by trespassing on disputed territory."

Just then the wail of a siren cut through the desert air, and a black-and-white state police car turned off the highway onto the dirt track. A moment later, the patrol vehicle pulled up beside the leading van. "Is there a problem here?" the officer said as he emerged.

Marla looked at the reporter. "It's your move."

The woman glanced at the officer, then back at Marla. "You think you'll keep what's going on here from the public, but you're wrong. I hope you realize that."

Marla thanked the officer as soon as the reporters had gone, then watched him leave, as well.

Sam came up and joined her. "I think you're going to have to hurry to make your meeting," he said, glancing at the setting sun.

Marla looked at her watch. "Oh, darn! You're right." She glanced at his jeans. "Since you'll need to change, too, would you like to meet me up at the college in Farmington?"

"I have a suit in the pickup. It'll only take me a few minutes to change."

"Come on then. We'll both use the RV. There are curtains there and you'll be able to wash up. We'll make better time."

Marla cleaned up, then went to her compartment. As she changed, she could hear Sam moving around on the other side of the fabric. It was disconcerting to undress, knowing he was so close. The scent of his cologne reached her as she hooked her bra, and she was suddenly acutely aware of the way the cloth brushed her nipples. Her imagination strayed, and for a delicious moment she wondered what it would have been like to feel his hands caressing her breasts.

"You almost ready?"

The sound of his voice pulled her thoughts abruptly back to the present. "Yeah," she managed. "Just about." She tried to sound casual, but suspected her voice had been too high-pitched to pass as normal.

By the time she pushed the curtain aside, Sam was already waiting. His eyes seared over her, taking her in from head to toe. Her tailored dress gave her a professional look, yet the embroidered white-on-white accents that edged the open collar and the front pocket softened the image. She looked competent and extremely feminine. The combination packed an incredible sensual wallop, and for a moment he was at a loss for words.

"Shall we take the college's van?" she asked.

He stared at her uncomprehendingly for a moment. Then realizing he'd said absolutely nothing, Sam nodded. "Yeah, sure. It's probably a smoother ride than my pickup."

She smiled. "I wouldn't count on that, but the box with the club is already loaded in the van." She paused for a moment. "On second thought, it might be better if you drove your truck, and I put the box on my lap. Even though everything we pack is heavily padded, I still prefer not to have it bounced around."

"Okay. Let me go pull up closer so you won't have to walk as far in heels in the sand."

"These aren't very high. I can manage."

He shook his head. It was more than gallantry, but he wasn't going to admit it. The truth was, he had no intention of carrying the box with the club any farther than absolutely necessary. Pottery sherds made him uncomfortable enough, but there was no comparison between those and the club. It was like the difference between a chihuahua and a wolf. "I insist. Let me go get the truck."

Marla watched Sam leave. He looked spectacular in a Western-cut suit and bolo tie with an eagle carved from turquoise at its center. She'd often fantasized about what it would have been like to live in the past, with all the adventure and romance. The lure of history had always intrigued her. And here she was, exploring a setting from another time alongside a man like Sam. He was a walking testimony to traditions she'd learned about only through books. He was the stuff her dreams were made of, come to vivid life.

Marla sighed. She was losing her mind. Too many hours working in the sun had finally baked her brain. That was the only possible explanation. Climbing down out of the RV, she walked over to the van.

Lena came over just as Sam pulled up. "Hey, you two look great!"

"Are you sure you don't mind staying here tonight?" Marla asked. "Carmen and Dulce don't have special plans...."

"I'll be fine. There's the guard the college is sending over, remember? Don't give it another thought."

Marla unlocked the side door of the van and picked up the box with the artifact.

"If that's too heavy, leave it there, and I'll get it in a minute." Sam jumped out of his truck, and hurried around to the passenger side to unlock the door.

"I've got it," she answered, and slipped inside the cab of his truck.

He smiled, closing the door for her. Good. He'd have carried the box reluctantly in order to help her, but was glad it hadn't been necessary. Seeking protection for the journey and whatever came afterward, he went over a few lines of the Blessing Way a *hataalii* had taught him, then got into the truck. With a final wave to Lena, they started down the track leading to the highway.

Sam glanced at the box, then back to the road. "Whatever made you go into something like archaeology?"

"It fascinates me. It's a process that helps all of us find our links to the past, and sometimes even learn from it." She hesitated, wanting to ask him something, but uncertain if she should. Gathering her courage, she continued. "Does knowing that I handle objects you consider dangerous make you feel uneasy around me?"

"It bothers me," he said carefully, "but not so much that I'll run away from you." The fire that all too often raced through his veins whenever she was near commanded too much of his attention.

"I'm going to need an ally close at hand if we have more problems with those reporters."

"I'll be here, but Saffron is the one you'll have to worry about most. He's determined to get a story no matter what."

"That's why we need extra funds. We have to tighten security."

"The evil in that place breeds trouble," he answered. "No amount of security will be enough," he added, his voice whisper soft.

ALMOST FOUR HOURS LATER, they headed back. The moon added a pale indigo cast to the stark terrain, and the clear air rendered distinct the outlines of each mesa. Marla turned to look at Sam, noting how his eyes glistened in the half light. "I told you that the artifact would be handled with respect, and you saw that for yourself tonight," Marla finally said, breaking the silence. "Everyone there was eager to look at it, but no one even touched the glass case it's in."

"Smart people. Have you ever considered the possibility that there might be truth in the teachings of my people, that those objects do carry a danger?"

She paused, gathering her thoughts. "There are many archaeological sites with objects believed to be cursed. We do the best we can not to offend anyone."

"That's a nonanswer," he countered. "Do you believe that certain things are inherently evil?"

"I think that some things like jealousy, money and power corrupt. But the evil isn't in things, it's in the people."

"But you *do* believe that certain things bring out, or attract evil." Seeing her nod, he continued. "Then why can't you admit the possibility that there's danger in what you're doing at that site?"

"Even if I felt that the place was evil, it wouldn't be reason enough for me to back away from what's there. You fight evil, you don't give in to it."

Sam shook his head. "Is what you might find there really worth the danger you might confront or release?"

"I won't know for sure until I finish my work, but so far I'd say yes. The knowledge we're gaining is definitely worth it."

Time hung heavy between them. Marla could sense that she hadn't swayed his opinion. The matter of the security fencing had been settled tonight because she'd managed to get the funds, but that hadn't addressed the real problem that lay at the root of his concerns.

The pickup's headlights cut through the pitch-black darkness as the moon disappeared behind a thick layer of clouds. They finished the drive in silence, each lost in their own concerns and questions.

As they approached the site, Marla began to feel uneasy. "Now that Lena and I have the RV, you're more than welcome to either of the tents."

"Thanks, but I prefer to sleep outside." He felt much more comfortable with an unrestricted view of everything around them. He wasn't sure what to expect out here anymore, but he certainly wasn't going to leave himself open to surprises.

As he parked, he glanced around in the darkness. There were no lights in either the RV or the tents. "The guard's pickup is here, but where's your graduate student? Could she be working inside the cave or hogan alone?"

"I doubt it. She probably went to sleep already."

"I'll walk you to the RV, and wait while you make sure," he said, keeping his voice low. He was glad when the moon peered out from behind a cloud, lighting their way once again. "Stay alert, just in case." Something wasn't right. Even the night sounds from the crickets were gone. The air was still and oppressive. His muscles tensed sharply.

As Marla started to climb inside the door of the RV, he placed a hand on her shoulder, stopping her. Wordlessly, he went inside first, looked around the main room, and listened. Finally, he offered her a hand up the step. "See if she's asleep," he whispered.

Marla walked to the end of the small compartment, where one bed was positioned. "She's not here. She must be outside somewhere."

"Is your cellular phone in here?" Seeing her nod, he added, "Give the state police a call now. Then we'll go look."

She dialed quickly, a feeling of foreboding pressing down on her. Taking the phone with her, she walked outside with Sam, glad for the nighttime shadows that gave them some protection. "The guard must be here someplace, we saw his truck. Where could they be?" she whispered urgently. "It's so quiet."

"Let's try the cave first." As they passed the storage shed, a low, long shape lying behind a clump of brush caught Sam's eye. He took a step closer, wanting a better look, then suddenly stopped. "Don't come any closer," he said in a harsh whisper.

"Don't tell me what to do," she snapped, annoyed. Moving up beside him, she followed his line of vision. Her breathing suddenly caught in her throat. Not even her worst nightmares could have prepared her for the sight. One of the digging trowels had been plunged deeply into Lena's back. Only the handle remained visible.

Oblivious to the blood, and swallowing the bitterness that touched the back of her throat, Marla knelt beside her student. "She's still alive," she said, feeling for a pulse at her neck. "We've got to call an ambulance."

He picked up the phone she'd set down, and dialed 911. After making a hurried request for a medical team, he handed it back to her. "I'm going to find the guard."

She nodded. "Be careful."

As Sam moved away, she stayed still, listening to the darkness. She knew he was heading for the cave, but he moved with such stealth across the ground it was impossible to say exactly where he was at any given moment. The minutes passed by slowly.

Marla took Lena's hand, wanting to offer silent comfort though she suspected the gesture was futile. As she waited, she slowly grew aware of a soft, scraping sound. She stayed low, trying to pinpoint the source. There was no way she could call Sam for help; he was too far away. Peering into the darkness, she saw movement about twenty feet to her left. She craned her neck, using a boulder as cover, and caught a glimpse of another prostrate figure. Her heart froze in her chest. She feared the guard had been struck down, too.

Placing Lena's hand gently down, Marla reluctantly left cover. As she drew near, her worst fears were confirmed. The guard lay on his back, his leg caught in the jaws of a massive steel bear trap. A shiny red substance coated the ground around his boot. She felt her knees start to buckle, but she steadied herself against a boulder until the dizziness passed. The man, barely conscious, hardly moved his eyes when he saw her standing there in the dark. "It won't come loose. I tried to pry it open," he said in an agonized whisper.

She made a second call to the emergency number, then knelt beside him. "They don't want me to pry the trap open. I may end up doing even more damage. But help will be here soon. They've dispatched a helicopter. Can you tell me what happened?"

He groaned, his breath coming in shallow gasps. "I heard a noise, and came to investigate. Before I knew it, I'd stepped right in the middle of this thing, and it snapped shut. I yelled for help until I passed out, but no one came. Where's the woman who was here?"

"Lena's been injured, too," Marla said, avoiding the details.

She listened for Sam, afraid to call out, but he failed to appear. Finally unable to stand the wait, she shifted to a crouch. "I'll be back in a minute. I've got to check on Lena, and see if Sam's returned."

As she crept away from cover, she caught a brief flash of movement out of the corner of her eye. She turned quickly, her heart hammering. The spectral Indian warrior that stood about fifty yards away made her blood turn to ice.

An unearthly glow emanated from him and the ornate flint armor covering his torso.

"Slayer," she said, her voice a stunned whisper in the night.

Chapter Nine

Marla's mind went blank until she heard the guard moan. The sound broke through her fears. She glanced back, and quickly positioned herself in front of the injured people. He would have to get past her to get to them. Ready to confront the apparition, she searched the darkness fearfully, but the warrior had vanished.

Suddenly hearing a noise behind her, she turned instantly, but it was Sam. He'd returned and was kneeling beside Lena. She hurried over to him.

"Her heart is still beating," he said, "but they better make it here fast. She's still unconscious, and her life spirit may not return."

Marla told him about the guard. She started to mention seeing the warrior, but abruptly changed her mind. Maybe she'd tell him later. The last thing she needed to do was give him reason to think that she was crumbling under the pressure.

"What were you about to say?" he asked, noting her lapse.

"Nothing. I better get back to the guard, and see how he's doing."

"Did you see something?"

"Nothing that would explain what happened here," she answered, moving away quickly before he could ask anything else.

The ambulance helicopter arrived ten minutes later. While the paramedics tended to the injured, Marla tried to locate Lena's parents, but their telephone number was unlisted. Finally in frustration, she reached the college chaplain who offered to keep trying for her. By the time she finished her telephone conversation, the police had arrived. Leading her and Sam away from the area where the paramedics were working, the officer spoke to them.

"Our crime scene unit is on the way, and this area will be sealed off for tonight, maybe longer," he said.

"I won't touch anything, but I'd like to take a look around," Marla asked. "Do you have any objections?"

"Not at all. Maybe you could tell me if anything's missing or disturbed."

"The RV looked okay, so let's look at the campsite," Marla said.

The officer accompanied them as they walked toward the tents. As they approached the one Sam used to stow some of his gear, they saw that nothing had been left intact. The bedroll had been slashed open and the stuffing scattered everywhere. Papers had been torn, and a small laptop computer smashed.

Sam stared at the mess. "I can replace all of this, but I can't understand what they thought they'd accomplish."

"Is it possible they were looking for something?" the officer suggested.

"I don't know what," Sam answered, then added, "unless they thought that some of the artifacts or the records of their discovery would be here. But inside my sleeping bag?"

"Maybe they got angry when they didn't find whatever it was they were after," the officer ventured.

"I think we better look in the hogan next," Marla said. She thought about the apparition she'd seen. If the Slayer armor was gone, then it would prove to her that she'd been tricked. Why would a *chindi* take the armor out of the hogan, or steal it?

Making sure the ladder was steady, she descended into the hogan, followed by Sam and the officer. Though she'd been prepared for the worst, what she saw there still took her by surprise.

"The armor is gone," Sam observed, glancing at the scattered bones. "But they didn't take everything. The other artifacts are still here."

Marla swallowed, fighting off a horrible sinking feeling in her stomach. "That atlatl, that spear thrower, shouldn't be here. It's one of the first objects I found in the cave . . . and one of the artifacts stolen from us before you came."

"You mean an atlatl *like* the one that was stolen," Sam said, attempting to clarify.

"No. That's the *same one*," she replied quietly. "I recognize the spur and finger loops."

"Wait a minute," the officer said. "Are you saying that they stole the flint breastplate, but brought something back in exchange, like pack rats?"

"That's a good way to put it," Marla conceded.

"But why would they do that?" Sam insisted.

"Who knows? But it's a good way to make me look inept. It's also going to rob some of the artifacts of context. We can't substantiate the atlatl's original location now, so there's no way to verify that it came from this site. Its return and repositioning will cast doubts on the authenticity of anything we find from now on."

"We'll have to take that spear thrower in as evidence, then. With some luck, we'll be able to lift some prints off it," the officer said.

As they climbed up the ladder and came away from the cave, Marla's attention was captured by the swirl of dust the helicopter blades were generating. Looking through it, she discerned Lena and the guard being loaded into the helicopter. She ran over to the medical team, ducking low as she approached. "Can I ride with them to the hospital?" she yelled.

"No, ma'am. That's against regulations." The medic continued to load his gear.

"We can drive in together," Sam, who'd followed her, yelled. "The county hospital in Farmington is less than thirty miles from here."

She nodded, and they ran over to the officer, who'd remained out of the dust. "I'm going to the hospital in Farmington. If you need me, you can reach me there."

"A detective with the county will meet the copter, and an officer will be assigned to guard the injured," the state policeman said.

"You think the attacker will try again?" Marla asked fearfully.

"It's possible, it depends on what they witnessed. Or what the perpetrators think they might have seen."

As Sam and Marla left in his truck, Sam's gut instinct told him there was something Marla was holding back. "What's on your mind?" he finally asked as the silence stretched out for several minutes.

"The discovery of the Slayer armor wasn't public knowledge. Either someone knew exactly where to find it, or they got lucky."

"Are you thinking of Lena's theory that I'm leaking information?" he demanded, his voice suddenly as cold as a February morning.

"It's a possibility," she answered calmly. "Or it could be that one of the people you told decided to take matters into his own hand."

"You mean Begay?"

"Why not? He's organized protesters, called a press conference, and created trouble any way he could. Maybe he got tired of methods that weren't giving him the results he wanted."

"On the reservation we get to know each other very well. I don't particularly like Begay, but he's no more likely to commit murder than I would."

"He might not plan it. But what if Lena walked in on what he was doing? A man in his position has lots to lose."

"Begay's a politician through and through. He'd fight for the right to close the site down, but he'd never approach it himself. It goes against his character. You see, that would create opposition from those who believe that *no one* should go near there, and he doesn't want Navajo enemies."

Lost in thought, Marla stared at the highway lines as they rushed past them. The possibility Lena had raised stayed in her mind, refusing to be brushed aside. She gave Sam a furtive glance, then sighed. In her heart, she just couldn't bring herself to believe that he'd been involved in any way.

"There's something else you're not telling me, isn't there?" He glanced over for a second, then returned his eyes to the road.

It bothered her that he could read her so well. What else had he guessed about her thoughts? "There is one more piece of information, but I need time to sort it out in my mind," she answered. "Otherwise, I could end up sounding like I've gone off the deep end."

He remembered the warrior he'd seen the day they'd been trapped in the shed. "No matter what you tell me, I won't think you've gone crazy."

"Thank you, I think," she answered after a moment. "Don't worry. I intend to talk to the police as soon as we get to the hospital."

Respecting her desire to keep her thoughts to herself, he concentrated on his driving. He hadn't exactly been eager to tell anyone about his own unprovable experience.

By the time they arrived at the county hospital, he was more curious than ever. As they walked through the entrance doors, a plainclothes detective rose from a chair and approached them.

"I'm Detective John Gomez. We've got a guard with each one of your people, but I need to ask you a few questions."

"Fine. There's something I also wanted to tell you." Marla studied him carefully, wondering how he'd take what she had to say. Gomez was a big man with the self-assurance of one who knew he was good at his job. His face was long and thin, giving his features a hard, chiseled look.

"There was one thing I neglected to tell the officer at the site," she admitted slowly. "At first I wasn't even sure I'd really seen it." She explained about the spectral warrior, and saw the look of disbelief that crossed the detective's face.

"This was right after you'd seen the two injured people?" Gomez asked.

"I know what you're thinking. I also thought I might have imagined it, but then when the armor turned up missing, I figured it was a trick. If the people involved wanted to keep their identity a secret, and maybe destroy the credibility of any witness at the same time, that would have been the perfect disguise."

Sam gave Marla a speculative look. He wasn't sure he bought that explanation, but it was certainly possible. He remembered the warrior he'd seen, and wondered. "We better do all we can to keep this piece of information out of the papers," he cautioned. "The press would have a field day."

"I'll keep this under wraps. Count on it," Gomez assured. "No way I'll help them sensationalize this case even more."

After the detective left, Marla hurried to the nurses' station. A young R.N. quickly brought her up-to-date.

"Ms. Mendez is still in surgery. The college chaplain called. He's still trying to locate her family, but has been unsuccessful so far. The guard, Mike Ryan, required some stitches, but should be just fine. His wife is with him now. We'll be keeping him here for observation for a day or so, but we don't expect any complications."

"How soon will there be some news about Lena?"

The nurse shook her head. "That's hard to say. Several hours at least, I would imagine."

Marla walked to the reception area and sat down wearily next to Sam. "I'm glad to hear about the guard, but I'm really frightened for Lena. I wish I'd stayed with her. This wouldn't have happened."

"What happened was beyond your control. What on earth do you think you could have done?"

She shook her head, feeling more helpless than ever, and hating it. "I don't know. Something."

"Or maybe nothing, except end up in the hospital with both of them." He wasn't insensitive to the pain and confusion she felt, but what she needed right now wasn't sympathy. She had to focus on a constructive plan of action. "What has happened can't be changed. Let's concentrate on what we can do about it. The thief apparently expected to find only one person at the site—the guard. Lena took him by surprise. The trap could have taken care of only one person. Whoever we're dealing with may not be very familiar with your operations there."

"I'll call my students after Lena comes out of surgery, and find out who they've spoken to recently," she answered. "But until then, I'm not moving from this hospital."

"You can't do anything here. If you at least try to get some sleep, your thinking will be clearer."

She hesitated, torn between the logic of what he was saying and her need to stay. "And what will you do in the meantime?"

"Notify the tribal chairman, then pay a visit to Begay."

"I thought you didn't believe he had anything to do with this."

"I don't, but it wouldn't hurt to verify his whereabouts tonight. It's also possible he knows something that could help us now. He's been in contact with quite a few people who are opposed to the dig."

Marla told the nurses where they could reach her, then arranged for another guard to protect the site after the police left. With one last glance back at the empty hospital corridor, she left with Sam.

The motel was down the street. They arrived in minutes. Sam waited until she checked in, then said goodbye while she waited for the key. Standing at the lobby window, she watched him drive off. They both had duties to attend to tonight.

Marla walked down to a small, simply furnished room at the end of a long hall. Sitting on the bed, the phone in her lap, she called the college chaplain. She was told Lena's parents were on a camping trip in Colorado, and highway patrolmen were attempting to find them. After thanking the chaplain, Marla then began the process of notifying her students. As casually as possible, she questioned each about their whereabouts, and checked to see if they'd told anyone about the guard or their discoveries.

Tony and Hector had solid alibis since they'd both been at work. Carmen had been with her parents, but Liz and Dulce had both been alone at home. She hoped that the police would have enough sense to know that neither of the students would have been capable of violence. Learning nothing that could help, she finally prepared to make her last call.

She'd been dreading having to notify Dr. Hartman. He'd been looking for a chance to shut her down, and she had no doubt that this would be it. Without her position at the college, the grant and the pilot program for her students would be suspended until someone else reapplied for the funds. And even then there was no guarantee they'd be able to obtain the money. So she'd have to fight him now, more than ever, if he tried to make things impossible for her. After what Lena and the guard had gone through, there was no way she was going to give up.

Hartman's silence was unnerving as she recounted the events. "I haven't reached Lena's parents yet. The college chaplain has the police's cooperation and they'll find them for us," Marla said. "Can you check in her file and see if there's anyone else we can try, another relative or her ex-husband, then call me back?"

"I'll take care of letting them know. You've done quite enough already."

Before she could answer, she heard the dial tone. Marla slammed the receiver down, then lay back on the bed staring at the ceiling, whispering a prayer for Lena.

She wasn't sure when she drifted off to sleep, but the ringing of the telephone suddenly jolted her awake. A nurse's cool professional voice informed her that Lena had died after coming out of surgery. Her parents had arrived just before she passed away.

For the first time she was glad she'd left the hospital. Alone in the motel, there was no reason to hold back her emotions. Placing the receiver back, she allowed the tears to fall freely down her cheeks. She cried for the loss of a woman who'd been on the brink of making a new start in her life, she cried for the loss of someone she'd known, and she cried for herself and her inability to protect someone who'd been under her care. Eventually weariness exacted its price, and sent her into a mercifully deep and dreamless sleep.

She woke up early the following morning, and got ready to go back to the hospital. As she was about to leave, Sam came to her door.

The lines on his face had deepened, making him seem older. "You look as if you've had a bad night," she commented.

"I spoke to the tribal chairman, then had a meeting with Begay."

"Could he account for his whereabouts last night?"

"No, and that's the reason I think he's telling the truth. Begay's wife died a year ago in a car accident, and since then he spends his nights alone in his home. If he'd had several people corroborate an alibi, I would have wondered."

"Maybe you're right."

"I stopped by the hospital and heard about your student. They said you'd been notified." He saw her nod. "I'm very sorry."

"I was on my way over there now."

"Your department chairman is there with her parents, although the police won't release the body just yet."

The tears were about to appear again, but Marla quickly forced herself to swallow, keeping herself in check. "I better get over there and see if there's any way I can help."

"Come on. I'll take you."

They entered the hospital ten minutes later. As they approached the information desk, Lena's parents came from down the hall. Marla went up to offer her condolences, but the hurt and anger in their eyes struck her with the impact of a physical blow. Pulling herself together, she started to speak.

John Mendez held up one hand to stop her, then placed his arm around his wife's shoulders. "Your words don't mean anything to us now. You left my daughter there to die. You knew of the danger."

Marla glanced at Hartman but all she saw in his eyes was contempt. She took a step back and allowed them to pass. They were understandably distraught, but Lena hadn't been there alone. And there was no way anyone could have foreseen what happened. She wanted to shout at them, wishing desperately to decrease her own pain, but she remained silent.

"Let's go check on the guard," Sam suggested, noting the pain etched on her face. There wasn't any way he could have spared her the unexpected cruelty brought about by someone else's grief.

As she walked with Sam down the hall, Detective Gomez caught up with them from behind. "Would you mind visiting Mike Ryan later? I want to question him right now. I'm hoping he'll remember something useful to us. At this point we have very little to go on."

"Lena never recovered consciousness?" Marla asked.

"She said one word in the helicopter. The medic couldn't figure out if she was referring to what had happened to her, or something to do with the dig. Does the word 'Slayer' mean anything special to you?"

Chapter Ten

Marla fought a feeling of vertigo. Every time she thought that nothing else could come as a shock, she invariably found out she was wrong. "Maybe Lena saw the same guy I did. I told you about the warrior," she suggested in an unsteady voice.

"I remember," the detective answered, unconvinced.

Sam felt a prickle at the back of his scalp. If only the *bilagáanas* had left that site alone. But it was too late now. "What's your next step?"

"Trying to figure out what's been going on at that dig, and searching to see if Lena Mendez had any enemies. I suspect that she was killed because she got in the way, but we've got to cover all the bases." He looked at Marla. "Did anyone you know dislike her enough to want her dead?"

"No. I think you'll do far better pursuing the other angle. There're quite a few who want us to stop the excavation and abandon the site," Marla added.

"Will you abandon it now?"

"Not if I can help it. In fact, I'd like to know when I can go back."

"My guess is around noon today. We had teams out there last night and since dawn this morning. The security guard the college sent over is there, too. But let me warn you, the area is crawling with reporters. We've had to run a few back away from the site."

"Then I should be out there right now."

Gomez shrugged. "You won't be allowed past the yellow tape line unless someone needs you for something. And outside it, you'll be mobbed. Have you seen the morning papers?"

She shook her head. "But from your expression, I think that maybe I should."

"Take a look at the *Grapevine*. I don't recommend that rag normally, but you should see the worst first. Then the rest won't seem half as bad."

Sam walked outside with her. "Let's pick up some newspapers then have breakfast. By the time we're through and drive to the site, the police should be finished."

They stopped at a convenience store on the way out of Farmington and Marla picked up two local newspapers and a copy of *Grapevine*. The headline made her cringe. It read Redskin Ghosts Exact Bloody Revenge.

She groaned. "They're making a mockery of everything."

"Including our beliefs," he answered, then walked with her back to his pickup. "Let's go to the *Yah'eh-teh'* Café. I could use something to eat."

"Okay, but I hope you'll excuse me if I don't eat. I'm just not very hungry."

"Well, maybe something on the menu will tempt you. If not, you can have some coffee and we can talk."

Sam pulled out onto the highway and drove west. The New Mexico equivalent of urban sprawl extended for a few miles, then as the road dropped back down into the San Juan River valley, a small café appeared on the right side of the highway.

They went inside and seated themselves in a booth facing south. The mesa above the river was dotted with tall black hills of coal extracted from an open pit mine. Sam ordered Navajo tacos: "fry" bread stuffed with scrambled eggs, red chili and chunks of potato. "You're going to have to make some changes at the site in terms of security. You might consider increasing the number of guards, and arranging to have a shift present all the time. This would also make it possible for you to leave the site at night since you'll have your people there patrolling the area.''

"I can't do that, but I am going to keep at least one guard there all the time. I'll also make sure the RV is double-locked.''

"That's not a bad idea.'' Sam's food arrived, and he ate in silence for several long moments. "The tribe will expect me to file an injunction in district court to try to shut you down.''

"I'll handle things as they come. Whether you like it or not, the law is on my side.''

He stirred his coffee, lost in thought. "I'm worried about *you*. It's more than business.''

Her heart quickened, and she hated herself for the reaction. "Don't say things like that.'' Sam was determined to stop her; she couldn't believe anything he said.

"I think that you must have overheard some gossip about me at the government center. There's always gossip going on at the Rez. You shouldn't pay attention to it.'' He glanced at her, then out the window. Why was he bothering to defend himself? Her opinion of him didn't matter. The way things were now, they could barely accept each other as friends.

"Are you saying that your reputation is undeserved?''

"Yes. I'm considered an eligible bachelor among my tribe, but I don't make conquests to prove my manhood. I don't play games, never have.''

She found herself listening and wanting to believe him, though she'd promised herself she wouldn't. "Then how did the gossip get started?''

He smiled. Direct, just like him. Well, at least she cared enough to listen. "I think the married men I work around envy my life-style. It reminds them of the way they were once, so they embellish it. If nothing else, it's a lot of fun for them.''

"So you're nothing like they say.''

"Find out for yourself,'' he countered, a twinkle in his eye.

"Maybe I will."

Their hands were less than six inches apart, and she had to fight the urge to touch him. She didn't want to trust him as even his friendship was laced with danger. But she couldn't quite make herself back away.

She stared at the tabloid headline, forcing herself to focus on that. "This kind of story is going to bring out curiosity seekers in droves. I'm going to need round-the-clock guards. Maybe the college will agree to fund them."

"*If* they allow you to continue, I'm sure they'll be glad to do that."

He had a point, but she'd deal with that when she had to. Seeing he had finished eating, she glanced at her watch. "It's still early, but I really need to go back to the site. Even if the police team isn't done yet, I'd like to see the crowd and get an idea what we're dealing with."

A half hour later they pulled up to the site. The gathering of reporters and protesters was even bigger than she'd imagined. As Sam drove up the track, someone must have recognized them because the press quickly surrounded the pickup.

"We heard about mysterious voices inside the cave. What did they sound like?" a woman shouted. "Do you think Navajo spirits are at work here?"

Before there was a chance to reply, a uniformed state policeman came up. "This is a restricted area," he said, then recognized Marla.

"You can drive through, but you'll have to stay in the RV until we're finished here."

Sam continued forward as the police officer cleared the way. "That yellow tape line will keep the reporters back only until the police leave. I'd make sure that guard is going to stay."

As soon as they reached the RV, Marla called and made arrangements with the security chief at the college. "He'll contact some of his men, and set up shifts with those who want to make some extra money. We should have two here later to relieve the man who's been here all night. I'll dip into my savings account and pay for them myself, if I have to."

Marla watched the crime scene unit from the RV window. The team had apparently worked for a few hours last night, then returned at daylight to finish up. Now they finally appeared ready to leave. "I hope the guards get here soon. The reporters don't look like they're prepared to be reasonable."

He placed a hand on her shoulder. "Don't worry. I've been told I can be very intimidating when I go into my prosecuting attorney mode," he said, smiling.

As they watched the police vehicles disappear one by one, Marla felt as if she were tottering on the edge of a precipice. She had no idea how one weary guard would be able to restrain the waiting crowd.

As the last police vehicle disappeared down the highway, two trucks turned off and headed up the track. "That's Carmen's truck," she said, surprised, "but I don't recognize the one with the tall camper shell."

"Let's go meet it then," he said, clenching his jaw. The college guard, keeping the crowd at bay, looked uneasy at the arrival of the new vehicles.

As they drew closer, Marla sighed in relief, recognizing Tony at the wheel and Hector beside him on the passenger side. "What on earth are they doing in that thing? It looks like it's about to fall apart. More to the point, what are they doing here? I thought I'd never see any of them at this site again after what happened!"

"Maybe they care about you, even when the going gets tough. Do you find that so hard to believe?"

"Yes," she replied somberly. "All my life I've seen people do the opposite. When my mom and I moved out of the old neighborhood into a tiny apartment, and we weren't in such a nice home anymore, all our friends eventually stopped coming over. I learned back then never to expect much from people. You avoid a lot of disappointment that way."

"They're here..." He paused, then continued, "And so am I." He brushed her shoulder with his hand, and felt the shivers that cascaded down her spine. "But I'd still like to hear you say that you're glad I'm with you." He wanted her to admit the very thing she'd avoided acknowledging.

"Please don't ask me that."

"It's too late, woman. I already have."

She watched him for a moment, marveling at the depth of caring she could see in his gaze. She felt the silken web of emotion that drew her to him tighten ever so slightly. "There are questions that shouldn't be asked because the answers shouldn't be given," she said quietly.

Hearing the vehicles approach, she walked toward the yellow tape line the police had put up. Just then, she saw a third vehicle, one she didn't recognize, coming up the dirt track. She walked down the road, intending to block their way, when she spotted more uniformed guards inside.

The one on the passenger side stepped out of the Jeep and came toward her. "All three of us will remain until the situation here quiets down." He strode over to the other guard, had a quick conversation, then went to meet the noisy crowd. "This area is restricted," he said in a loud voice. "Please do not attempt to trespass." He pulled a pair of handcuffs from his belt. "Anyone who fails to comply will be detained for the police."

The reporters started to move away, although their grumbles made it clear they weren't happy with the situation. Satisfied, Marla went to greet her students. Carmen rushed to her, a worried look on her face, and threw her arms around her, hugging her tightly. "We're so sorry about what happened to Lena! But we knew you'd need us here so we came as fast as we could."

Dulce glanced at the reporters. "Are we going to continue the dig?"

"For the record, we think you should," Tony said firmly before she could answer. "We realize that it'll be dangerous, but we'll take precautions and stay alert. Criminals shouldn't be allowed to dictate what we do."

"I agree," Hector added. "I spoke to my dad, and he's loaned us his old camper. We'll be staying at the site as often as we can, but the camper will be here round the clock. That way no one can tell how many of us are around."

Carmen nodded in agreement. "We'll stay overnight as often as we can, too. Dulce and I are taking night courses, but we'll work around it." She hesitated. "Liz won't be coming back. She called, and is trying to find another way to stay in school."

Marla nodded. "I can't blame her. She has to do whatever she thinks is right for herself."

"The extra guards took care of the vultures," Tony said, gesturing at the crowd of reporters now moving toward the highway. "What needs to be done next?"

"I think we should all go and check our work areas very carefully," Marla said, leading the way up the hill.

Sam studied the ground as they entered the cave. "Well, if they came in here, they didn't go any farther than the area you've been excavating. There are no footprints leading into the heart of the cave."

Marla and the students verified that nothing seemed to have been disturbed. "There are no indications that they tampered with anything here at all."

"Maybe the murderer was satisfied after he found the armor," Sam suggested. The oblique reference to Lena's death settled over everyone like a heavy weight. A thick, tense silence hung in the air, and everyone stood there awkwardly for a moment.

"Let's go to the hogan and take another look," Marla finally said. "The police and I checked in there last night, but if other artifacts were damaged or missing we didn't notice them at the time."

Without warning, a low, whistling sound tore through the cave. It echoed through the passageway like a mournful wail and lingered in the air. Leaves and dust from a passing whirlwind rattled noisily near the entrance as if accompanying the sound, and then the cave was silent again.

"That was more than the wind," Tony said nervously. "I've been in several caves, and I've never heard anything like that."

The sound had sent its reverberations right through Sam, sharpening his concern. "I think it came from one of the chambers. Wait here. Those places don't have a quick exit." He sprinted toward it. He wasn't sure what he'd find. But he was certain that he was the only one capable of handling the entire gamut of trouble this site held for them.

Hearing footsteps behind him, he quickly turned his head. Both Marla and her students were right behind him. He smiled despite himself, realizing that he should have expected nothing else.

"We're in this together, remember?" Marla whispered as she drew near.

The trilling noise began again, reverberating around the narrow passageway. They stopped, confused by the shifting nature of the high-pitched sound.

"Maybe it's coming from deeper inside the cave," Tony said thoughtfully.

"No, it's just being distorted," Marla answered. "Let's go back toward the entrance."

They made their way slowly to the mouth of the cave. Once they were outside, the echoing seemed to stop, making the sound more directional and easier to pinpoint. A large dust devil hovered outside the cave.

Sam stared at it hard. "S-s-su!" he whispered. The dust devil shifted directions and continued in a wide arc past their camp, shaking the canvas awning.

"What did you just say?" Carmen asked.

"Dust devils are an ill wind. I told it to leave," he answered simply.

Carmen raised her eyebrows. "It worked."

Sam listened as the noise lowered in pitch. "It's out there, in line with the cave, but beyond the camp."

As the tautness left his muscles, he took a deep breath. *Chindi* weren't supposed to appear in daylight, particularly in the middle of a deserted mesa. This had the earmarks of a human trick, or maybe a diversion. The thought brought him to an abrupt stop.

"Let's split up," he said quickly. "I'm getting a strange feeling about this."

"You think it's a trick?" Hector asked quickly.

"Like the one that lured the guard away?" Carmen's voice rose slightly.

"Split up," he repeated.

Marla glanced at her students. "No. All of you go to the RV now. We'll handle this."

Hector shook his head. "No way, Professor. We're here to help, not run away at the first sign of trouble," he insisted. He glanced at the others, who nodded in agreement.

Sam looked at Marla, conveying silently that there was no time to argue. Marla sighed, understanding. "Okay, but let's stay in pairs. Tony, take Dulce with you and go over to the rise just beyond us. You'll have a clear view of the whole area. If you see anything or anyone, whistle, but keep your heads down.

"Hector, Carmen," Marla continued, "circle behind the cave. You'll be on high ground, and close enough to see anyone we flush out. Don't try to stop them, but try to get a good look and remember as much as you can."

"What about you two?" Dulce asked.

"We'll go around the vehicles, and circle behind that cluster of junipers near the arroyo," Sam answered. "We'll approach the sound directly, taking it slowly and cautiously."

Sam crept forward, staying behind cover as much as possible. Without looking, he was aware of Marla behind him; he could *feel* her presence. It was as if an invisible cord had bound them together in some spiritual sense. He brushed the thought aside, concentrating on what he had to do. A skilled hunter, he edged through the camp, listening to every nuance of the desert. He'd just reached the vehicles when some sixth sense warned him of danger.

Something whistled through the air just as he reached for Marla and dived to the ground. An instant later, a loud crash shattered the stillness.

Chapter Eleven

Glass showered down over them, then there was an unnerving silence. Sam remained still, listening, and suddenly heard rapid footsteps. Glancing up, he saw the students running in their direction.

"No! Stay down!" They scattered immediately and took cover.

Relieved, Sam waited for time to pass. When everything remained calm around them, he finally moved away from Marla's side and stood. "Are you okay?" he asked, his eyes taking her in quickly and thoroughly.

"Yes." She brushed the tiny cubes of glass from her hair and got to her feet. "Good thing windshields have safety glass nowadays." She glanced up at him curiously. "You grabbed me before Carmen's windshield burst. How did you know?"

"Something seemed wrong, then I heard a whistling in the air. I wasn't sure what it was, but there wasn't time to debate the probabilities." He waved his arm, gesturing an all clear to the students.

As they rose and started to come forward, Sam walked to the damaged truck. A large, round rock lay on the front seat along with broken glass. "That couldn't have come from very far away, unless we have an Olympian shot-putter out there." His gaze took in every inch of the terrain facing the broken window, as he estimated the trajectory of the rock.

Carmen approached and saw her windshield. "Aw, jeez! Just what I needed. I hope my insurance will cover it."

"Let's try to find him," Tony said, his face set with determination. "I'm tired of this cat-and-mouse game."

"Wait a second," Marla said sternly. "This isn't a prank. We're dealing with someone who's very dangerous."

"And by now he's undoubtedly long gone," Sam reminded her. "But it's possible we might be able to find tracks or something that will give us some clues," he said, careful to leave the decision to her.

Marla considered his suggestion for a moment, then nodded. "Go," she told the students. "But stay together, tread carefully and keep your eyes wide open. Clues, like artifacts, can be obliterated in the blink of an eye. And remember, we're also looking for whatever made the wailing sound we heard inside the cave. I don't think we can attribute that to the rocks."

Sam studied the rock that had smashed the windshield. It was so large it must have been thrown from somewhere nearby. But where?

The feel of her hand on his arm jolted him out of his musings. The warmth ripped through him stoking the fires in him and making them burn even hotter.

"Thanks for not trying to usurp my authority with the students."

As she moved her hand, he was able to think again. "They answer to you, so I would have been out of line. I'm not here to create problems, but to try and contain them," he added, wondering if she'd understand what he meant.

She walked with him to the reservation side. The ground there was thick with brush, and littered with rocks about the size of the one that had been hurled at them. "And what do you think? Can we contain the problems?" she added, her voice barely a whisper.

"I'm not sure, but we have to try. There's nothing else we can do at this point. I'll tell you one thing—that high-pitched trill was a diversion meant to bring us out here."

Thirty minutes later, they all met back at the camp. One look at the downcast faces told Marla their luck hadn't been any better than hers and Sam's. "It's okay, guys. We did our best—that's all we can do."

"We found nothing that would explain the wailing sound," Carmen said. "As for the other..." She shrugged helplessly. "Look around. There are lots of shallow arroyos crisscrossing this area, and rocky ground everywhere. We could look for days and never find anything. Heck, until I saw all the footprints around here, I never realized how many protesters we've had."

Hearing a vehicle coming up the path, Marla turned around. The two remaining guards would have stopped any unauthorized personnel, and since the students were all here, that left only one person. "It's Dr. Hartman," she said, trying to keep her feelings from showing through her words.

As the students walked back to the site to return to work, Sam waited. "I have to make a phone call to the tribal government center. So unless you'd like me to stick around, I'll leave you to your business."

"Go ahead. Use the phone in the RV if you want." As Sam walked toward the RV, Marla turned and watched Hartman approaching. The anger on his face was easy to detect. She'd known that reopening the site would lead to a confrontation, though she hadn't expected it to happen quite so soon. She took a deep breath, bracing herself.

"How on earth did you get any of the students to come back here?" He held up a hand, stemming her answer. "Never mind. The real question is how you can even consider continuing this project after what has happened."

"It's *because* of what has happened that we will continue," she explained, then added one final point. "That's what Lena would have wanted, I'm sure."

"And how do you think the coal company sponsoring your scholarship program will react when they learn that the items you're uncovering are phony?" He handed her the report from the college lab. "The ceremonial ax you found is a fake, less than a year old, probably. The clay pots also seem to be of recent make, but those tests haven't been completed yet."

"Someone is trying to discredit me. We've already questioned the authenticity of that ax. It was in the field report I wrote."

"These faked artifacts compromise the site's integrity, throw suspicion on everything, and threaten the reputation of the college." He ran a hand through his hair in a gesture of exasperation. "And Lena's death is on your hands. It's a direct result of your incompetence."

"That's not fair," she said, struggling to stay calm. "You have no basis for an accusation like that."

Hartman stared at her coldly. "You could easily be next," he added undeterred. "Have you thought of that?"

"I'm aware of the risks, and I've done everything I can to minimize them."

"And you're willing to gamble with their lives, as well?" He gestured toward the site where the students were working.

"They know what's happened, and they're here because they choose to be."

He shook his head in exasperation. "If you won't close the dig, then sign it over to me. I have a lot more experience with fieldwork," he said. "You can continue as my assistant. That'll show the public we're trying to take steps to improve the situation here."

"No." There was no anger in her voice. "The fact remains that my name is on the grant, not yours. I owe it to Lena and the students in this program to see this through, and I have every intention of doing that. If my motives are in question, maybe you should remind those concerned that I'm an unpaid volunteer."

"I can't intercede officially for you if you're set on this disastrous course. I just hope that no one else has to pay for your mistakes." He walked to his vehicle and returned, holding an accordion file of documents. "These are some additional reports I want you to complete, retroactive to the first day here."

She saw the two-inch-thick stack of forms. "What are those?"

"You'll use them to explain everything—supplies, hourly reports for each student, and every step you carry out as long as you're here."

"You can't be serious. If I do all of these, I won't have time for anything else."

"You better find a way. These will be read by me, the college president and the Southwest Archaeological Society. We want specific details of *everything* that goes on here."

She exhaled softly. "All right. I'll get it done."

"One more thing. There's been gossip intimating that you and the tribal representative have something personal going on. You better wake up and smell the coffee, Garrett. He's trying to manipulate you, and it looks to me like he's doing a great job of it. Nez's 'ghost' stories and his charm are ruining what's left of your professional reputation."

As Hartman strode off, Sam returned from making his calls. "I'm sorry, but he was so loud, I couldn't help but overhear a lot of what he said."

"That's okay," she answered, fighting to keep her voice steady. Hartman's words had cut right through her. He seemed more concerned about running the project than about their work or Lena's death. The man was jealous and callous beyond words. Marla turned away, trying to avoid tears in front of Sam.

"For the record, I am not trying to manipulate you with 'ghost' stories," he flung out, as if the accusation had left a bad taste in his mouth.

"I know that," she answered calmly, facing him with an attempt at a reassuring smile.

"He hurt you badly with his words," Sam said in a quiet voice, "yet your defense was just enough to hold him off."

"Spoken like a lawyer," she noted.

"It's an observation," he answered, his voice gentle, "not a challenge. How well do you know him? I got the feeling you were trying to be very diplomatic when he threw that paperwork at you."

"I didn't think fighting with him was the right approach," she admitted. "People I'm responsible for are being threatened right now, and one paid with her life. I *know* how much that hurts. He went through a lot worse. I can't go on the offensive with someone like him."

"What do you mean?" Sam asked. "Can you tell me?"

Marla nodded then glanced up as she heard the students' voices. "Come on. Let's go for a short walk." As they headed away from camp, she continued. "Several years ago when I'd just started teaching here, Hartman fell in love with one of his students, a young woman named Brianne. After a short courtship, he married her. Soon Brianne graduated and got a teaching position of her own. For a while things were just fine, then the gossip started. Brianne was apparently having an affair with one of the other associate professors, and in a small college town news travels fast. Hartman found out and they separated."

"But weren't divorced?"

"No, he refused to give up on her. After the affair ran its course, Brianne went back to Hartman. It looked to everyone like they'd resolved their differences. Then about six months afterward, Brianne left to go on a dig. She was working alone when there was a sudden cave-in. She was crushed under tons of rubble. Hartman blamed himself for not supervising the work at that site more closely."

She gazed off into the distance, jamming her hands into her jeans pockets. "Nowadays his career is the most important thing in his life. He was very upset when I challenged his status by competing for the departmental chair. But I don't think he took my chances too seriously until I got the scholarship grant. He was angrier than ever then, and wouldn't even speak to me unless others were around. Of course, I'm hardly a competitor for the chair now. His concern is that my failures here will reflect on him since he's still the department chairman. He's trying to cover himself by claiming I'm incompetent.''

"You're not.''

"I've got to prove that, though, and the best way is to nail whoever killed Lena. I'm certain it's the same person who's been sabotaging everything we're trying to accomplish here.'' Her voice grew hard. "The killer has to be caught.''

"I have a meeting with Billy Todacheene today. I'll check with the police in Window Rock while I'm there. Maybe they'll have heard something from the state police on either the Slayer armor or the murder.''

"When you first reported what happened to the tribal leaders, what was their reaction?''

"They understand that it's this place, not you, that's creating the problem. But they feel that circumstances have proven out what they've said all along. You'll find nothing good here, and as long as you remain, the troubles will continue, and maybe even worsen.''

"They couldn't possibly get any worse.''

"I'm a stubborn fighter. I don't run away—my actions prove my words. But I doubt that either of us has ever been in a more dangerous situation than the one we're facing here.''

Marla knew he was thinking of the evil the *chindi* awakened in some mortal hearts. Yet she knew that evil had one weakness. It could only exist in the shadows. What they had to do was bring it out into the open and expose it. Then it would never threaten anyone again. "I'm staying and fighting with everything I've got.''

"Sometimes fighting exacts an even higher price. Are you sure you're prepared to face whatever comes?''

"I believe in what we're doing—'' The ear-piercing scream of sirens stopped her before she could finish. Heart racing, she turned toward the dirt track and saw two police cars and a fire truck racing up. She ran as fast as she could to the road, then glanced back up at the site. Now what? Her team was here and all accounted for.

The officer emerged quickly, then jogged toward her. "You have to evacuate everyone immediately. We've had a report that there's a bomb hidden somewhere on this site."

Chapter Twelve

Moving instantly, Marla headed toward the group of students. Carmen and Dulce, coming down the hill because of the excitement, had overheard the officer. Their eyes were wide with fear, and as easy to read as a page from a book. Tony and Hector were also approaching, apprehension etched in their features.

"What do you want us to do, Professor?" Tony asked, after Marla told them of the threat.

"Follow the officer, and get away from here. You'll know when it's safe to come back in."

Marla saw a man in protective gear leading a dog wearing a flak jacket. Terror gnawed into her. "Go," she urged her students. As they headed to one of the patrol cars, she turned and faced the officers. "I'm staying. You'll need someone familiar with this site to help you find all our excavations. The less time spent searching, the safer all of you will be, correct?"

"Well, yes, but—"

"I can help, and you're short of manpower."

The officer glanced at Sam, who stood a half step behind her. "Let me guess, you're staying too?"

"I'm here to make sure this site is protected. That includes helping you now."

"I don't want to argue with you two." The officer's voice was firm.

"Then don't and let's get started. We don't want to jeopardize the bomb team and you by wasting time," Sam answered calmly.

They fanned out, advancing carefully, but Marla saw that Sam was never far from her. She didn't want him here now; she wanted him with the students where he'd be safe. A hundred conflicting emotions raced through her head as she continued searching for a telltale shape on the ground or beneath a vehicle. Had he risked his life because of her, or was he more concerned for the site? It seemed unlikely that either he or the tribe would regret an explosion that would destroy the artifacts and cave forever.

That left concern for her as the answer. The knowledge wrapped itself around her, making her feel protected and wanted. The emotions were even more powerful because they'd been so rare in her life. But now she was more worried about him than ever. He needed her protection, too.

Marla kept checking on Sam as the police dog worked quickly, going from the RV and vehicles to the tents, missing nothing. Yet there was lots of ground around the site to cover, and they didn't know how much time they had. Fear made her hands tremble, and she pushed them inside her pockets, closing them into tight fists. The danger was real to everyone because of what had already happened at the site.

Unexpectedly cutting through her thoughts, Sam called out a warning, gesturing to something on the ground ahead of him. She moved toward him, not having a clue as to how she could protect him, but wanting him to know she was there.

"Stop, woman," Sam hissed through his teeth. "Don't come any closer." What had she been thinking? Had she wanted to share in whatever fate lay in store for him? Dark, heated emotions fired his blood as he berated himself for not having been able to protect her better than this.

The officer in protective gear, his dog on a short leash, approached the object hidden in the center of a cluster of grass. The dog sniffed and sat, indicating the scent was there. Waving everyone back, the officer crouched down, and carefully examined the object. After a minute, he reached over and carefully picked it up. "You can breathe easy, guys. It's a hoax. It's three emergency road flares taped together."

Her legs almost buckled with relief, and she reached out to Sam for support.

Sam took her hand gently, and as their eyes met he felt himself drowning in the shimmering mistiness of her eyes. The woman cared for him, and was as torn by the emotion as he was.

"It's over. For now."

"Who called it in, Officer?" Marla asked. "Were they able to trace the phone call or record it?"

"The call didn't come to the police station. The threat was telephoned to a Farmington newspaper. They called us."

"Another coup for the papers," she said, swallowing fast.

As Sam moved away to talk with the bomb-squad officer, Marla answered the state policeman's questions. A sense of futility almost overwhelmed her, but that feeling was quickly replaced by the acid taste of fear as she saw her students approaching.

"You guys shouldn't stay. Despite the guards, someone managed to place that phony bomb there."

"It could have been there for days," Tony answered, "and the guy phoned it in now to unnerve us."

Carmen looked Marla squarely in the eye. "Don't let this scare you. Things are just starting to go our way. Everything that's happened has put pressure on the state officials. We're going to have more police protection than ever and the college is paying for the two round-the-clock guards as long as we need them. I heard it over the radio while we were waiting to come back in."

Dulce cleared her throat. "There are also some terrible stories about you coming up in the evening papers, so you might as well be prepared. The reporters who were here earlier are really cutting loose. A guy from the tribe, a senator or something, suggested that you could have arranged for the theft of the Slayer armor. He implied that would be a way to get it to the college lab without letting the tribe know.''

"Begay," Sam muttered.

"That was the guy's name," Carmen said. "Apparently he talked to almost every reporter with a pencil."

"Begay should have a chat with the staff at the college," Marla said wearily. "They'd love it if the Slayer armor was safely there in our labs."

"Well, since I'm the one giving you all the bad news," Dulce added, "I might as well tell you that there are more reporters at the end of the dirt track waiting for you to come out. The guards have kept them at bay."

"Okay. Then I suggest those of you who'll be leaving for town tonight do so now. That situation will only get worse. Don't give any statements to the press. I'll do that myself."

"Dulce and I will return after our evening class, but it won't be until late," Carmen said.

"Look, I worry about you guys traveling these roads late at night. They're pretty much deserted. You don't have to come back."

"But we will," Dulce answered. "So there's no sense in you arguing with us."

"All right, but be very careful, okay?" Marla insisted.

As the students left, Marla glanced at Sam. "Why don't you come to the RV and have something to eat? It's close to dinnertime, and we both need some food."

"You'll cook supper for me?" Sam asked, a bemused smile on his face.

"Sure, if you like. We have dehydrated stew, dehydrated tuna casserole and dehydrated lasagna. Your choice."

He cringed. "Some choice." He paused. "I'll take the stew. It sounds the least revolting."

"What a rotten guest you're turning out to be!" she said with a smile.

It felt good to kid around with him, even it was just in passing. The tension of the last few days had held her in a stranglehold that didn't seem to want to let go. As she opened the door to the RV, she heard the cellular phone ring. She rushed over and picked up the receiver.

Hearing Hartman's voice, she tried not to cringe. He hadn't missed the radio broadcast about the bomb threat. "It was a hoax, Dr. Hartman."

"Like half the artifacts you've uncovered?" His words came over in a jumble of static.

"What do you mean?"

"Some of the pots you found. They were of recent Navajo manufacture. You might ask the tribal representative if he knows of a potter whose mark consists of a simple arrow and something else. We couldn't make out the rest from the sherd."

"I'll check it out," she said, her voice taut.

"By the way, the alumni you met with in Farmington also heard of your problems," he snapped. "You'll have your security fencing up by the end of tomorrow."

She placed the receiver down, and told Sam what Hartman had said. She watched him as he considered the matter of the pottery. "I know there are lots of artisans on the reservation," she said. "No one expects you to know just off the top of your head."

"The reservation is a big place, but I do know quite a few people. The mark you described sounds familiar."

"Whose is it?"

"I can't say for certain, but Begay does fire some pottery as a hobby. His marks are an arrow and a willow. They're indicative of his mother's and father's clans."

"Shouldn't we tell someone?"

"I'll talk to him tomorrow, but I can tell you that as far as evidence goes, that's not worth much. His daughter sells whatever pots he makes to the tourists. Although that might have been one of his originally, he can't be expected to keep track of every single piece he's sold. I'm sure that's what he'll say, too."

"He'd have a point," she admitted.

"There's something I want to tell you," he said as she brought out the stew she'd promised him. "You're not going to like it."

She braced herself, wondering if she could take any more bad news. "Go on."

"You're not supposed to know this yet, but I'm filing a suit on behalf of the tribe. We're going to try to stop the dig, citing everything that has happened here."

She stood up so fast that she almost knocked over the chair. "You know what this site means not only to me, but to the students. Couldn't you talk them out of it?"

"No. Those decisions are not up to me. You and I are each loyal to our jobs. You've known that all along." Sam forced himself to remain calm. He wanted her out of this place, and somewhere with him, alone. He wanted to haul her into his arms and kiss her until she forgot everything except his touch. Yet every word that came out of his mouth seemed to be putting more distance between them.

"It's a no-win situation for us, isn't it?" she whispered, moving to the window and staring outside.

"I feel so strongly about you. Don't treat me like the enemy. I've been here when you needed me. What binds me here is much more than my duty to the tribe." Sam gently turned her until she faced him. "For just this one moment, listen to your feelings and let them guide you."

The flash in his eyes kindled a fire deep within her center. Sam stepped closer and brushed her face with his palm. She couldn't even remember her name as desire ribboned through her.

"Let my heart speak to yours," he whispered, and his breath caressed her lips.

The simmering in her blood turned to fire. Needs too powerful to deny spiraled down her, making her body flush with heat. Instinct guiding her, she touched his face gently, tracing his jaw, then his lips.

His mouth parted, his tongue coming forward to touch her fingertips in a feather-light caress. Her body trembled in response.

Need clawed at him. He drew her against his body, spreading his hand over the small of her back, and pressing her into his hardness. He wanted her to know the passion he'd kept under control for her. Her soft whimpers pounded through him like the searing winds that stripped the desert bare. Tangling his fingers into her hair, he drew her head back, taking her mouth with his own. Her lips were so soft, he had to have more. He teased them apart hungrily until she yielded.

Her surrender fueled the fires burning in his blood. He thrust his tongue deep inside her mouth, claiming her, wanting her to understand the possession.

Her mouth was so sweet, and wet. He tried to memorize everything about her, the way she tasted, her scent, her softness. But his body burned white hot, like open flames under the midday sun. He'd never wanted anything as badly as he wanted this woman now. Yet something held him back. Shuddering with the effort it took, he forced himself to pull away. He needed more than the comforts of her body. The knowledge stunned him. He wanted her trust and her love.

Marla stared at him in confusion as he stepped back. Feeling the sharp sense of loss and disappointment stabbing through her, she began to understand. It had been too hot, too intense.

He nodded, acknowledging without words what they both knew. "I'll be sleeping outside if you need me."

"I won't need you," she answered in a ragged whisper.

She watched him walk across the site, her heart breaking. How could she feel so strongly about someone whose loyalties would never be wholly hers? She cleared the tiny lunch table, and picked up the stack of paperwork Dr. Hartman had left for her. Some things hurt too much to think about. Shutting everything out except the papers before her, she began to work.

THE NEXT MORNING, Dulce came to the trailer, a large manila envelope in her hand. "Dr. Hartman gave me this after class last night."

Marla opened it quickly. "It's the lab reports on the other artifacts." She leafed through the papers. "And the wood from the hogan has been dated."

"What's it say?" Dulce leaned over, trying to read upside down.

Marla smiled. She couldn't fault her enthusiasm. "The weapons belonging to the three warriors we found at Slayer's feet have been identified as Anasazi, not Navajo like the Slayer figure seems to be. The Anasazi weapons and what's left of their clothing seems similar to those found in the Chaco Canyon–era community near Aztec, New Mexico. So far, everything checks out."

"What about the tree-ring dating?" Dulce asked, trying to peek without seeming to do so at the other papers.

It felt wonderful to share good news for a change. "Dendrochronology data indicates that the timbers for the roof were cut in 1251 A.D. Our work here, thanks to the scholarship pilot program, has uncovered the earliest Navajo site in the Southwest. Up to now, it was believed to be the ruins near Gobernador, New Mexico, dated around 1540.

"What about the ones around Quemado?" Tony asked, appearing from behind Dulce.

"That dates back to 1387, but although they're linked to the Athapaskans, they're not conclusively Navajo." Marla glanced at Sam, who had come up and was standing a few feet away from the open RV door. "Evidence from this site places your ancestors here in New Mexico much earlier than anyone believed. We've uncovered knowledge that will fill in some gaps in your tribe's cultural history."

"Be prepared, then. It'll be argued now more than ever that the site should be turned over to our tribe."

"It will be, after our work is completed and the knowledge is shared," she added calmly, then turned to her students. "We've finished for now on the hogan. Let's get started on those grids leading farther into the cave."

The morning proved productive. With the guards outside, and workmen erecting a six-foot chain-link fence, they were able to concentrate solely on their tasks. The work progressed at a steady pace, and they found an increasing number of objects as they dug deeper and farther back into the cave.

A small blanket was spread on the cave floor in a place not yet excavated. Weapons of determinate origin, and pottery sherds were placed on top of it. They were cataloguing the morning's discoveries when an officer approached the mouth of the cave and called out for Marla.

She sighed, and walked to the entrance. This had been the first morning when everything had gone well. She fervently hoped this wasn't more bad news.

The officer stood holding a sturdy cardboard box. "We've finished with this artifact so we're returning it to you."

She took it from him and found the spear thrower nestled within the shredded brown paper. "What did the crime lab say?" Marla asked.

"The results aren't in yet. And I'm afraid the bomb components weren't much help, either. The flares could have come from any of a dozen auto parts stores in the area. They're the most common brand."

The officer glanced down at the objects spread on the blanket. "What kind of site is this?" he asked. "Did people live or fight here?"

Tony and Hector came forward. "Good question. We've been wondering if you've come up with a theory yet, Professor."

She nodded. "The Anasazi were nonviolent, but they would defend themselves, and sometimes, rarely, took the initiative. My theory is that they pursued a Navajo raiding party back to their base camp—this place—and laid siege. A rock slide, probably initiated by the Anasazi, engulfed the hogan where the Slayer impersonator and his victims were found, and also blocked the cave entrance. Those unfortunate enough to be in the area were killed instantly by tons of sand and rocks, much like what we found blocking the cave entrance. That's what leads me to believe that we'll be finding more bodies in the cave, and hopefully many well-preserved artifacts. The items that we found near the entrance and in the hogan were covered mostly in dry, loose sand, and that helped preserve them.''

The officer glanced into the cave and shuddered. "I don't see how you do it, Professor. If I spent every day digging for things left behind a gazillion years ago, I'd go nuts.''

She smiled. "Well, it isn't a job for everyone.''

Sam took a position near them as they returned to work. He watched Marla and her students in guarded silence, sketching and photographing each and every article found just as they did. Finally late that afternoon, too tired to continue, Marla and the others stopped for a long break.

Sam approached her as she stood alone outside the cave entrance. "I've told the tribal leaders what you've learned about the site. They're quite upset that you're still working here, knowing it's a place where Navajos died.''

Marla was resolute. "Even if we left, what makes you think looters wouldn't take over?''

"The cave would be sealed,'' he answered.

She opened her hands in a gesture of resignation. "For how long? People would sneak out here with shovels, destroying half of what they dug up. The truth of this place would be lost forever.''

"You wonder why our tribe is so cautious? Why we fight attempts to, as you say, 'share' our culture? The reason is that your people very often come here with the best of intentions, then leave us with a mess we have to live with. You don't know enough about us to really understand.''

"That's not a fair statement. I've studied your tribe for years.''

"You've studied through books, with the clinician's detachment. Come with me now. See it through my eyes and through the eyes of the Dineh. Will you do that?''

"I *know* your people haven't always been treated ethically...."

"Will you come with me?" he repeated. "I want you to see us as more than words in a book. I want you to see with your heart."

He was asking her to understand him as well as his tribe, since to know one was to know the other. His heart had spoken to hers in a way that only another heart could understand. She couldn't refuse. "All right."

She walked with him to his vehicle. "I've studied your tribe's history. The Long Walk to Bosque Redondo in 1863 killed a lot of people. Your tribe was starved into surrender, then forced into a march that you were ill equipped to make. Then you were starved again after being promised food and a new life. All this took place while bureaucrats squabbled back and forth in Washington."

"Yes, you know *facts*, of that I'm very sure. But now take a look at this land they allowed us to keep," he said as he got the pickup under way and drove through a cattle guard onto the reservation. "With so little water, the land couldn't yield very much. Water was a constant problem. Still is. In those years where there's little rainfall, crops continue to wither and die and animals go hungry."

"But you've built schools here, and modernized. Nowadays there are fine communities with roads, bridges and hospitals on the reservation."

"True, but take a closer look," he urged. "Jobs are scarce, and poverty is still very much a part of our daily life. The kids grow up torn between their culture and the Anglo world. They learn their own traditions from us, but then the Anglo world tells them their knowledge is worthless pagan superstition. So they try to blend the two cultures, but what they end up with is a crazy patchwork. In other words, a disaster."

"But many Navajos do quite well, and keep their culture. You did."

"Yeah, but so many others don't. The Anglos tried for decades to make us forget our past, and be ashamed of who

we were. Did you know they would force Navajos to send
their children away to boarding schools, and then beat the
kids when they spoke their own language?''

Sam drove the pickup down toward the San Juan River,
then along a road which topped a wide levee. A large irrigation canal half-full of water was just below them.

"But things are no longer that way. That's what's important. You have quality schools, and government and
tribal funding that allows anyone to get a tuition-paid college education. That all spells progress.''

"Does it? Our culture and our rights get stolen at every
turn unless we fight constantly. Anglo companies come into
the reservation to extract minerals, but they don't protect
the land and the air. Most of the profit leaves with them.
We get a royalty, that's all. Almost every family has learned
a bitter lesson that reminds us to remain constantly on our
guard.''

"What is yours?'' Marla asked, wanting to know everything that she could about him.

"In the late sixties the uranium mill in Shiprock was
closed down. But they didn't clean up the radioactive tail-
ings the processing left behind. Home builders mixed it in
with cement, winds blew it everywhere, and the rains carried it into the river. Kids played in that area for twenty
years. Finally, experts were brought in and said we were in
real trouble. Our home, one we had built room by room as
the family grew, had to be torn down, along with the homes
my friends lived in. We won't know what the radiation did
to our health until years from now. My uncle's family knew
right away. He worked in a uranium mine without a dust
mask, and died of lung cancer before he was forty. They
said it wasn't the radiation, so his family didn't get any
compensation.''

"Most Anglos don't treat your people that way. Be fair.''

"That's true. We have good public services, better roads,
and some people in government now that really care. And
we have made progress in some areas. My ancestors had to
dig by hand canals to irrigate the corn and melons. Now we

have irrigation canals made of concrete in some areas. But water's still a problem, so some things remain the same," he added with a wry smile.

He parked off the side of the road, and guided her toward the deep ditches that lined the edge of an alfalfa field. "We've made the land work for us, though farming wasn't what we did best." He picked up a handful of dry sand, and allowed it to drift away in the hot summer breeze. "But years of mistakes that continue to extract a price made us tougher and much more skeptical."

He met her eyes. "Now you come along and tell us to trust you, that your work will benefit everyone. But our beliefs assure us that what you're doing will cause this tribe untold harm. That's why we fight you—you've left us no other choice."

"Some Eastern and Western tribes have all but disappeared in the last two hundred years, leaving almost no traces behind," she protested. "Out of two hundred Atsugewi Indians who used to live and hunt in California, only one woman remembers the native tongue. Their history is all but forgotten. What my colleagues and I do is preserve what could otherwise be lost forever." They walked around in silence for a long time. "We both have valid points," she said. "I just don't know how to compromise on this."

"There isn't any way to do that."

"If we have a *hataalii* conduct a sing to exorcise any evil, would that help?"

"They won't come unless you agree to leave the site to the tribe. What you continue to do would undermine their efforts." Sam glanced down into a dry arroyo that bordered the field. Beyond that lay Marla's camp.

"What are you looking at?" she asked, following his line of vision.

"Those two holes. They've been recently dug."

"What do you think made them?"

Sam walked ahead, then studied the next section of arroyo. "Not animals. Two more are over here. I'm going down there to take a closer look."

"The site is about what, say two hundred and fifty yards from here?"

"More like three hundred." As he searched for an easy spot to climb down, he caught a glimpse of someone several yards behind them. He continued down into the arroyo as if nothing out of the ordinary had happened, took a quick look around, then climbed out.

"That was fast. Did you figure out what they were?"

"Not really, but something more important's come up," he said quietly. "Don't turn around now, but we're being followed."

"Can you see who it is?" she asked, resisting the urge to look for herself.

"No, they ducked the second they saw me glance in that direction."

"We're out in the open. Maybe we should head back to your pickup."

"Excellent idea, but first let's go down into that irrigation ditch up ahead. The water there is only about ankle deep right now. If we use the ditch as cover, and follow the direction it winds in, we'll come up behind the guy. He won't risk coming up close and having us spot him, so that gives us all the advantage."

"Are you sure that's a good idea? I mean do we really want to confront someone who might be responsible for the death of one person already?"

"I'm a good ally," he said without any particular emphasis. "I wouldn't let any harm come to you, if there was a confrontation. But that's not what we're after. We want to get close enough to identify him, that's all. Are you willing to try? I don't want to force this on you. There is some risk."

"Let's do it," she said after a moment's pause. "I'm tired of the deadly games this guy's playing."

He walked a few more feet ahead, then started descending at an angle into the steep-sided ditch. Marla stayed a little to his left as she made her way down, not wanting to fall over him if she slipped.

As he reached the bottom, he turned to offer her a hand. His touch sent a ripple of pleasure through her as their fingers entwined and she descended those last few steps. Although she knew he'd felt it, his expression remained guarded, his emotions in check.

The water that touched her ankles was cold, and as her feet hit the muddy bottom, her boots began to squish. Marla wasn't sure how he managed, but somehow Sam's boots weren't making the same repulsive noise. She tried to minimize the sound, and was partially successful by staying on the balls of her feet and never quite placing her whole foot down. But she'd never been a ballet dancer, and the rough going was making her calves ache.

They hadn't gone far when he turned, held a finger to his lips, and stopped. He listened carefully, hearing a metallic squeak somewhere up ahead.

In a few seconds the high-pitched noise stopped, replaced by an ominous rumble. It was like distant thunder, only it held a strange undertone. "Climb!" He grabbed her by the waist and threw her upward against the side of the ditch. "Faster!"

But before she could anchor herself in the mud long enough to take another step, a wall of angry water came rushing around a curve of the channel. She barely had time to take a breath when the torrent slammed against them.

Chapter Thirteen

There'd been no time to prepare. One second she'd been clinging to the muddy side of the ditch, the next she'd been swept away. Sputtering and holding her breath, Marla fought to get her head above the water as she was tossed downstream like a piece of driftwood.

Marla threw her arms out in a desperate attempt to reach the bank, but discovered that something had taken hold of her wrist. She tried to pull away, but she couldn't get loose. An instant later, Sam's head bobbed to the surface beside her, and she realized he'd never let go of her hand.

"Don't fight it. Bob like a cork in the water," he managed to gasp as the powerful current carried them down the irrigation ditch.

Choking as she swallowed tiny mouthfuls of muddy water, Marla gripped his arm tightly. Water closed in over her head, swirling around her, yet she could feel Sam. He was a lifeline to sanity, keeping her terror at bay.

Yielding to every survival instinct she possessed, Marla gasped for air every time her head reached the surface, then held it again as she was drawn back under. Her lungs continued to scream for oxygen, but she refused to give in. She concentrated only on one thing: staying alive until they reached calmer water. Intent on breathing, she tried to ignore the pain as she was bounced against rocks and roots projecting from the embankment. The water pushed her forward ahead of Sam, but he continued to hold on to her.

As the current forced him away and her arm stretched out, his grip on her wrist tightened.

His head broke the surface of the water an instant later, and he gasped for air. He looked directly at her for a split second, then the current pulled him down again. There'd been no time for words, but the intensity mirrored in that one look assured her he'd never let go. Pushing away her fears, she forced herself to think. She had to move to the side. If she could grasp hold of something solid, a root or a rock, then maybe she could get them out.

Miraculously, as her head broke the surface, a branch appeared out of nowhere in front of her. "Grab it!" she heard a faraway voice urge.

Twice she tried, but each time she was too tired and slow, and the swirling current propelled her farther down the ditch. Then she heard a woman shout. "It'll be in front of you in another second. Reach for it fast!"

Marla did. Her fingers clenched the wood in a death grip, and she pulled herself closer. Sam grabbed it a heartbeat later with his free hand. Slowly they were dragged through the water toward the side of the ditch by an old Navajo man and woman.

The elderly couple, surprisingly strong, helped them up out of the water and onto dry ground. They lay there, exhausted, for several long moments. Marla was both laughing and crying, but so much mud and water covered her face she knew no one would be able to see the tears. She glanced up at their smiling saviors, and resisted the urge to hug them out of deference to their customs.

Sam rolled over onto his back and looked up. He recognized them as neighbors of his parents from the time he was a child. "*Ah-sheh'heh*, Uncle," he said.

"We saw someone running away, then heard the water. He opened the gate to the big ditch. We had already irrigated this morning, so we came to shut off the water. Then we saw you two in there. What happened?"

Sam explained, making the incident out to be a prank. Marla could tell that their benefactors were far from convinced. "Did you know the person who ran away?" she asked.

"*Doh-tah.*"

She felt her spirits plummet, understanding the term for no. "I thought we'd never get out of there," she said, staring down at the ditch. The flow of water had evened out now, and it looked almost peaceful.

Sam and the Navajo man exchanged a few words. Then as the couple started back to shut off the irrigation gate, Sam turned to Marla. "They don't know what to make of this, but they suspect it wasn't an accident. I think they were also a bit afraid our enemies would become theirs, so before they offered hospitality, I told them we had to be leaving."

"That was a good idea." She was walking beside him when she realized they weren't heading toward his pickup. "Where are we going?" she asked, pulling her wet shirt away from her body. Her ponytail hung limply, sending a small stream of muddy water running down her back.

"I know most of the ground bordering the field is covered with wild grasses and rocks, but I want to look for footprints."

As they searched, the hot desert air absorbed the moisture right out of their clothing. It was almost like standing in a dryer. By the time Sam had finished checking the ground, their clothing had dried into brittle hardness, chafing them as they walked.

"There's nothing conclusive here," he said at last. "This stretch must be used as a shortcut to the main road." They slowly headed back to the pickup. "We're also close to the border of the Rez," he added, "so it's impossible to say whether we're dealing with a trespasser or one of the tribe. The Navajo police will ask around, though. Maybe they'll turn up something."

He started the engine, then rolled down the window. "Do you mind if we stop at my house? I really need a shower." He gave her a wry grin. "Actually, I think your students might also be very grateful if you stopped long enough to clean up.''

"Oh thanks. I thought I'd impressed you with my Eau de Scum." She touched her blouse and grimaced. "I'd love to stand beneath an honest-to-gosh shower and clean off, but then I'd have to get into these clothes again.''

"You could borrow a pair of my jeans and one of my shirts.''

"How far is your house?''

"It's just ahead. See against the hillside? It's the only house around. The neighbors hardly ever gossip,'' he joked.

She laughed. "Yeah, I hear cottontail rabbits and prairie dogs are lousy at idle chitchat.''

Moments later, they arrived at a medium-size cinder-block house. Leaving their muddy shoes and socks near the door, they walked inside. The first thing that caught her attention was the simplicity and openness of his home. In the living room a window encompassed the entire south wall, with a window seat invitingly beneath it. Marla had the impression that the desert outside was part of the decor. She walked across the orange-red tiled floor to take a closer look at an intricately woven Navajo rug hanging on the wall. Suddenly she stopped and glanced down at the floor, making sure the caked mud on her clothing hadn't left a trail.

"Don't worry. You're fine," he assured, joining her. "That's a *Yeibitchai,* or sandpainting rug.''

"They use the same images for healing too, right?''

He nodded. "It's said that it's dangerous to make permanent copies. To protect himself, the artisan always leaves something out. It's the same with the sandpaintings that are sold commercially.''

"It's beautiful,'' she said. The background color was a golden tan. Blues representative of sacred turquoise, yellow and black were woven into a pattern that incorporated dancers, Talking God and Water Sprinkler, two major deities of the Navajo people.

As she admired the rug, he went to a linen closet in the hall, and pulled out several clean towels. "You better take the bathroom in my study. It's small, but it has the better shower." He showed her the way to the office, which was down the hall from the bedroom. "Holler if you need anything. I'm going to report our 'swim' to the police before I shower."

"Clothes?"

"I'll bring them in while you're still in the shower, okay?" He glanced at her speculatively. "My jeans should fit you well enough, except you'll have to roll up the cuffs. And I have a sweatshirt with short sleeves."

"Thanks. I appreciate it and I promise to return them as soon as possible."

"Great! How about thirty minutes from now in my living room?" he teased.

"In your dreams, mister," she countered.

As he closed the door, the room seemed to watch her. This was his domain and everything in here, from the Washington Redskins coffee cup to the law textbook on his desk, attested to Sam. His cologne hung lightly in the air, surrounding her with that maleness she'd come to identify as part of him.

Shaking her head at the direction her thoughts had taken, she walked to the bathroom and allowed her clothes to fall to the floor. The shower felt wonderful, but halfway through, the hot water turned ice-cold. Figuring it was an omen, she allowed the ice-cold droplets to rain down her body and rinse off the soap.

After drying off, she opened the bathroom door just a crack and peered out. He'd said he'd bring in clean clothing while she showered, but if he'd been slow she didn't want to walk out and find him there. As she looked around, she saw the jeans and sweatshirt he'd promised placed on a chair.

Marla walked out naked, feeling awkward, yet knowing she was being foolish. No one could see her. Yet there was an inescapable intimacy about using this room that was so much his. She pulled on his red-and-silver sweatshirt and smoothed it down over her naked skin. A shudder ran over her. That was the problem with an active libido and a creative imagination. The two could mix and become as volatile as gasoline around matches.

She sighed, resolving to put a firm clamp on her wildly inappropriate thoughts. Then she pulled on his jeans. She felt the well-worn fabric touch her in places no one had in years. There hadn't been anyone special in her life since college, and that was more years ago than she cared to remember.

Hearing him walking around in the living room, she finished dressing quickly and went out to meet him. As she stepped inside his living room, she felt the impact of his gaze. It traveled over her leisurely and thoroughly, making her mouth go completely dry. "Thanks for the loan of the clothes," she managed. "I feel one hundred percent better." Standing there in his clothing, so near to him, she could match the searing heat of the desert surrounding them.

"My clothes look good on you," he said, his voice a husky murmur.

Her heart began to pound frantically. Restless, she moved around the room and walked to a *nicho,* a recessed shelf, that held several small fetishes. "They're so small, yet the carvings are really detailed."

"That was my father's work." He ran his finger over one piece. "Each fetish is considered to possess life. The powers associated with the animal the fetish represents are magnified in the human that 'feeds' it corn pollen and cares for it."

She studied the small figures, then her gaze fastened on the smallest one. "Tell me about this creature."

"This one's the badger. Its qualities are courage, tenacity and self-confidence. When they have to fight, they usually give an account of themselves all out of proportion to their size." He picked it up and stretched out his hand. "Take it. A gesture of friendship." He placed it in her palm, then closed her fingers around it, his own hand encircling hers.

She swallowed. If he truly thought that they could be just friends, then he overestimated her self-control. "I'll treasure it always."

His eyes burned as they held hers. "Whenever you look at it, remember me," he whispered.

She couldn't tear her gaze away. She was sinking into the twin black pools that created such sweet secret fires inside her. "I could never forget you." Aching with longing, she felt the warmth of his body as he stepped closer.

"Then kiss me. Give us something more to remember," he murmured, his arms encircling her waist.

She caressed his face slowly and tenderly, dazed by the onslaught of emotions erupting within her. Moistening the tip of her finger, she traced the outline of his mouth.

Sam sucked in his breath. Taking her hand, he placed a kiss in the center of her palm, then traced the imprint with the tip of his tongue.

Desire made her burn with need. An instinct as primitive as the desert guided her as she drew his lips down to meet hers. As they touched in a hot, wet greeting, his restraint seemed to shatter. His mouth moved on hers, hard, hungry and demanding.

Marla clung to his shoulders, feeling his body thrumming beneath her hands. There was no sense of time or place, only needs that were sweeping her away into a world of wonderful sensations. She whimpered into his mouth, desperately wanting more, and knowing that a kiss would never be enough to satisfy her.

It was that knowledge that gave her the courage to pull away. For several long moments, they stared at each other, chests heaving, lips still moist. She saw herself reflected in his eyes, and knew that the intensity of their feelings had also taken him by storm.

"I think I'd better go back to the excavation now," she said, though her knees felt liquid and fire pulsed through her veins.

THE RIDE BACK was filled with a tension neither dared voice. When they arrived at the site, Sam parked near the RV. "I filed a report with the police. They may want to question you or have you sign a statement," he said.

"No problem. I'm sure they know where to find me."

"I'll be back later. I have some other business to attend to."

"All right." She started to get out, then stopped. "Thanks for the clothes, and for the gift."

"You're welcome, to both," he added with a half grin. "Will you be taking the rest of the day off?"

Marla shook her head. "I'll work. It's good for me."

"You just escaped death, and now you're going to spend time with it," Sam murmured, shaking his head. "I just don't understand you."

"Maybe it's easier for you not to." Marla walked away sadly, knowing there was no remedy for the sharp ache in her heart.

Taking a few minutes to compose herself, she approached the cave slowly. Her students, seeing her return in clothing that was clearly not hers, approached her quickly, but the questions didn't go any farther than their eyes.

"Your restraint is admirable," Marla teased, "but you have a right to know what happened." She recounted the events.

"I guess we should all start being very careful, even when we're *away* from the site," Carmen commented.

"Definitely," Marla answered, then shifted the conversation back to their work. They were worried for each other more than themselves, but what they needed now was to concentrate on their work.

The hours passed slowly that afternoon. They found two dart foreshafts with the points still attached, carefully recorded their location, and packed them in newspaper. As they finished, Sam walked up. It was almost dark now, but even in the faint light it was easy to see how tired he was.

"We have to talk," he said, approaching Marla.

"Professor," Tony interrupted, "it's almost time for us to leave for our jobs in town, but we'll be back later."

"Don't worry, guys," she assured. "Everything will be fine."

Dulce and Carmen placed their tools aside. "We have a class tonight, but we can skip it. After what happened to you today, you're bound to want company."

"No, don't let anything interfere with your classes. That's your future. I'm going to take a look around the rest of the cave, and make plans for the remaining excavation."

Sam spoke after the others left. "I wouldn't count on having the opportunity to excavate the rest. I've filed for a court order to stop you until our lawsuit is settled. The tribal leaders have also increased the pressure on state and Federal agencies. We have a very good chance of getting your permits rescinded."

"If that's so, then time is even more crucial than I thought. Now I *really* have to work tonight." She glanced around for the largest flashlight. "Since I'm just going to take a look around, would you like to come with me?"

"If I trust your knowledge to guide us in and out of the cave, will you trust mine and promise not to touch anything you find until daylight at least?"

"Done," Marla replied. She took a flashlight from a backpack of supplies near the entrance. "Let's go."

They went inside the cave, Marla leading the way. As they entered the rocky tunnels, she sensed the tension in him. His concern hadn't been for the artifacts; it had been for her. Even though this was the last place he would have gone on his own, he'd come along to protect her from an evil he believed to be there. The gesture touched her deeply.

As she moved through the network of tunnels, sketching a map on a small clipboard and consulting a compass, the air seemed to grow stale. Sam shoved his hands into his jacket pockets, his face set with determination. "How can you stand it?" he hissed through his teeth. "It's like being buried alive."

"You're experiencing a little claustrophobia," Marla said with a shrug. "It happens in places like this."

"It's not claustrophobia," he protested. "My tribe defines death as a failure to grow and be productive. What awaits after death, if anything, is a shadowy underworld. This place fits both descriptions."

She glanced around. "But things do grow here." She pointed to a daddy longlegs spider. "Some caves harbor bats and even fish, though I doubt this one does. There's plenty of insect life, like crickets."

He pointed to something small crawling through the sand. "Like that scorpion? Death is all Surface People can find here."

Marla started to answer, when she caught a glimpse of several small lights that shimmered in the midst of the darkness ahead. "What on earth...? It's not the right place, or part of the country, for fireflies."

Sam felt a prickling that made the hairs at the back of his scalp stand on end. He suppressed a shudder. It was said that the *chindi* often appeared as spots of fire in the night.

"I'm going to go see what that is," Marla said. "Why don't you wait for me here?" She slipped her flashlight into his hands, taking a small pocket one from her jacket. Without waiting for an answer, she moved on.

"Wait," Sam said, then realized he was talking to himself. Using her flashlight to pick his way along the rocky tunnel floor, he went after her. Marla was like a child who needed protecting because she was totally unaware of danger. And that perhaps frightened him the most. Her unwillingness to recognize it did not lessen the threat one bit.

As he progressed down the tunnel, he wondered how she'd managed to cross ground like this so quickly without ending up flat on her face. Large boulders and narrow openings were scattered everywhere, ready to ambush an unsuspecting intruder.

He slowed down as he reached an area stacked high with loose boulders that had fallen from above. He climbed over the rubble and worked his way down the other side carefully, going from rock to rock. Then, coming to a cross-roads of sorts, he stopped abruptly. To his left lay a narrow passageway about five feet high. To his right was the continuation of the tunnel. He hoped she'd gone down the wider passageway, but a second later, saw the tiny beam of her pocket flashlight cutting through the darkness of the narrow one.

Muttering to himself, he bent over and made his way slowly to a high walled chamber. Marla stood at one end, the narrow beam of her light illuminating the bones of several skeletons. He shuddered, and instinctively stepped back.

"I was trying to find the lights, but found this instead. They must have been trapped here after the cave-in, or maybe this was a burial place," she said quietly.

"The lights might have come from here," he said, his voice taut, "but you won't find the explanation inside a science book."

Marla made a quick sketch and added it to her simple map. "Let's go. There's no need for us to stay here right now. My team and I will return when we're ready to work on this section."

The words hung in the air with a life of their own. He wished she hadn't said that, but it was already too late. His skin prickled again, and his body tensed in anticipation of trouble.

By the time they left the chamber, every nerve in his body seemed to scream with the need for caution. He turned to see if she felt it, and to his surprise saw her shaking. "Are you all right?" he whispered.

"It doesn't feel right in here," she said, her voice low. "I can't explain it any better than that."

"Seal off this area, Marla," he urged.

"I can't. It's not my right."

He would have argued the point more vehemently, but all his instincts told him it was imperative they leave quickly. He stepped aside, waiting for her to take the lead, but she hesitated. His gut tightened. "Don't tell me you're not sure how to get out of here."

"I know the way," she answered after a momentary pause. "Go straight ahead, then turn to your left. Stay in the larger main passageway." She started up the pile of boulders blocking their path, but as she put her foot on a wide slab, it tilted up and slid down. Marla stumbled back into Sam.

He caught her, almost dropping his flashlight, but then another large boulder fell from the top of the pile and bounced down toward them. They jumped aside quickly and the rock just missed their feet.

"Now what?" he asked.

"We have two choices," she answered. "Either we try to pick our way over this and maybe break an ankle, or we check the tunnel that seems to run parallel to this one. It might connect with the main passageway a little farther up."

He aimed his light at the rubble heap. "We can always come back, so let's try the tunnel. Here, better take back the big flashlight. Save the pocket one for now."

Marla nodded in agreement and led the way. The area ahead was inky black, and the beam of the flashlight seemed dwarfed by the oppressive gloom. They followed the passageway's curving pattern, carefully keeping track of any landmarks.

Marla checked her compass at every turn, and continued drawing her map. If this failed to work out, then they could always retrace their steps. She noted the curve of the rock floor, making sure they continued following an upward slope. Then, as the beam of her flashlight sliced through the black interior, Marla stopped in midstride.

Sam, who'd been concentrating on his footing, almost ran into her. Sensing danger, he glanced up quickly. His gaze fastened on the indistinct shadow that blocked their way. The shape seemed to absorb the light from her flashlight, consuming it like a black hole in the vastness of interstellar space. It remained in their path, neither advancing nor retreating.

Fear enveloped him when he realized Marla was moving toward it, curiosity driving her. "No!" He grasped her shoulder and pulled her back behind him.

A gust of wind rose from nowhere, filling the air with the rotting stench of a slaughterhouse. Then a sharp, earsplitting whistle seemed to reverberate against the rock walls, gaining in intensity with each breath he took.

An awareness based on instinct, rather than recollection, swept through him. He knew then he was confronting evil in its purest and deadliest form.

Chapter Fourteen

Marla's flashlight flickered, then suddenly went out. The only light in the tunnel came from the erratic blue sparks radiating from the blackness in front of them. The vague shape began to slowly move toward them. She reached for the smaller pocket light in her pocket, but it slipped through her fingers and fell with a clatter onto the cave floor. She quickly bent to retrieve it, feeling around on the ground, but it was impossible to find.

Marla scrambled to her feet. The lights were less than ten feet away. "Come on, let's get out of here." She grabbed for Sam's shirtsleeve and tugged. "Let's move!" When he didn't react, she gripped his arm hard, and practically yanked him after her. "You can't keep it from advancing! It has no substance!"

"We can't run away. We're trapped in here."

"Follow me." Marla led the way, feeling along the side of the tunnel with her fingers. She had no idea where she was going, but she was determined to put as much distance as she could between the source of the lights and them. Luck kept them both on their feet as they hurried through the passages, stumbling on small rocks littering the cave floor.

Trying to outrun the bluish sparks, she looked over her shoulder often. She was certain it had something to do with trapped gases, but gases inside a cave could be lethal. She wouldn't question the intuition that assured her the void held only death.

They finally slowed a minute later, then stopped in the blackness. She glanced back, but no blue sparks lit up the tunnel. In fact, she couldn't see anything at all, not even her hand in front of her face. "Hang on, I know these batteries are fresh. Maybe there's a loose connection, and if I tighten the top..." A second later, the beam flickered and came back on. "There!"

Sam looked around. This passageway looked like every other one in this nightmarish place. "Where are we?"

"I'm not sure," she admitted after looking at her compass, then her map. "My priority was getting both of us as far from those gases as possible. I was afraid they could be deadly."

"Gases? Is that what you think?" he said, his voice a whisper. "When's the last time you saw anything like that in your work?"

"Well, never, actually." Marla started to move forward, trying to get her bearings. "But I didn't want to risk coming into contact with it."

"That's exactly what I've been telling you all along," he admonished. "Not being able to explain something doesn't mean it isn't a threat."

She glanced up at him, understanding. "If you also believed that whatever we were facing was deadly, then why didn't you run right away? It was as if you wanted to square off with it."

"I was hoping to divert it and give you time to escape."

His words made a lump form at the back of her throat. He firmly believed that he'd come face-to-face with the *chindi*. Yet he'd confronted his worst fears, and been willing to fight to the death so that she might have a chance. What he'd done was akin to a Christian confronting one of Satan's strongest demons. Her throat tightened as emotions too raw to contain welled inside her. "What you did..."

Sam shook his head. "I did nothing that you didn't do for me. I wanted to stay, but you forced me to go. Until I moved, you refused to leave my side. Although you interpreted what you saw differently, you were as convinced as I was that it was deadly."

His voice penetrated her skin, touching her nerve endings and leaving her trembling. He'd awakened her to a truth she'd tried to hide from herself. She'd fallen in love with Sam. It was that complicated, and that simple.

"We had a duty to each other," he continued softly. "Neither of us could willingly betray the pact we made when we came in here together."

His statement jolted her. The realization that he'd acted out of a sense of responsibility rather than love chilled the warm feelings that had flowed through her moments before.

"But now I've got to defer to you. I can't find my way out of here without you to guide us."

He'd hoped to spare her any injury so they *both* could escape. Flawlessly logical. She chided herself for allowing romantic fantasies to delude her into thinking it might have been more.

She forced herself to concentrate on the slant of the rocky tunnel. "If you remember, the entrance is slightly uphill from the recesses of the cave. The trick is to elect passages that lead upward."

She moved as quickly as she could. Though she'd blamed that infernal bluish light on gases, something told her that it was far more than that. She had no desire to meet up with it again.

"You're not really convinced it *was* gases, are you?" he observed, seeing her checking the area behind them.

Marla hesitated. "I'm not discounting it," she answered. "I don't know what we saw."

"That's a beginning."

"If you're relying on your court orders to shut me down, what does it matter what I think?" she countered, still nursing the hurt inside her.

"*I* care what you think, woman. Does that require an explanation?"

She wanted to turn around and demand that he do just that. If she hadn't needed explanations, then she wouldn't have asked!

He gave her a puzzled look in response to her silence. "Human beings operate on several levels," he said gently. "We're capable of many emotions, and often they conflict." He stopped abruptly, and stood with rocklike stillness. "Do you feel that?"

"It's a breeze!" she said, as it brushed against her skin.

"And it smells fresh, not like before," he said with relief.

"We must be near an opening." Marla quickened her steps, aiming the flashlight farther ahead. "There's light somewhere close by. It's no longer completely black in these tunnels."

Hope filled her as she hurried forward. Finally she recognized the chambers where they'd been working. The entrance was just ahead. There was a full moon outside, and after the oppressive tomblike blackness of the cave, it seemed as bright as the sun.

Sam took a deep breath. "It's over." He stepped out into the open and stared at the star-filled sky. As his glance drifted down to the camp, his gut knotted. They'd left one problem, but emerged to another.

She saw it at the same time he did. The tools left near the entrance had been vandalized, practically destroyed. The handle of one shovel had been snapped in two, while several lanterns had been struck with a blunt object.

"Where are the security guards?" she managed, a panic she could barely contain rising up inside her. Her breath was coming in shallow gasps as she tried to brace herself for whatever was out there.

"Let's go find out." He gathered strength from the cold night air of the desert. Focused on protecting both of them, he paused to pick up a four-foot piece of oak handle.

As they walked down the hillside, they first saw a flashlight beam, then a security guard running toward them. "Are you both all right?" he asked, panting from exertion.

Relief washed the tension from her muscles, and she felt as limp as a rag doll. "We're fine. What about you and your partner?"

"I heard something near that arroyo, then saw lights moving back and forth. I figured that a group was trying to sneak up here, so I notified my partner and went to check it out. He stayed at the beginning of the dirt track leading up here, watching for cars, in case it was a diversion."

"Good plan," Sam acknowledged.

"But when I went out to the arroyo, I found absolutely nothing. I figured we'd been right to assume it was a trick so I headed back quickly. Only by then it was too late. Someone had cut a hole in our fence near the reservation side, and left everything in the condition you see now. They tried to break into the camper and trailer, too, but all they did was bang up the locks. They did trash the supplies stored in the shed, though. We've notified the state police, but they only took the report on the phone. They won't be out until tomorrow."

"Where's your partner now?" she asked.

"He's still at his post. No one approached from that side," he answered.

To Marla, it seemed so trivial in comparison to what might have been, the news was actually a relief of sorts. "Well, we can replace supplies, and we'll patch up the fence the best way we can."

Sam stared across at the arroyo, deep in thought. "Tell me about the lights," he asked the guard.

"It was the weirdest sight you've ever seen. It was like a cluster of fireflies. I figured they must have blacked out their flashlights until only pinpoints of light remained. I tried to count the lights, figuring I'd get an idea of how many people were out there, but in the distance they seemed to shift and bounce around. I couldn't keep track."

Marla knew what Sam was thinking. "What about footprints?"

The guard shrugged. "In that section? There's scrub brush and grasses all over the place, and footprints from everything else that's gone on here. Maybe in the daylight we'll be able to see more, but I doubt it."

"I'm going to take a look at the shed," she said, glancing at Sam.

"I'll check out the area around the arroyo and right near the fence."

Borrowing the guard's spare flashlight, Sam walked away, unable to shake off the uneasiness he felt about the guard's report. Pinpoints of light. That's how the nightmare inside the cave had started. Out here a different kind of nightmare, but one all the same.

He walked pensively to the fence. Making sure he didn't obliterate any tracks that may have been there, he carefully picked his way around.

A skilled tracker, he searched the ground methodically, looking for an imprint. From the faint marks he could make out, he knew they'd worn soft moccasins that would minimize their footprints. Any Navajo would have known to do that, but then so would many *bilagáanas*. The evidence was scarcely conclusive.

Questions multiplied in his head and remained unanswered. He was on his way back when he saw Marla coming toward him. "The sherds and dart foreshafts we'd packed and left in the shed are gone now. Do you think the same person who killed Lena is responsible for this?"

"It's possible," he said.

"Did you find any footprints?"

"No, just very light impressions that make me believe the person or persons knew what they were doing."

"Well, we've scored at least a partial victory tonight. What happened out here could have been far worse if it hadn't been for the guards."

"What about inside the cave? Evil contaminates this area, and you know that now as well as I do. Don't try to avoid the truth."

Marla headed back to the trailer. "I'm not avoiding anything." She clamped her mouth shut, realizing that wasn't precisely true. She was avoiding her feelings for him. But certainly nothing else. "I can't explain what we saw in the cave, but that doesn't mean someone else couldn't. Have you considered the possibility that someone might be trying hard to make us believe in spirits?"

"It's always more comforting, and less frightening, to search for rational explanations." He waited by the front of her trailer.

She opened the door. "Would you like to come inside?"

Sam shook his head. "I'm going to take a walk, then call it a night."

"Wait. Before you go, there's something I want you to know." She struggled to find the right words. "I don't share your religious beliefs, but I do respect them. Most religions are rooted in metaphysics, and those concepts never lend themselves easily to explanations. I was just suggesting that there are some who might be willing to confront anything, including that cave at night, in order to stop my work here. To them, it might simply be their way of protecting the tribe."

Sam nodded slowly. "There could be some truth to that." He glanced up at the moon. For now, Father Sky watched over them in peace. "Something happened to me beside the Hogback a long time ago, and I'd like to tell you about it. It'll help you understand. Will you come for a walk with me?"

As they walked around in the shadowy gray light, Sam felt the familiar pull of the empty desert as it welcomed him, and asserted the ties that bound them together. He told her his story, attuned to her without having to check her reaction. "I've tried to tell myself that the experience was mostly my imagination, but deep down I know that's not true."

His candor touched her deeply, and for a few moments she didn't speak. He'd opened himself up to her, and risked a part of his soul he'd bared to no one before. "There are many things science can't explain. I know this, though it's something that has always made me uneasy. I'm much more comfortable with solid facts that I can touch, and feel, and measure. To me that's *real*. Lights that I can't explain, or an intangible evil that I can sense but can't prove, scare me because they open a crack in my thinking. It's like being shown another time or place where sand talks, and the sun rises in the west. Ideas that you took for granted, that kept your world stable, no longer apply. And without those, there are no sturdy pillars to lean against for support.

"My father used to say that as long as we can bend, we survive. The small tree, for instance, yields to the desert winds and lives. But the thick pine that is too rigid to comply gets uprooted and dies."

"Life has taught me how to fight, but never how to yield," Marla answered with a shrug. "I've had to struggle for everything I've ever attained. That meant always looking for and facing facts. It was the only way I could make the most out of whatever opportunities came my way. And that's how I managed to finish college, though the odds had been against me from the start."

"What do you mean?"

"My grades were good, but not good enough to get me a full scholarship. I had to hold two jobs, sometimes three, to make ends meet and still send some money home. Six months before I was ready to graduate, the bookstore where I'd worked for three years shut down. By then, all the other jobs on or around campus were taken for the semester. I went everywhere looking for work, but it didn't do me any good. I had a job waiting for me after graduation, but without the degree, I'd lose it.

"Then I got an idea. I went to an alumnus whose photo was plastered everywhere in the college's small archaeological museum. He'd made generous donations to the archaeology department in the past. I figured I'd give him the chance to invest in a different way—not in a building, but in a person." She smiled. "I waited outside his office for three days before I ever got a chance to see him. But he liked my tenacity. In the end, he loaned me the funds I needed interest free, and told me to consider it a scholarship. I graduated on time, and went on to my job."

Understanding flickered in his eyes. "You received a hardship scholarship, like those you've managed to obtain for your archaeological team here," he observed.

"Exactly, only this one is funded by a private corporation, and promises to continue in the future if our work is completed successfully."

"I can see why this project means so much to you. It's natural to want to help those who keep trying no matter what, especially if you've been there yourself."

They'd been allies inside the cave, and now despite the differences that separated them, that bond remained unsevered. "But you know, my one problem is that although life has made me tough, I'm not nearly as tough as I'd like people to think I am," Marla admitted before she'd realized it.

"That's true."

His arrogance made her glance up, but she suddenly chuckled. "Then again, neither are you."

He lifted one eyebrow, and regarded her coolly. "Woman, I am extremely tough." A smile touched the corners of his mouth. "It's only when I'm around you that the other side emerges. You bring out the gentleness in me."

His eyes shimmered in the moonlight, like coal turned to diamonds. She tried to ignore the sensations rippling through her, but her efforts were futile.

He brushed her cheek with his palm, then pulled his hand away. "I better take you back, *sawe*. You need my protection now more than my love."

Her body tingled with wanting as they returned to the trailer. "What was that word you used?" she asked, her voice unsteady. "I never heard it before."

"Roughly, it means darling." He said good-night quickly, as if worried about the temptation that lingering would pose.

Marla went inside the trailer, then stood by the window and watched him walk toward the tents. There was raw masculine power in the rigid set of his shoulders and the confident way he carried himself. A longing she no longer bothered to deny spiraled through her.

As she turned away, the hollow feeling inside her intensified. Why couldn't her heart see what her mind understood so clearly? It was better not to want something she could never truly have.

SHORTLY AFTER seven-thirty the following morning, Marla prepared to start the new work day. As she opened the door of the trailer, she saw Sam standing there.

"I was getting ready to knock," he said with a chuckle, and lowered his hand.

"You almost did, on my forehead, from the looks of it," she teased. "Come in. I was about to invite the students in for coffee. Will you join us?"

"First, there's something I need to ask you. Who, besides your students and the tribal leaders know when an artifact is uncovered here?"

"That's hard to determine. I make out my report to Dr. Hartman, and that in turn is scanned into the computer records at the college. Assessing the right data banks shouldn't be that difficult for someone with a password or who's savvy with computers."

Dulce knocked on the open trailer door and came in. "Professor, this morning when I stopped by the grocery to pick up some supplies for us, I saw this." She dropped a copy of *Grapevine* on the breakfast table.

Chapter Fifteen

The cover displayed a fuzzy photo of the vandalized equipment from the night before, and another grainy photo of Sam and her emerging from the cave. The story maintained that they'd tried to contact the evil spirits, but had incurred their wrath instead.

"Where does Saffron get this stuff?" Marla cried out in exasperation, then gestured for the other students to come in.

"He makes it up. There's no basis for this piece of garbage," Sam answered. "But there's something that bothers me even more. Those photos had to have been taken last night. That means he was around here somewhere." Sam studied the photo. "From the angle, I'd say he was on the reservation side."

"Begay's land," Marla said angrily. "That man always seems to be involved somehow."

Hearing the cellular phone ring, she picked it up. The second she identified Dr. Hartman's voice, her stomach tightened. Seeing the story had considerably soured his disposition. "I have no idea how long he's been watching us, Dr. Hartman."

"Aren't you aware of *anything* that happens there?" His voice, despite the static, came through perfectly clear. "Was anything else taken?"

"Yes, unfortunately." She filled him in. "I've made out a report."

"Bring it. I'd like to see you here in my office this morning."

"All right. I'll be there as soon as I can," she answered.

Marla hung up, and explained the situation to the others. "I'll leave the cellular phone with you in case there's a problem. You can also expect the state police to come around sometime today."

"Would you like me to drive you in my pickup?" Sam offered. "You can plan how you want to approach your meeting without being distracted by the road."

"I'd appreciate that," she answered.

Carmen poured Marla a mug of coffee and handed it to her. "We'll work in the first chamber while you're gone. The guys can help us catalog any finds."

"Fine, but don't go farther in until I return."

Sam walked with her to the pickup. "Are you going to tell them?"

She seated herself in the passenger seat and waited for him to get under way. "Eventually, but first I have to do more research on that distortion and the twinkling lights. After I talk to Hartman, I'll check with the geology professor and see if he has a scientific explanation."

"And if he doesn't?"

"I don't know. The students need to be warned, but I have to do my homework before I can figure out exactly what to tell them."

"Speaking of homework, I've been thinking about everyone's alibis for the night of Lena's death. Begay's whereabouts, of course, are impossible to verify for any night, just as Hartman's are since he doesn't teach evenings."

"Hartman? You're reaching," she scoffed.

"That's my opinion, too, when you go after Begay."

"Fair enough," she conceded. "We'll dig deeper into both, and keep our minds open for others. I've got the contacts at the college, and you've got them at the reservation. We'll use each other's strengths and make that work for us."

Marla watched the changing landscape out her window. The farmland of rural Kirtland was slowly growing into a bedroom community for larger Farmington. Housing tracts littered the river valley to their right.

Her personal life, however, was changing much more rapidly than northern New Mexico. Her feelings for Sam were deepening with each passing day as her admiration and respect for him grew. Affirmative action programs would have practically insured him a top-notch job with any firm in the state. Yet he'd returned to his own people, ready to defend them, and reconnect with the land and the beliefs that sustained him.

"When you came back, was it hard?" She said the words before she realized that she'd spoken out loud.

"Was *what* hard?" He gave her a startled glance.

She chuckled softly, realizing the slant he'd taken, and justifiably so. The tension in the car was there. Beneath all her other thoughts, more basic instincts clamored for her attention. He'd sensed it, too, judging from the way he was gripping the wheel, his knuckles pearly white. "I was thinking of your return to the reservation after living away for so long at college."

"For a long time I thought of it as a sacrifice I would perform out of duty. But you know, it never was that way. When I crossed back into the Navajo Nation after getting my degree, I knew I'd done what was right for me. I was home to stay."

"I've never felt that way about any particular place. I feel most at home when I'm working. I guess it's a state of mind for me."

"It shouldn't be that way. Your Wind Breath demands that you do more with your life than work. You can't find harmony without balance."

"Not so. My work is a big source of satisfaction. I shape the minds of the students I teach. I broaden their knowledge and horizons."

"But in the meantime, you're limiting your own. Your world of science, facts and absolutes deceives you into thinking that's all there is. Open yourself to possibilities, even if it means taking a few knocks. That's what 'walking in beauty' is all about. It's seeking all of life, and embracing it. It's learning to value the darkness because without it, you can't fully appreciate the light.''

WHEN THEY REACHED Durango forty-five minutes later, she led him through the old but revitalized mining town and up the hill to the college. From here, within the forests of southern Colorado, the site and the reservation seemed almost like a different planet.

"Park here." She gestured to a space with her name on it, located beside a modern-looking building. Pine trees lined the sidewalks leading to other classrooms and laboratories.

Marla went inside with him, but as they approached Hartman's office she slowed her steps. Lost in thought, she tried to prepare mentally for the confrontation.

Sam matched her pace wordlessly, then glanced around. "He'll want to see you alone, so I'll wait out here."

Marla nodded. "There's a soft-drink machine nearby."

As he watched her stride down the hall, he could see Marla had retained her stubborn courage. She stood tall, her hair was tossed back, and her strides were filled with confidence.

He finally turned and walked back down the corridor. Passing a secretary's desk, he smiled. The short, dark-haired woman watched him go by, then casually followed him to the vending machine. "Hi," she greeted, fishing two coins out of her purse.

"Hello." He picked up the can of soda that fell at the bottom, then held it out to her. "This is the only choice, since the rest are sold out."

She laughed. "Thanks. It's what I was after, anyway."

Sam inserted two more quarters, then retrieved the second can. "Is there anyplace around here I can sit down and relax while I wait?"

"Yeah, the department lounge. It's for staff only, but you're working with Professor Garrett at the dig. That's close enough."

He chuckled. "Am I that high profile around here?"

"Sorta," she hedged. "Well, we've all heard about you, and that you're there to stop us."

"I am trying to halt the digging, but all I'm doing at the site is observing," he corrected good-naturedly.

The vivacious woman led him to a small lounge. It was unfurnished except for a large folding table, several chairs and a small table holding a coffeepot and several mugs. A picture window offered a magnificent view of the San Juan Mountains.

"Are they any closer to finding whoever murdered Lena Mendez?" she asked.

"I don't think so. An investigation can be a long process, though. People tell half truths, or don't come forward with information, and the facts have to be gleaned from the stories."

She glanced down, as if disturbed by his answer.

Every instinct he'd sharpened in the courtroom came to life. "Sometimes people hold back, and it has nothing whatsoever to do with the crime under investigation. What they don't realize is that little details seemingly unrelated to the crime sometimes turn out to be crucial. When that happens, the criminals are one step closer to getting away with it."

She turned to the window, gazing out as she took a sip of soda. "Can someone who knows a witness is lying get in trouble?"

"Not if they come forward in time," he assured, forcing himself to be patient. "Otherwise it could be considered obstructing justice."

She traced a pattern on the frost covering the soda can. "Look, if I tell you something that helps, will you keep my name out of it?"

"I can't guarantee it, but I promise to do my best," he added with a nod of encouragement.

She gave him a nervous smile. "Check into Hartman's alibi. He's no murderer, but he's protecting someone."

"Can you help me figure out who that might be?" He flashed her his most charming smile. Mercifully it worked.

"He leads a very private life. The only person he sees day in and day out is his secretary, June Moore." Not waiting, she stood and walked back down the hall.

Sam waited a moment before leaving, knowing it would be better for her if they weren't seen together. After a few minutes he left the lounge. He was halfway down the hall when he saw Marla coming around the corner.

"I hope you didn't get bored waiting. Just as I was leaving Dr. Hartman's office, I saw Dr. Wilson, one of our geology professors. I stopped to ask him a few questions about what we saw in the cave."

"And?"

She shrugged. "He said he'd never heard of anything quite like that, but he'd check it out with experts at the Bureau of Mines."

Sam smiled. "I was also busy while you conducted business." He waited until they were outside the building before telling her what he'd learned.

"That sounds like something Dr. Hartman might do, but to protect himself, not necessarily June. His status means a lot to him."

"Well, if he was with his secretary, then his alibi becomes a lot more solid. I think it's worth checking out."

Marla glanced at her watch. "It's nearly one, so June's probably out to lunch. Her desk was empty when I passed by a few minutes ago. We could try the cafeteria, or the coffee shop across campus."

Twenty-five minutes later, unable to find her at either place, Marla suggested they stop by the anthro building one more time. As they pulled into the parking lot, Marla sat forward in the seat. "There she is! She's just getting out of that blue sedan."

Sam stopped beside it, and Marla got out. "Hi, June!" she greeted.

In her mid-forties, June seemed very concerned about her appearance. Every hair was in place, and her clothing was always impeccable. She and Hartman were suited in that respect. "Hi, Marla. Have you seen Dr. Hartman? I know he was eager to speak to you."

Marla nodded. "We've already had our meeting."

June gave her a sympathetic smile. "I know that you two don't always see eye to eye on things, but remember that he has the good of the department in mind."

"I know that, and I also know how protective you are about him," Marla said gently.

June shrugged. "He's a great boss. He treats me like an equal, and trusts me to carry out whatever needs to be done."

"Loyalty is very rare nowadays. The professor is lucky to have you," Sam interjected as he approached. "But misplaced loyalty can sometimes create trouble that was never intended."

June gave Sam a wary look, then glanced at Marla. "I better go. I'm going to be late."

"June, there's something I think you should know. Dr. Hartman claims that he was alone the night Lena Mendez was killed. That placed him on the police's suspect list."

"Surely no one really thinks he could have harmed that woman!" Her eyes grew wide, and her face paled.

"The police only care about the facts. Since they don't have many leads, Dr. Hartman could be in for a great deal of unpleasantness," Marla said.

"But he's innocent."

"I believe you have information that could clear him completely. If you do, won't you help him by telling us? You'll be keeping the police from embarrassing him when they have to ask the college staff all kinds of questions," Marla insisted.

"I don't know...."

"If they start looking into his background and questioning people around here, how do you think that's going to sit with the regents? They're bound to hear of it."

She nodded. "It never occurred to me that he might lie about us."

"Was he with you?"

She nodded. "We had dinner at my place." She bit her bottom lip, and shifted nervously. "He didn't leave until morning," she added. "Is there any way you can let just the police know?"

"You'll both have to go in and tell them. They won't be pleased, but having you come forward now of your own free will is going to go a long way in placating them."

"I'll talk to Dr. Hartman."

Marla watched June hurry inside. "Hartman is going to go ballistic when he hears about this."

"Maybe not. It'll depend on how she presents it to him. Maybe he'll see you as having his best interests at heart."

Marla's eyes opened wide. "You don't honestly believe that!"

Sam chuckled. "No, I suppose not. But I don't think he's going to be in a position to give you a hard time about it."

"You're probably right," she said, thinking it over.

As they got under way, Marla glanced at her watch. "Before we leave Durango, would you mind making a quick stop by my cottage? It isn't far from here, and I'd like to pick up a few things."

"Not at all. How do we get there?"

She guided him to a small, wood-framed two-bedroom home not far from campus. The house had a fresh coat of sky blue paint trimmed in white, and red miniature roses had been set in a planter on the large porch. It looked well cared for, though admittedly it was far from being sumptuous. "I hope you're not disappointed, but professors and teachers never make much money," she said. "That's reserved for athletic coaches, who lead the academic community, building character and new stadiums," she added cynically.

Sam remembered what she'd said about work being home. That meant this was the place where she lived, nothing more. As she unlocked the front door, he was prepared for almost anything, except the sight that greeted them.

Marla gasped, and fell back a step. "What the heck—" Drawers and their contents were scattered all over the living room. Papers and office supplies covered almost every inch of floor space. She stepped inside and glanced around. "I don't get it! What were they looking for? Treasure maps? The TV is still there, and so's the VCR. Don't they usually go for those?"

"Maybe it wasn't an ordinary thief." Sam grasped Marla's shoulder, holding her back. "Why don't you let me take a look around first?" Seeing her nod, he went farther into the house. When he returned a few minutes later, he saw her crouched among the papers.

"These are mostly grant proposals. Why would they bother looking through them?"

"Don't touch them. We have to call the police. Maybe they can lift some prints."

She stood up slowly. "What's the rest of the house like?"

"Things are scattered everywhere, but the bedroom and this room took the worst of it."

She walked down the hallway to her bedroom. The nightstand had been overturned, and her dresser drawers had been up upended onto the floor. "Okay, they were obviously looking for something, but what?" she muttered to herself. She stared at the disarray, trying to make some sense of it. "Did they think that *I'd* stolen the artifacts from the site, and hidden them here?"

"If that's what they were doing, then why search the drawers? The valuable pieces like the Slayer armor would never have fit in any of those."

"Maybe they thought I'd left a safety deposit key or a storage building receipt where I'd stashed the loot," she replied cynically.

Sam considered it, then finally shrugged. "Who knows? Come on. You have to phone the police. I doubt they would have touched the telephone."

After making the call, they sat down on the porch steps and waited. "They won't find anything, you know," Marla said dejectedly. "That's the way our luck's been running."

"We can't afford to make that assumption."

It took twenty-five minutes for the officers to finish going over her house, and then take her prints for comparison. "Did you find anything that will lead you to whoever did this?" Marla asked.

"I found several good prints, but they could all end up being yours," the officer answered candidly.

She struggled to keep her disappointment from showing. Her biggest problem was being forced to admit that she wasn't safe anywhere. Up to now, she'd believed all she'd have to do was abandon the site. Now she wasn't so sure.

After the officers left, Marla and Sam started picking things up from the floor. They were halfway through when she glanced at the wall clock and shook her head. "Forget it. This'll keep. We have to go back. We've been away for too long."

"Okay, let's go."

Sam pulled out of the small driveway and headed back. It wasn't late; the sun was still warming the interior of the car despite the air conditioner. After a short time, Marla leaned back in the seat and shut her eyes. He turned on the radio but kept the sound low.

As the miles stretched out, he found himself growing unbearably sleepy. He shook his head, trying to stay alert, then turned up the air conditioner a click. It was so warm, maybe that was the problem. By the time they'd passed through Farmington onto a stretch of open desert, his eyelids felt as if they were being weighed down with rocks.

He'd have to pull over; he was just too tired to keep driving. At the moment, even his brain felt as if it had been packed in cotton gauze. If he could only close his eyes for a while, he knew he'd be fine.

He slowed down and drove to the shoulder, barely able to stay awake. Vaguely aware of a small object ahead, he swerved sluggishly to avoid striking it. But his reaction time was off. He heard something crunch, then felt the vehicle shudder as a loud bang came from the front end.

The truck suddenly lurched, then bounded off the road onto the desert floor. Sam gripped the steering wheel hard as he forged an uncertain, bone-jarring path through the tumbleweeds and rocks.

Chapter Sixteen

The vehicle bounced heavily over the thin clusters of sage-brush, and rocks hammered against the underside of the chassis. Sam fought to keep the steering wheel straight. He wasn't so sure there'd be much left of his pickup, or them, if he lost control now.

They traveled a few more yards when the pickup quickly bogged down in a patch of soft sand, and they came to a halt in a cloud of dust. It was the realization that Marla was still groggy and disoriented that made his brain click.

"Open your door!" he yelled, throwing his own open.

Blinking through heavy-lidded eyes, she slowly did as he asked.

"Get out of the truck."

Her expression left no doubt that she thought he'd lost his mind. "I'll explain in a minute," he answered. "Just get out of the truck and start walking."

"What are we doing here?" she asked dully. "Did someone run us off the road?"

Sam came around and grabbed her by the hand. "I hit something in the road and blew a tire. Now we're both taking a walk."

"Boy, I'm dizzy. Yeah, let's take a walk. I need some air." They took several uncertain steps. As the hot desert air hit her face, she breathed in deeply. The fuzziness that had settled over her like a thick fog lifted slowly, and she found herself feeling weak and a little sick to her stomach. A pounding headache throbbed at her temples.

A moment later she realized they were walking in a circle around the truck, a good fifty yards from the highway. Marla said nothing, suspecting she didn't really want to know the reason why they were baking out in the sun.

"We can't get back in that truck until we figure out how to fix what's wrong with it," Sam said. "And I'm not talking about the flat tire."

"Carbon monoxide?" she guessed.

"What else could explain both of us getting that sleepy?"

"And queasy and feeling as if your head's about to explode?" She saw him nod. "Do you think we should try to hitch a ride to get to a phone? One of my students can give us a lift."

"No. Let me see if I can figure out what's wrong first. Maybe it'll just be a matter of fixing the tire and driving with the windows down."

She watched him walk to his pickup and retrieve the bumper jack from behind the seat. Ten minutes later, the destroyed tire replaced with a spare, he scrambled beneath the truck. As she stood by, she heard him mutter something under his breath. She couldn't quite make out the word, but from the tone, it was easy to conclude he wasn't exactly blessing his luck.

"I found it," he said. "There's a big hole in the exhaust pipe, and another in the cab floor right above it." He slithered out from beneath the truck. "They could have been caused by hitting a rock or piece of scrap metal somewhere on one of these dirt roads. But it must have happened not too long ago, otherwise we would have noticed it on the way to the college. And since then we haven't been on any rough roads."

"Except for just now. You know, if this was done on purpose, it means we're both targets now." She took a deep breath. "Or maybe they saw you as expendable, providing they also got rid of me."

He considered it for a moment. "The tribal factions that are against the excavation might be blaming me because I haven't been able to stop you."

"What are you going to do?"

"About that possibility?" He shrugged. "There's nothing I can do. But I am going to have the punctures checked out by the police. My guess is they'll find they were actually made by rocks. The holes are jagged, not clean like you'd expect from a metal tool."

"And the dents that the rocks put on the underside of your truck when we veered off won't help convince them it was a murder attempt," she observed.

"Even without them we wouldn't have been able to prove anything. My truck isn't exactly brand-new, if you judge by the miles on it. Finding rock holes in the bottom won't even raise an eyebrow around here. On the reservation the highway's paved, but not most of the side roads."

"Yeah, you're right," she said with a sigh.

"I should have realized what was happening as soon as I started getting groggy."

"We should both have been quicker to act, but neither of us is at fault. I remember a story one of my professors told us. She said that when a horse shied at a snake, people blamed the horse, sometimes they blamed the rider, but they never stopped to think it might have been the snake who was responsible."

"I would have liked your professor." He stared at the truck, deep in thought. "I'll block off the hole in the floorboard with a piece of cardboard and some electrical tape. I think it'll be okay to drive it then as long as we keep all the windows down. Of course if either of us starts feeling sleepy, we'll pull off the road immediately."

"Okay, let's try it."

Sam managed to get them back through the sand without getting the truck stuck again, and minutes later they were on their way. Marla felt every nerve in her body on edge. To her, it seemed like standing out in an empty field during a thunderstorm and wondering if you'd be struck by lightning. As they continued down the highway, she realized she was leaning toward the window more than usual. But at least she felt alert.

"I think this is going to work," he said. "I'm not drowsy, and my headache is starting to fade."

"Well, the wind's blowing right in our faces." She held her hair back with one hand to keep it from flying everywhere.

"I'm going to meet Billy Todacheene this evening. I'll drive my pickup to his place, then borrow one of his trucks while the police check out mine. I won't be back until late."

"It's probably just as well," she answered wearily. "I have a feeling I'm going to have my hands full when Dr. Hartman reacts to our activities at the college today. He's probably already left a call for me at the site."

Their conversation was tentative, and toward the end of the ride they'd even given up any pretense of talking. After Sam dropped her off, she went to the RV, hoping to relax for a while. Before she could even take an aspirin, Carmen came to the door. "Dr. Hartman's coming up the dirt track. I just saw one of the guards wave him through."

She suppressed a groan, and her head started to throb again. "Okay. I'll go meet him."

Marla was near the parking area when he arrived. The moment she saw him leave his vehicle, she knew he'd come ready to do battle. She decided to let him bring up the subject of their talk with June and not mention it herself. There was a chance, however slim, he'd come on another matter.

His eyes were expressionless and almost glassy with intensity. "We need to talk—inside," he began.

"Sure."

She led the way to the RV, then offered him one of the chairs around the tiny table. "Can I get you something to drink?"

"Cut the amenities," he snapped. "I heard that the tribal rep, Sam Nez, was questioning my staff today. What's he after? Has he decided to force you out of here by harassing the entire anthropology department?"

"He's trying to find answers to what has been happening here, as I am."

Hartman watched her closely. "Do you realize that his job is to get you out of here any way he can? And this is the man you've chosen to give your trust to?" He shook his head in exasperation. "You've become emotionally involved. I can see it. And you can bet he knows that, too. He'll use it against you, Marla."

"The problems at this site have nothing to do with Sam Nez, nor are they my fault. Whatever's happening here goes deeper than anything we've managed to uncover. But I *will* find the truth."

"Now you intend to do the state police's job for them?" he scoffed. "You've been out in the sun too long."

"At least I'm doing something constructive, instead of just creating more problems," she snapped. Just as she started to regret her words, someone knocked at the door, and Carmen poked her head inside.

"We've got a problem out here, Professor," she said.

Marla bolted out of her chair. "What kind of problem?"

"Remember the kid's voice we all heard before?" Seeing Marla nod, she added, "Well, it's back."

"Were you able to pinpoint it?"

"No. That's why I thought you might want to come outside."

Hartman, who now stood behind her, looked outside. "What's this all about?"

Marla explained quickly. "But we never could find the source."

Hartman's expression changed to one of curiosity. "Let's go find out what's going on."

They met the other students by the cave entrance. "What exactly did you hear?" Hartman asked Carmen.

"It's like a cross between the mewing of a cat, and a kid's voice."

"Could it be the cry of a bird? That would explain why it seems to move before you can locate it."

Dulce shook her head. "No, that's not it. Wait a few more minutes. Maybe we'll hear it again."

Hartman shifted and leaned back against the cave wall. "This is ridiculous. You're in the middle of the desert, for Pete's sake! I'd be worried if you heard the blast of a foghorn, or something totally out of place. But the sound of a—"

"Listen," Marla interrupted. It only lasted a few seconds, then everything grew quiet again. "I think it came from near the arroyo."

Carmen nodded. "Yes, I think you're right."

Hartman stared at them incredulously. "You people aren't serious, are you? What's the big deal? It's either the wind playing a trick, or some animal like a feral tomcat."

"Neither the wind nor an animal could form words," Dulce snapped.

"I didn't make out one coherent syllable, did you?" Hartman challenged.

"Well, no," Dulce answered, "but it sounded like words. Maybe they're Indian words."

Hartman stared at her scornfully. "You're assuming they're Indian words because the sound didn't make sense to you?"

"I'm going to the arroyo, and see if I can find tracks or something," Marla said quickly. Dulce was no match for Hartman, and she had no intention of allowing an argument to get started. "Are you coming?" she added, looking at Dr. Hartman.

Marla led the way downhill. If there was no evidence to substantiate what they'd heard, Hartman would have a field day with her. He'd heard it, and Marla was certain that he knew it was more than just the cry of the wind, or the screech of a faraway hawk. But he'd probably never admit it, not without proof to back him up.

Hartman accompanied her. "You know, the desert does carry sounds for long distances. It might be a child in a nearby residential area. The wind is blowing from the reservation, and there are houses off in the distance."

"I've considered that," she admitted. "But I don't think it's the answer."

They searched the arroyo for tracks, then split up. After fifteen minutes, neither of them had managed to spot anything out of the ordinary. They started walking back to the cave. "Do yourself a favor, Garrett," Hartman said. "Don't let your enthusiasm and imagination carry you away. You have enough real problems to worry about."

"I'll keep it in mind," she answered tautly.

Marla saw Dr. Hartman off shortly after that. As he reached the end of the track, reporters swarmed around his vehicle. He stopped to talk, and Marla wondered what he was telling them. The press was out there just hoping for some disaster to strike so they could take advantage of it.

Turning away, she joined the students in the cave. They worked together for a few hours more, but then it was time for them to leave. As they went to their vehicles, Marla could sense their reluctance to drive past the reporters. "Don't worry, guys. Just tell them you have no comment. The guard posted there will keep them off your backs."

After all the students had left the site for the day, Marla went inside the RV. The myriad reports Hartman had saddled her with awaited. With a sigh, she picked up the first of many forms, and began filling it out.

SAM DIDN'T RETURN until after nightfall. Deep lines etched his face and formed a network around his eyes. "You look beat," she said, inviting him inside. "Tough meetings?"

"Yeah." He ran a hand through his hair. "The police found nothing they can prove was sabotage."

"What about your meeting with Todacheene?"

Sam hesitated, then shrugged. "He's not at all happy with the way things are going," he answered at last. "But from the look on your face, I'd say you also had a rough afternoon."

She told him about the child's voice. "It's so unnerving."

"But at least Hartman heard it for himself. That's another witness."

"Not really. He was very insistent on explaining it away." Marla gathered up some of her paperwork. "But I really didn't expect him to do anything else. He seldom sticks his neck out for anything." She walked to the two-burner stove, and started heating some water. "Want some coffee?"

He glanced at the stack of reports still on the table, and noted the redness that tinged her eyes. Marla was working much too hard. "No thanks. I can see that you've got plenty to do tonight."

"I am busy, but I can talk for a while if you'd like."

He shook his head. "I'm too tired to even think anymore. I'm going to walk around a bit, see if I can unwind, then go to bed early."

"Well, then I'll see you tomorrow morning."

Marla worked until midnight, then finally left the table. Restless, she glanced around the room, wondering if it had somehow grown bigger. It seemed very empty at the moment. Loneliness crowded in at the edges of her mind, demanding that she acknowledge it. Lately, she seemed to have discovered a gap in the life-style she'd so loved. Work just wasn't enough anymore.

She stood at the window, watching the moon. The real question was, what now? Sam had awakened a side of her she wished she'd never discovered. Emotions filled her with an acute yearning.

As she started to move away from the window, she noticed a flicker of motion near the cave. Her pulse quickened, and she leaned forward, trying to get a better view. Someone was standing in the shadows near the entrance.

Chapter Seventeen

Marla stared hard at the figure barely outlined in the moonlight. It was possible it was one of their guards, but she couldn't be sure. She grabbed her flashlight and a large broom, the only weapon around that would help her keep an intruder at arm's length while she yelled for help.

She slipped outside quietly and took a quick look around for the guards, keeping the flashlight off so she wouldn't reveal her own presence. The security men weren't in sight. That probably meant that it was one of them by the cave. Still alert just in case, she approached cautiously. As she got close, she turned on the flashlight. Sam stood a few feet from the cave entrance, arms on his knees, struggling to catch his breath.

"What on earth—" She aimed her light down and saw several objects on the ground in front of him. She recognized a well-preserved dart and wooden shaft that had been stolen a few days ago. Several projectile points and one large sherd she guessed had once been part of a ritual bowl also lay on the sand.

"It's not what you think," Sam said, still breathing hard. "I saw someone up here, and I ran over. The thief dropped these, and took off at full speed. I'm a fairly good runner, but there was no way I could keep up."

She studied the soft earth, but the only fresh tracks she could discern came from Sam's sneakers. "Where are this guy's tracks?"

"There'll be some around, but they won't be very distinctive. I think he was wearing moccasins."

She took a look inside the cave first, but too many people had come through, making it impossible to tell much of anything. Outside, the desert grasses, hard-packed sand and rocks made it impossible to track anything with certainty. Silence stretched out between them as her uneasiness grew.

"You're not sure you can believe me," he observed at last. "Why?"

"Because I neither heard nor saw anything except you. But all of a sudden some of the stolen artifacts are here."

"If I'd stolen them, why would I return them now when I could see from the lights in the trailer that you were still awake?"

"I thought you were planning to go to sleep," she countered.

"I couldn't. I was too restless."

Hartman's words and Lena's warning niggled at the back of her mind. Had her feelings blinded her to the realities? She wanted to believe him, but she wasn't sure anymore. "Give me your word that you're not keeping anything from me, and I'll believe you." She stopped and faced him.

He paused for a long moment. "I can't do that," he said at last. "I have other loyalties. You've always known that."

She nodded slowly. The realization that he wouldn't confide in her hurt more than she ever imagined possible. Obviously she'd misjudged the strength of his feelings for her. She'd been prepared to trust him with everything. But as he'd said, his loyalties were elsewhere.

She returned to the cave entrance and retrieved the artifacts, placing them carefully inside one of their packing boxes. "I'm taking these to the RV. When the state police arrive, I'll turn them over to them so they can check for prints and whatever else they might want to look for."

"I had nothing to do with the theft or return of these objects."

She gave him a sharp look. "What's this, more word games? You've admitted that you're holding something back, and that loyalty to your tribe exceeds any friendship that existed between us," she added, deliberately using the past tense.

"Yes," he admitted. His gut twisted, knowing the pain he was causing her.

"What do you expect me to do? Congratulate you for being such a good spy?" She picked up the box. "Get out of my way, please."

He didn't move. "Trust your instincts. Do you honestly think I had anything to do with what's happened at this site?"

"You're trying to work with me *and* against me. It can't be both ways. I'm just sorry I didn't really see that until now." She stepped around him and headed back to the RV.

As she went inside and shut the door, she felt empty and lost. She'd wanted to force Sam to see what he'd thrown away. But maybe the loss had been greater for her because she'd truly opened her heart and trusted him.

Leaving the box safely inside the RV, Marla went out to look for the guards. She found one patrolling near the vehicles. Quickly she recounted what had happened. The surprise on the man's face was evident. It wasn't hard to guess the direction of his thoughts.

"I never saw anyone, and I've been alert and all over this site tonight," the man said slowly. "I'll go check with my partner out by the highway."

"If it's any consolation, I didn't hear anything, either," she muttered.

The man nodded. "It looks like you'll have your hands full looking into other possibilities then," he said obliquely.

She went inside the RV, called the police, and made out a report. They weren't pleased she'd handled the objects, but she hadn't had a choice. She couldn't have left them there on the cave floor. The guards couldn't have been expected to watch the artifacts exclusively. They had to protect access to the site, and that required mobility.

As she waited for the patrol car that would collect the items, she tried to go back to her papers. It made little sense to just sit there and waste her time. Yet at one-thirty in the morning, she was simply too tired to concentrate. Finally, she threw her pen down in exasperation and went to lie down. She'd rest her eyes for a few moments, then maybe she'd feel better.

She wasn't sure how long she'd been dozing, when she suddenly felt the RV being rocked back and forth. It seemed as if giant hands were trying to topple it right onto its side. As she grasped the sides of the cot tightly, she heard heavy footsteps running across the metal roof. Marla jumped out of bed, but the swaying motion brought her crashing to her knees. Struggling to her feet, she made her way to the door. She'd just reached for the knob when everything abruptly grew still.

Marla threw the door open, and seeing the guard near the women's camper, ran to him. Quickly, she explained what had happened.

"Ma'am, I've been right around here for the last fifteen minutes. If anyone had been walking on top of your trailer, or shaking it from side to side, I'd have noticed." He smiled benignly. "Maybe you had a bad dream."

She saw Sam approaching. "Trouble?" he asked.

"Did you see anyone?" she demanded, after a brief explanation.

"No. In case you might think I'm somehow to blame, I've been within sight of this guard for the last quarter of an hour at least."

The guard nodded in corroboration.

"But I *felt* that trailer rocking...."

"Dreams can seem very real," the guard said. "And after everything else tonight, I wouldn't doubt that you'd have a nightmare or two."

She saw the expression on Sam's face, and knew he wasn't buying the nightmare story anymore than she was.

The guard used his flashlight to check all around the RV. "To rock this baby back and forth, you'd need a team of people, Professor." He studied the ground. "And in case you're wondering, there's no indication of anything other than normal traffic around your RV."

He sounded so logical that it was tempting to believe him. But she knew it hadn't been a dream.

As the guard left, she looked at Sam. "You don't buy the theory that I was dreaming. How come?"

"I'm not sure you can accept the explanation I could offer you. Maybe you should stick to the guard's."

"If you know something, then just tell me, okay?" she snapped. "I'm in no mood for games."

His eyes darkened like storm clouds moving over the face of the moon. "I remember stories my grandmother told," he said simply. "What you described isn't uncommon when you're dealing with the abilities of the ones you have disturbed," he said, avoiding using the word *chindi* so close to the site and at night.

She started to deny his explanation, then clamped her mouth shut. Right now, she had a choice between his theory and the guard's. The answer the security guard had suggested just wasn't true, no matter how plausible. Sam's wasn't plausible according to everything she'd ever learned, yet the explanation seemed to fit. She shook her head. She was too tired to even think straight.

"I told you that the guard's would satisfy you more."

"I'm going to get some sleep, then in the morning—" she glanced at her watch and groaned "—which is about four hours away, I'll give this some thought."

Sam jammed his hands into his pockets. "When I tell you what is, you refuse to believe me. Yet you blame me for not being more direct with you." He held her gaze for a second, then turned and walked away.

Marla ran a hand through her hair. Swearing she didn't understand anything anymore, not men, not archaeology, not Indian religion, she strode back inside her portable office and slammed the door shut.

SHE WAS UP by 6:00 a.m. the following morning filling out reports when the state police arrived to retrieve the artifacts. She answered the officer's questions, then was told that the detective in charge of the case would let her know the results of their examination of the items. As the officer headed back to his vehicle, she saw Sam standing near the tent he'd chosen to use.

He gave her a hard, accusatory look, then came over. "Whether through theft or through legalities, all I see is more of our artifacts being taken from this site."

"Unavoidable," she returned sharply.

"Is it?" he challenged, his gaze stony.

She walked away from him, feeling his disappointment in her more keenly than she would have liked. He'd let her down, too; she couldn't trust him anymore. What could be worse? A blackness of spirit engulfed her.

"Morning, Professor," Carmen greeted, emerging from the camper.

Dulce came out to join them. She started to stretch, then stopped abruptly. "Why is that Navajo man over there staring at us?" She gestured toward Begay, who was watching from beyond the fence on the reservation side. "It's creepy."

"I don't know. Maybe it's got something to do with last night." Marla told them about the artifacts being returned. "Sam could be telling the truth about chasing someone, but until I know for certain, we've got to watch him very carefully."

"I know you can't ask him to leave, but surely you can restrict where he goes," Dulce said.

"Not really. There's an agreement between the college and the tribe that has to be honored, otherwise we're going to create even bigger problems than those we're attempting to resolve."

"We'll keep an eye on him, Professor, don't you worry about that," Carmen answered.

"And what are we going to do about *that* guy," Dulce said, her attention focused on Begay.

"Ignore him as much as we can. He might be trying to unnerve us, and we can't let him know that he's succeeding."

An hour later, ready to begin working, Marla met the others at the cave entrance. Her expression hardened as she saw Sam approach, but she said nothing.

Marla trapped her feelings for him deep inside herself. She avoided looking at him, afraid that she'd reveal too much in her gaze. She wanted to plead with him, to make him see that he could trust her completely, but her nerve failed. You couldn't make someone trust you by begging.

They worked all morning with few breaks. The tension was thick in the air, evidenced by the uncomfortable silence between them. That afternoon as the wind swept the mesa with a drying heat, a strange sound, like one shrill note played on a flute, drifted through the cave.

"That's the first time we've heard that sound," Dulce whispered.

A second later, the strange trill rang out again. Marla suppressed the shiver that coursed through her. She glanced at Sam. "Any theories?"

He shook his head. "It's coming from farther inside the cave, no doubt about it."

Remembering the lights and the distortion they'd found within the tunnels, she quickly took the lead. There was no reason to expose the graduate students to something like that. She'd stay alert and be ready to make a run for it the second she spotted any blue sparks.

As she traveled farther into the cave, she noticed the sound coincided with the gusts of wind. She studied the rock walls that encased them. "Search for any opening in the rock face that air could whistle through," she advised.

Carmen ran her hand down the cave wall. "It's got to be too small to see, or light would be streaming in."

"When you're driving on the highway, the car window doesn't have to be down more than a crack to make a loud squeal," Dulce said pensively. She, too, began to run her hand over the rock.

Hector, well over six foot four, concentrated on the top of the cavern walls. "If the wind would cooperate and rise up again, maybe we'd hear it."

"Or not," Carmen said glumly. "This place always seems to toss us a curve ball when we least expect it."

Hector suddenly stopped moving. Marla, immediately aware of it, felt a prickle of fear course up her spine. She knew enough about snakes to realize it was dangerous to blindly poke a hand inside a hole in a rock. She'd assumed that Hector, born and raised in the Southwest, would exercise caution, but now she wasn't so sure. "What's wrong?" she said quietly.

Hector's expression was edged with wariness, but then he relaxed. "I thought for a moment that I'd stuck my hand in the wrong place," he answered, not bothering to explain. "But it's okay. What's in here can't harm me or anyone else."

"Careful," Marla said, always uneasy with assurances like those.

A heartbeat later, he extracted a blue plastic tube about three feet long. It was corrugated, and the diameter of a vacuum-cleaner hose. "Here's what was causing that high-pitched sound." He twirled it through the air quickly, and the wail echoed loudly in the interior of the cavern. "You can pick these up at almost any novelty shop."

Carmen shuddered. "It's a very unpleasant sound, but it's not nearly as bad as the little kid's voice we hear from time to time."

Marla nodded. "I agree, but if this is a trick, the other probably is, too." She glanced at Sam. "So much for the theory that any of the events are supernatural."

"You can discount *this* one," he said quietly. "With that much I agree."

Marla held out a grocery bag. "Drop it in here, Hector. Maybe the police can figure out who left it in the cave."

"Wouldn't count on it," he observed wryly. "I probably smudged all the prints, if there were any to begin with.

It was really wedged. Besides, with all those ridges, it wouldn't leave complete prints."

"Can't hurt to try," she answered.

As they arrived back at the mouth of the cave, one of the security guards, new on the shift, came inside. "About thirty minutes ago I found a reporter prowling near the back of the rise taking photos. I chased him off, but I didn't catch him," he admitted. "The guy jumped over our security fence and ran for the reservation."

"Well, at least you chased him off," Marla said with relief.

"For all the good it did. We just received a call from Dr. Hartman. I'm not sure how you'd like us to handle this, but he said he's meeting with a few of the press people, then bringing them here."

Marla schooled her face into neutrality, mostly because she was incredibly furious. Hartman had overstepped his bounds. This site, and the grant funding the work, were hers. Though he was the department chairman, she should have been consulted about this. "When's he coming?"

"Right now." The guard gestured toward the dirt track.

Marla jogged out to the parking area and waited, arms crossed, for Hartman's van to pull up. He had made it impossible for her to stop him with any semblance of diplomacy. As he and three reporters, including Saffron, stepped out of the vehicle, she motioned for them to wait, and called Hartman aside. "Why are you doing this?" she demanded.

"The stories that have appeared so far in the papers and on TV are killing us. The press is totally in sympathy with the tribe, and making us appear like insensitive fools, at best. The dean of arts and sciences is coming down hard on me, and the regents on him. If you plan to keep your job, you've got to help me make sure this trend doesn't continue. Our best bet is to let these reporters take a look around. Maybe if they don't feel we're shutting them out, they'll start treating us a little better."

"Or not," she countered, noting the two men and the woman were laden with cameras and tape recorders. "What exactly do you want us to show them?"

"Let them ask their questions, and give them a chance to tour portions of the site as you see fit. Be friendly, but make sure you're aware of everything they photograph." Seeing her expression of disapproval, he continued patiently. "Look, they've been using long-range lenses to take photos anyway. This way you have *some* idea of what they're doing."

She pursed her lips, struggling hard to keep her temper. "Do you realize they might take this as a precedent and expect to be asked back whenever it suits them?"

"No, that won't happen. I told them that we'd escort them around today, and then maybe again in the future—if they deal fairly with us. This way, I've given them some incentive to behave themselves."

Marla sighed, glancing at the three reporters. "Keep them with you until I speak to the students."

As Marla explained the circumstances to the others, she saw Sam's expression harden. "I don't have a choice about this," she continued. "If I did, they wouldn't be here. But maybe Dr. Hartman has a point and this will make things easier for us around here."

"Does the tribe know?" Sam challenged.

Before she could answer, Dr. Hartman approached. "I couldn't help but overhear your question. I telephoned the tribal government center this morning. They've been notified."

"And they agreed?"

Hartman hesitated. "Not exactly. But they said that it wouldn't hurt if the press saw that this site clearly shows traces of Navajo culture. They asked that you speak on their behalf and clearly present the tribe's viewpoint to the reporters."

"Who did you talk to?"

"A tribal councillor named Begay."

Sam bristled at the thought that the request had come from Begay, not Todacheene. There'd be heated discussions on this later, but for now he had no choice except to do as one of the tribal leaders had asked.

Marla assigned one student per reporter, then stationed Hector at the cave, just in case. As the reporters walked around, Hartman joined her. "There's a reason why I chose to do this now. I wasn't going to tell you just yet, but it might induce you to cooperate a little more gracefully." He rubbed the back of his neck in a weary gesture. "Yesterday the main road to campus was closed down to one lane to fix a storm-drain problem, so I detoured and came in the back way. That takes me right past your cottage, and I saw someone looking around on your front porch. By the time I parked and got out, he'd driven off, but I did see his face. It was Fred Saffron from *Grapevine*." Hartman nodded toward Saffron.

"Do you know if he tried to get inside my house?" she asked, her mind on the break-in.

"I doubt it. I saw one of your neighbors outside watering her plants, and I asked her what he'd been up to. She said that he'd walked up and down the block asking questions about you, and then looked in all your front windows."

That made sense, considering that almost everything he printed was based on innuendo. "So you decided to let him in *here* today?"

"Under your supervision," he answered. "You can control the information he has access to." He watched the reporters and their student guides heading toward the excavated hogan and cave. "It's not just you they're targeting, you know. I found out they've also been trying to get background material on your grad students and our department. They've started looking into my private life, as well."

Marla saw the reporters start toward the cave entrance. "They're not going inside," she said, jogging uphill.

Hartman hurried to catch up. "They won't. I told them they can take photos from the entrance, that's all."

Sam moved over beside Hector, who still barred the entrance, and began to give them a statement. Those precious seconds allowed her to catch up and join them.

As she approached, she heard Saffron ask Sam about the *chindi*. To Sam's credit, he didn't even flinch.

"Do you believe these evil spirits, whaddya call them, *chindi*, are on the warpath here?"

Sam's expression was as cold as the rock walls within the cave. "My religious beliefs are intensely personal, and not to be shared with you. The fact exists that this excavation has exacted a high price. Any conclusions made from that must be your own."

No one had to ask to what he referred. Lena's memory hung over all of them like a moonless night.

"You proceed from the basis of your own beliefs to judge ours," Sam continued. "Your archaeologists do the same. They never come with an open mind to learn about other cultures. Instead, they judge our ways and compare them to what they consider the truth."

"Hey, no offense meant," Saffron added, then continued with another question.

It seemed a very long time before all the reporters left the site, and by that time Marla was exhausted. Gathering the students and guards, she thanked them for their cooperation. "We'll know by this evening, at least in two of the cases, what kind of stories they're going to print. Let's hope they don't turn people against us."

On the way to the supply tent, Marla stopped by the plastic water barrel that stored their drinking water, but found it empty. "One of us is going to have to take this back before dark and get it refilled," she told the group.

Sam picked up a plastic cup from a nearby table and joined her as she went to the second, smaller barrel and filled her glass.

As she lifted the cup to her lips, Sam suddenly knocked it out of her hand.

Chapter Eighteen

Water splattered everywhere, and Marla turned to glare at him. "What do you think you're doing?"

"There's a rainbow-colored bubble forming on the nozzle of the water spout," he said, calling her attention to it. He touched it, then sniffed his fingertips cautiously. "It's detergent."

Marla glanced at Carmen. "Who washed out the container last?"

Dulce cringed. "Me. But I did rinse it out, honest! I'm always especially careful with that!"

Sam crouched by the back of the container. "There are footprints here, soft-heeled shoes of some kind."

"There are footprints all around the front, too," Carmen countered. "We all use this area."

"Yes, but these tracks are the only ones approaching the container from the back, and they're fresh." He glanced at Marla, the students, then the guard. "Did any of you come up from this direction?" When no one answered, he stood up. "Then I'm going to see where these lead."

"I'm going with you," Marla volunteered, then looked at the others. "I want you to check everything else. Then try to remember if any of the reporters came over to this area."

"They didn't, Professor," the guard replied. "I watched all of them very carefully."

"Then maybe while we were all busy with them, someone else took advantage of the diversion," Sam countered flatly.

"Let's go and follow these tracks," Marla said. "If they head around to the parking area, there are only two possibilities. Either the container was never rinsed properly, or the reporters sneaked in someone else who put detergent in our water."

"But why? It's such a dumb prank!" Carmen protested.

"If all of us were suddenly sick, the press would have had a field day," Marla answered with a wry grimace. "Their long-range lenses would have revealed that no one was working, and they would have had quite a story."

"Good thing none of us used the water to cook with," Sam added as he started following the footprints. "We wouldn't have even known what hit us, since the food would have masked the soapy taste."

Marla studied the ground intently. "Good point. And thanks for knocking the water out of my hand, by the way."

"You're welcome."

Marla walked with Sam past the arroyo. "This person isn't very skilled at hiding his tracks."

"Or maybe he didn't care that we found out. There's no way we can link this to anyone in particular, and what could you tell the police? That you think someone must have poured some detergent in the drinking water?"

"It's harassment—effective harassment."

"Yeah, what some of the press does best." He wiped the perspiration from his brow. "These tracks lead away from the parking area," he said, heading out toward the fence.

"They go right to the reservation," she said, "or more precisely to Begay's property. Isn't he the one who okayed Dr. Hartman's plans to bring in reporters?"

"Yes, but these tracks are too small for him."

They started back in silence. The rift between her and Sam was growing, and the knowledge filled her with sadness. "Why can't you be honest with me, and trust my discretion?'' she blurted impulsively. ''I don't want to treat you like the enemy!''

''I wish you wouldn't. I don't deserve it,'' he answered calmly.

''Then tell me what you're holding back.''

Sam shook his head slowly. ''Our Way teaches us that although it's good to pass on knowledge, it's just as important to know which portions should be withheld. To share all is degrading.'' He paused, measuring his words carefully. ''Would you share privileged information about your college with me, even if it had to do with something I was working on?''

''That depends on the information,'' she replied after a moment.

''Exactly. You would judge whether or not it was something so critical it was worth the cost of betraying a trust to divulge it. Like me, you have your own loyalties.'' He captured her gaze for a second. ''Revelations don't necessarily mean greater intimacy.''

''Your way also tells you to find harmony and balance. There must be some way for us to stop working at cross purposes.''

''I don't see how. What really mystifies me, is why you and your people fail to understand our position. Can you imagine how loud the public outcry would be if someone dug up Civil War graves so they could get what was left of the uniforms?''

''But what I'm doing is more than that.''

''Okay. If they dug up the graves so they could speculate on how they lived and died.''

Marla lapsed into a thoughtful silence. ''You've given me an idea.''

''You're going to dig up graves and study the corpses?''

''No,'' she answered irately, ''but I have a suggestion as to how we can work things out. What if we changed our approach to the excavation? If we find artifacts that have religious significance, a prayer bowl, or prayer sticks, or anything a *hataalii* would use, we'll take extensive photos and make sketches. That way we can make copies of the originals without removing them from here. Then after we finish our work, we'll arrange for this site to be put under Navajo stewardship. I'll have to check, but I'm sure the college would agree to all this, if you think your tribe might find it acceptable."

Sam considered her proposal. "The hard part will be getting them to trust your word."

"What if I met with them personally?"

He considered it. "Your best chance would be for me to take you to Billy Todacheene's place. His father is a highly respected *hataalii*. If you can persuade both those men, I'm certain the others will go along with it."

"Then let's give it a try."

"What I'm proposing won't be easy for you. Be prepared. First, I'd recommend that you bring native tobacco with you as a gift for Wallace, Billy's father. It's a courtesy to an elder, particularly a *hataalii*. Then if you're asked to smoke from Wallace's pipe, don't decline. That signifies peace, but it's also said that it's impossible to lie or hold back anything during a smoke."

"What's in the tobacco?" she asked nervously.

"It's a mixture of wide- and narrow-leafed tobacco. What makes it different from regular commercial mixes is how we blend it. But you don't have to worry about it being a narcotic of some type, or Mexican leaf."

"Okay," she agreed. "I'll make a few calls to the college and get my plan cleared. Then can we go soon after that, before I lose my nerve?"

He smiled. "Sure, but it's not like you're facing a firing squad, you know."

Marla telephoned Dr. Hartman as soon as she got back into the RV. Thirty minutes later, she was assured the dean not only approved of her plan, but eagerly encouraged it. The coal company responsible for the grant also supported it. Everyone was ready to compromise in exchange for a peaceful settlement.

Instead of relief, Marla felt more nervous than ever. Now it was up to her to carry it off. They left for Todacheene's an hour and a half later.

"I've made the arrangements, and they'll be expecting us at Billy's," Sam assured her.

"We'll have to stop someplace so I can pick up the tobacco you mentioned. Do you know where?"

He reached into the glove compartment, and extracted a small pouch. "Here. Stick it in your purse, and stop worrying. If they sense you're nervous, they'll think you're trying to hide something."

"How can I *not* be nervous!"

"Even if they agree," he warned, "this won't solve all the problems, you know. There'll still be fringe groups who'll oppose what's going on."

"Maybe, but it would make things easier."

He nodded, conceding. "On you and me, too. Have you thought much about that?"

She said nothing for a long moment; his words lay heavy on her mind. "There is no 'us' for you and me," she finally answered softly. "Your heart is here with your own people. I would never fit in. Knowing about your culture doesn't make me Navajo. I'd always be on the outside looking in."

"Yes, you're an outsider here, just as I am out there beyond the boundary fence. I earn respect in the Anglo world. Yet, when they look at me, they see someone whose skin is a different color from theirs. But you can't expect one hundred percent approval from others no matter where you are."

"True," she answered. "But we'd be foolish to try to build on ground that's already undermined." Sadness pressed in on her, making her heart ache. "Let's not talk about this right now. The present needs our attention." She let the words hang in the air, knowing that there was more than one meaning to what she'd said.

The drive was a pleasant one, but Marla was much too nervous about her upcoming meeting with Todacheene to enjoy it. At the town of Shiprock, they turned west near the new high school and drove a few miles down the road toward Teec Nos Pos, Arizona. Then they left the paved road and passed numerous small Navajo farms which lined the San Juan River. Soon they came to Billy Todacheene's home.

From the outside, the house appeared to be a modern and fairly ordinary wood-and-stucco-framed structure set among a stand of old cottonwoods. Yet toward the back was an unmistakable sign that the old ways were not forgotten here. A six-sided log hogan stood a short walk behind the main house, a blanket covering the entrance.

According to custom, she and Sam remained in the truck, waiting for their host to appear at the door and invite them in. As time passed, she wondered if they'd noticed their arrival.

"They know," Sam answered in response to her unspoken question.

She smiled. "Okay. I was just curious."

A moment or two later, Billy Todacheene appeared at the door, and waved them inside. She took her first full breath then. She'd begun to think that they'd changed their minds, and wouldn't even let them in to discuss her idea.

The interior was as modern as any middle-class home outside the reservation. The walls were decorated with oil paintings illustrating Navajo life, and Marla could see into a room that had been set aside as a small office. A glass-front cabinet in the living room held many kinds of artwork, from pottery to kachina figures depicting Navajo and Pueblo deities. A beautiful Two Gray Hills rug hung on a wall, setting off the entire room in a bold black, gray and white geometric pattern.

"Those are gifts from other tribal leaders," Billy explained, noting her interest.

She started to comment, when another man came into the room. He was older than Billy, but she couldn't make an accurate guess of his age. His gray hair hung loosely around his shoulders in the traditional style, and he wore a simple blue handkerchief as a headband. Gentle lines framed his face in a complex pattern. A large silver-and-turquoise squash blossom necklace hung around his neck.

He stood with his back erect, and watched her for a moment. Finally, he nodded, using the Navajo word for greeting. "'*Aháláane.*"

"This is my father," Billy said, introducing him.

She remembered not to shake hands, nor make direct eye contact with the elderly man, out of respect. "*Yah'ehteh'*," she answered, using the word for "how do you do." It was the only expression she felt reasonably sure she wouldn't butcher beyond recognition. She handed him the packet of tobacco. "For you, Uncle," she said respectfully.

"*Ah-sheh'heh*" he said, thanking her.

They sat in comfortable chairs in the living room and waited for her to begin. Marla took a deep breath. She knew she would have to sound confident, but at the moment that was the last thing she felt. Gathering her courage, she explained her idea. "I know there's been trouble and misunderstandings between us," she added, "but I believe this could help put an end to that."

Billy said nothing for what seemed an eternity, and the silence stretched out uninterrupted. She studied the rug on the wall, determined to wait patiently. She couldn't read anything from Todacheene's expression, and suspense gnawed at her.

"You've disregarded our warnings to shut down, and consequently experienced nothing but evil," Billy said. "Then, as a further offense, things of extreme value to our tribe have been stolen from you. But now you want our trust and cooperation."

"Yes," she said, unable to argue with the facts. "But we now have security guards around the site. You also have your representative there with us at all times. We've done all we can to safeguard against the danger." She paused, knowing it was imperative that she find a way to reach them. "Your ways teach the importance of finding a balance and striving for harmony. That's what I'm trying to do."

"It's a contaminated place," Wallace Todacheene said quietly. "You can't change that. None of us can. There's danger there. And what if, despite your precautions, the thefts continue? Those objects belong to the dead. You anger them when you take what is theirs, but soon *you'll* leave. Our people will remain and they're the ones who'll have to face the aftermath."

"I can't guarantee that there won't be more trouble," she said honestly, "only that I've done all in my power to prevent it. You will be gaining much of what you wanted. The items of religious importance will remain there, and everything else will be returned when we've finished our studies."

Mulling over her words, Wallace filled the long pipe with tobacco, then offered it to her. She accepted, hoping she could show some grace even though she'd never smoked in her life. The taste of tobacco in her mouth almost made her choke, but she stifled the impulse with a burst of willpower, then passed the pipe back to him.

He smiled, as if sensing her reaction. He took a long puff, then passed it to his son. "You don't believe in our ways, but neither have you discounted them. That speaks well for you," he observed. His expression grew thoughtful. "But you have made some powerful enemies."

"Well, the dig sure has," she said slowly.

"That, too."

Marla smiled ruefully. "I'm not important enough to have made powerful enemies."

Billy regarded her speculatively as he passed the pipe to Sam. "My father is quite intuitive about these things. You can rely on whatever he tells you."

Her skin prickled with unease. There was a luminous intensity in Wallace's eyes that chilled her to the marrow. "I'll remember your warning."

"You want our tribe's cooperation very much. Why?" Wallace pressed.

"I need help. The trouble hasn't stopped. But it's wrong to run from anyone or anything that uses violence to impose their will. I have to resist. There are also other futures at stake." She explained about the students' scholarships. "You know about resistance. When your children were taken away to boarding schools and beaten for speaking their own language, you didn't give up your native tongue. You withstood the pressures and held on to your culture. To give in to any form of evil only allows it to become stronger."

"There's a lot of truth in what you've said," Wallace answered.

Sam glanced at Billy. "The objects there are receiving the respect and the protection they merit. At first, the *bilagáanas* didn't know enough to expect trouble, and they were victimized. That isn't the case anymore. This woman is responsible for the changes made there and deserves to be trusted. I want to offer my word in addition to hers. She is making this compromise in good faith, and I believe we should accept."

Sam's words took Marla by surprise. He'd aligned himself to her, but now if anything did go wrong, he'd lose his standing with the tribe as well as their respect. The magnitude of what he'd done stunned her.

Billy Todacheene waited until his father placed the pipe down. "We'll speak to the others, and I will let you know what has been decided tomorrow."

"Thank you for listening to my proposal and for sharing your home with me," she said.

They left Billy Todacheene's house a short time later. The events had left her mind reeling. "Despite the way I've treated you at the site, and knowing the problems the dig has had, you still backed me in front of both Todacheenes." When he said nothing, she persisted, "Why?"

"I believe in you, and what you're trying to do with this new proposal of yours." He glanced over at her, then back at the road. "But there's something you should know. Our futures are now linked. Whatever happens at the site will no longer be seen as solely your responsibility. I will share in the blame if anything goes wrong, or the success if things go as well as we hope.''

"Now you've scared me," she admitted, brushing his arm with her fingertips. "Is there any way you can take it back before it goes any further?"

"I wouldn't even if I could. I've been at the site trying to control your actions, but without really sharing the burden. That wasn't fair." He reached for her hand, and enclosed it in his own. "But what was our weakness before can be our strength now, if you allow it."

The warmth of his hand and the gentleness of his touch filled her with a yearning more powerful than anything she'd ever known before. "We'll fight together." But even as she said the words, the feelings that surged inside her weren't of fighting; they were soft and filled with feminine needs.

He brought her hand up to his lips and brushed it with a kiss. "There's so much that is right between us. Let's not spend the time we have always concentrating on what keeps us apart." He looked out at the Shiprock, one of their sacred mountains. The sun was sinking slowly beneath the horizon, lighting up the sky in a blaze of crimson and lavender like a wild watercolor painting. "This is my home. My loyalty and my heart will always be linked to my tribe's. They're a part of who and what I am." He measured his words carefully. "But I'm a part of your culture, too. There's a lot of good in your world."

"Yes, there is."

"But it's the way of the Dineh that opens my eyes and lets me see that we're all interconnected. To find harmony, we have to honor the differences."

"There are times I truly envy you. You know where you belong and how you fit in." Marla leaned back in her seat looking out at the stillness of the desert countryside. "It's so peaceful out here. It's hard to believe there could be trouble so close by."

"Would you like to walk around a bit before we get back? This is the best time of day. It's cool, but not cold yet. I could even show you my favorite spot. We're near it now."

"Sure." At the moment what she wanted more than anything else was time alone with him. She felt wonderfully alive around Sam. It was a rush, a crazy jigsaw of emotions that fed off each other, taking her to dizzying heights. She knew she was skirting danger, but sometimes you just had to take a chance.

Sam pulled off the road, then recaptured her hand as they walked all the way around a steep arroyo, then toward a small rise on the other side. Nestled between several stunted piñons at the base were two large rocks. They leaned against the earthen sides of the hill, forming an inverted vee shape.

As they drew near, she could see where pollen had been scattered. A prayer stick protruded from the space between the rocks. "Is this your family's shrine?"

"It has been for years, since my great-great-grandfather found figures of Kokopelli drawn in the small place between the rocks."

"Kokopelli. He's the humpback god eternally playing his flute, right?"

"Yes. He was the god of fertility and love to the Anasazi, like Changing Woman is to us."

She watched him place a small turquoise bead inside the shrine. "This is for Changing Woman who gives power against all danger, though she stands for peace."

Taking her hand, he guided her around the rise and showed her the vast stretch of emptiness before them. In the distance, red clay bluffs gleamed as if on fire in the sunset. "The desert holds so much more than what you can see with your eyes. Unless you attune yourself to it, it'll defeat you. Yet it will welcome you, if you open your heart."

"You and this desert are one in spirit. Would you welcome me, too, if my heart was opened?" Her whispered words were spoken out of a need as primitive as the land.

"I've already welcomed you, *sawe*," he said. "But I can't provide you with the answers that you need in your life. And I won't take what I can't provide for."

"I'm not asking for promises that neither of us can make. I'm asking you to show me what you feel. If all that is in your heart is what I've created in my own imagination, then let's go back now."

He reached for her hand and pulled her against him. "You're playing with fire, *sawe*," he growled. "Don't tempt me. I'm a man with needs that could overwhelm yours." His hand cupped her neck as he slanted his mouth and kissed her hungrily. His tongue thrust forward, claiming her moistness and sweetness until she trembled against him.

An eternity later, he broke the kiss, but not his embrace. He was aroused almost beyond bearing. He wanted to feel her warmth sheathing him and hear her cry out with need for him. "Decide, *sawe*."

His eyes smoked in the fading light. The barely contained masculine power made her bones turn soft. She wanted to be loved by this man, even if all they could truly share were a few precious moments in time.

Her decision made, she guided his mouth back to hers and traced the outline of his lips with the tip of her tongue. Her kiss asked, and took from him, making the world alive with fire.

With a husky murmur, he pressed her to him. His body blazed like high noon in the desert as he dug his fingers into her buttocks, pulling her into the cradle of his thighs. The throbbing of his manhood against her center made her whimper and rub herself against him.

A long shudder traveled over him as he forced himself to ease his hold and step back. Her eyes were on him as he ripped away his shirt, baring his strong, bronzed body. Following his lead, she started to remove her blouse, but he shook his head. "No. Let me."

He stripped her slowly, his eyes drinking her in like a man dying of thirst. The red sun fell over her nakedness, playing over the soft curves, enticing him to love all the places its gentle beams touched.

"Sun was the father of Slayer," he murmured. "His rays found Changing Woman and caressed her as he does you now." His eyes seared over her. "But this is our time, and you are mine." For that moment he was jealous even of the sun. He thought of her belly growing someday and in that instant a possessiveness he'd never experienced burst through every cell of his body.

With his hand on the flat of her back, he pulled her closer and took her soft nipple into his mouth. He suckled it gently, teasing it with his teeth, then soothing it with his tongue.

She arched toward him, her fingers weaving through his hair. She was wildfire in his arms. The knowledge slashed through him like lightning. Impatient, he took a step back, snapped open his jeans, and slid them downward, kicking them brusquely aside. He saw her eyes widen, then grow misty, as she witnessed the ultimate proof of his desire.

Pride and male triumph rocketed through him as he guided her down onto the sand. He lay between her thighs and rained tiny, wet kisses down the center of her body. He loved her patiently, exploring and tasting all the hidden places that left her quivering and gasping his name.

Marla felt as if she were slowly drowning in a lake of fire. His caresses burned into her, making the world shatter and reform around her. An eternity later, he moved up beside her. He kissed her hard, his tongue claiming her mouth hungrily.

Her body trembled in anticipation of the ultimate act of possession that was yet to come. First she needed to know she held some mastery over him, that she was able to drive him wild as he'd done her.

"I want to give you pleasure," she managed, her voice unsteady.

"You do," he growled, kissing the pulse point at her neck.

She smiled at him tenderly. "I want to give you more."
She pressed her palm against his chest. As he drew back she
explored his body with her touch. His eyes closed when she
reached his manhood and encircled it gently. She could feel
it pulsing as she caressed him the way her body would soon.

He sucked in his breath and shuddered. "Please. I don't
know if I can stand it."

She felt the glorious power of her own femininity as she
continued to stroke him and love him, oblivious to his
words. His groans of pleasure fueled her desire.

Finally he took her hand away and pressed it to his lips.
"It's time." He parted her thighs, settling his body between them, and began a slow descent into her heated softness.

Her body welcomed him, and she closed her eyes, the
sensations almost too hot to bear.

"No, *sawe*." He stopped in midmotion. "Look at me. I
want you to know who's taking you. I need to see the surrender in your eyes."

He saw himself reflected in her passion-filled gaze as he
slowly pushed into her. He moved gently at first, restraint
making his body slick with perspiration. Even when he felt
her tighten and heard her whimper, he continued to hold
back. Not yet. She had higher pleasures waiting.

Heartbeats later, he saw the wildness in her eyes and
knew the desperation that drove her as she moved her hips
to meet his downward thrusts. His name on her lips, she
clung to him tightly. Then she cried out and he felt her
wetness encircling him.

At that moment the last of his control vanished. He began to move hard and fast, taking her with barely contained force. With every thrust, he felt a part of him
becoming hers. Passion and instinct combined forces, demanding a release. With a cry that rose and became one
with the desert, he spilled himself into her.

Peace filled them in the bittersweet aftermath. He held
her tightly, watching the sun edge closer to the horizon. "If
the memory of today ever dims from your mind, then Earth

Mother and Sky Father will conspire against you. They'l remind you of that afternoon in the desert when you gave yourself to me.''

THE SUN PEERED FROM behind the Chuska Mountain when Marla reluctantly moved away from him. They' shared a moment that would be hers for the rest of her life But it was too painful to remain here now, knowing that i was just a part of her past.

She walked back with him to the vehicle in silence. Wha they'd shared couldn't happen again. Like the old sayin went, a fish and a squirrel could fall in love, but where would they live?

A half hour later, after a tense ride back, they reached th site. Marla saw the reporter from *Grapevine* had parked hi vehicle across the road, blocking the entrance. ''Trouble,' she muttered.

Saffron stood in front of his car facing Hartman, wh was refusing to let him in. Hartman stood rigidly, clos enough to Saffron to make it a challenge.

''The guard's coming,'' Sam answered, ''and he mean business.''

The powerfully built security officer strode toward th two, his nightstick out and in full view.

Marla glanced back at Hartman who showed no signs o backing away from Saffron. ''We better get there befor this escalates into a major war.''

Chapter Nineteen

Marla jumped out of the pickup and went quickly toward the men. Fred Saffron turned toward her as eagerly as a rattler who'd found more appetizing prey. "We were told that we would be allowed back onto the site. I'm still waiting, so it's your call. Do I get to follow up on my story, or do you really want to settle for whatever I can get with my ingenuity and long-range lens?"

"Your story was an insult. You accused us of a whitewash," Hartman said, outraged.

Saffron motioned him to one side, and exchanged a few words with Hartman. Marla watched both men, puzzled when she saw the anger in Hartman's face disappear and give way to speculation.

Saffron returned to the others. "Let me inside that cave with my camera. Five minutes, that's all I'll need."

Marla signaled the guard to remain. "We can't do that. That site is sacred to the Navajo tribe, and not something they want exposed to the general public."

Saffron glanced at Sam, then back at her. "Okay. Then just let me in to look around."

Hartman looked at Marla, then pulled her aside. "He offered me story approval and a donation of two thousand dollars, though he wants me to keep it under wraps. If we watch him very carefully, this will work out in our favor. This deal guarantees us good press and additional funding for your project."

She didn't even have to think about it. "Nothing doing. He's already proven he can't be trusted by trying to sneak onto the site."

"Then how are you going to counter the horror stories he's been writing about you and the project? How much support will that drum up for your scholarship program?" Hartman said in a hard tone.

Marla looked over at the group of reporters while mulling over a plan that was forming in her mind. "Okay, I'll grant access to the site *one* time to *one* member of the press. But it must be someone with a more objective outlook—definitely not Saffron. Get Joe Sanchez from the Farmington paper—he's over by the fence. He's as conservative as they come. He'll balance out any story Saffron might be tempted to concoct later on."

Hartman nodded. "Fair enough." His eyes narrowed pensively as he studied the reporters standing in the road. "What we have to do is show people that we're the real victims here. We've lost a human life, a member of our team, not just artifacts. If we can make the public see that, then sentiment will shift in our favor."

"Go make the arrangements," she answered quietly, "including giving the bad news to Saffron. Afterward, I'll conduct the tour and you can deal with the press. You know what needs to be done, and you're better at dealing with them than I am," she admitted.

As Hartman moved off to talk to the reporters, Sam came to join her. "What's going on?"

Marla filled him in over the sudden noise of Saffron's protests. As the burly guard escorted the *Grapevine* reporter away, Hartman led Joe Sanchez to his van.

"Come on, Sam, let's get going. I want to be right there with them," Marla said.

Hartman kept Sanchez outside the cave until Marla and Sam arrived. After requiring the reporter to leave his camera outside the entrance, she escorted the men inside the lantern-illuminated site.

The students looked up from their work, and Sam explained what was happening. He could feel their tension as the reporter looked around, and knew that it matched his own.

"What about the rest of the cave?" Sanchez asked when Marla refused to lead him beyond the second chamber.

"That portion hasn't been adequately mapped yet, or excavated. You can see for yourself. There are no stake lines or equipment in that area."

Sanchez grudgingly started to go back outside, when a child's broken voice echoed clearly through the darkness. Marla's skin prickled, and she couldn't suppress the shudder that ran through her.

The gloomy shadows inside the cave heightened the impact of the sound, and for a moment it was as if everyone had stopped breathing. A disturbing quiet settled over them as they remained frozen, listening to the tomblike silence that followed. Then, as if feeding on their fear and the darkness, the tiny cry issued forth again. It was a plaintive whimper that touched her nerves like ice water dripping down her back.

"What the hell was that?" Hartman said quickly.

"Let's go find out," Sanchez suggested, and started to go farther into the cave.

Sam moved quickly to block his way. "It didn't come from the interior of the cave."

"Is this what Saffron's been describing as *chindi* activity?" Sanchez didn't wait for an answer. "I'd like to check it out."

Sam forced himself to relax, refusing to lose control. "Step back," he said, glancing at the others, as well. "That sound originated not far from where we're standing."

"But it wasn't very clear. Could a child have been buried alive in here?" Sanchez's face looked pale in the harsh lighting.

Marla remembered the chamber farther in, and shuddered violently.

"Thinking about it, I believe you're right about that sound being close by, though there's bound to be a certain amount of distortion here," Sanchez said. "What about that first chamber? Can we go in there? An enclosed area like that could have diffused the sound."

As the breeze picked up again, the sound echoed eerily around them. "Why is everything always connected to the breeze?" Marla muttered.

"Everything?" Sanchez's eyes gleamed as if a light bulb in his head had suddenly come on.

"The wind has a way of singing through these tunnels," she said, recovering quickly. "The sounds can be unpleasant enough to make your skin crawl."

"That was a voice, and you've heard it before," Sanchez observed. He looked over at Sam. "The cry is muffled, like it's beneath something, or maybe between something." He went to the cave entrance, picked up his camera, then skirted the small ledge that had obscured the alcove for so many years. "Maybe there's a chamber within a chamber. Are there any other entrances into the cave?"

"We've checked all around and haven't seen one," Marla answered. "And there's nothing on that ledge, unless it's been planted there since our last search."

"Let's make sure. What do you have to lose?" Sanchez insisted.

She pursed her lips thoughtfully. "Okay." Marla nodded to her students and Sam. "Go. Start examining the cave and entrance again."

After several minutes Carmen left the cave and joined Sanchez outside. Venturing onto the rim bordering the alcove, she went in the opposite direction from Sanchez.

She hadn't gone very far when her attention focused on a slender string directly in her path. She crouched on the two-foot ledge. "There's a trip wire in this scrub grass. It wasn't here last time we looked. Did somebody set it up to foil our intruder?" she yelled back at the others.

Sam and Marla exchanged glances. "No, so be careful," Marla answered. "That could be attached to almost anything. You and Joe better get off there."

"No way," Sanchez said, hurrying over to it. "Not until I find out what it is."

As Carmen made her way back and joined the others, Marla saw the reporter trying to balance and take photos at the same time. "Are you crazy? Get away from there! You'll either fall off or trip that mechanism!"

"Don't worry. I've shot photos while skydiving. I want to take a closer look." Sanchez slung the camera over his shoulder and leaned over the small tumbleweed that appeared to grow out of the rock itself. "I've got it."

"What? What do you have?" Marla asked.

"You're not going to believe this." Sanchez made his way back, camera against his side. He had something clutched in his free hand. "Or maybe you will. . . ."

As he stepped away from the ledge near the front of the cave, he opened his palm. Marla stared at the small plastic device and the string that dangled from the center of the mechanism. "What is it?"

"You don't know?" he challenged.

"I haven't got a clue," she answered honestly, then glanced at Sam, who shrugged.

Sanchez studied it further. "My mother used to repair kids' dolls to make extra money. It's one of the voice boxes." He pulled the string, and they all listened to a tiny, but familiar voice. "The mechanism was activated when the wind blew a leafy branch strong enough to release the string."

Sanchez stared at Hartman, then back at Marla. "Nice try, people, but the scheme won't work. I wasn't born yesterday. You've got to do better than this when you set *me* up."

Marla stared at him, aghast. Was he actually accusing them of trying to perpetrate a hoax? "What possible motive could anyone at this site have for doing something like that? You're way off base here, mister!"

He gave her a sanctimonious smile. "My guess is you want to make sure we don't pursue the truth—that the sounds coming from here *haven't* been explained. So you purposely leave something like this around to conveniently 'discover.' It would serve to discredit any articles, like Saffron's, of supernatural activity."

The words left her stunned. The theory was so outrageous she wasn't sure how to defend against it. She didn't know whether to laugh or cry. "Look, I have no idea who planted that there."

Hartman glowered at the reporter. "Someone's trying to discredit us further, and that person at least is no ghost. Keep in mind that falsifying anything at this site goes completely against what we're trying to do here."

Sanchez considered Hartman's words. "That's a good point. Okay then, so you *do* believe in the Indian spirits."

Marla saw it coming a second before Hartman did. Seeing Hartman's face turn puce, she decided to step in. "We're not here to prove or disprove any evidence of the supernatural. Our work is strictly archaeological."

"But if the spirits are trying to stop you, do you think you have a chance?" Sanchez said smugly.

"A chance for what? To catch a murderer? To catch vandals? That's police work, and has nothing to do with spiritual matters."

Hartman cleared his throat. "I think we've been more than fair with you. We've allowed you into the cave, and you've seen a good example of what we've been putting up with from the beginning," he said. "I sincerely hope you'll treat us with the same consideration you've been given." He started guiding the man back toward his van.

Marla stood by the cave, watching. Sam's gaze remained on the retreating men. "We've explained the voice and the hollow sounds, but there's much more than that at work here," he said firmly. "We both know it."

Marla started to answer, when the four graduate students approached. "I'd like to catch the creep who's doing this!" Carmen said through her teeth.

"Be grateful that we found the answer. At least we won't have to put up with it anymore," Marla said. She hoped that all the other questions plaguing them would prove to have answers as coolly logical as this. But she'd seen too much already to be able to convince herself of that.

After the students left for the evening forty minutes later, Marla sat outside her RV. Night had descended. Gray shadows dappled the ground, forming twisting, elusive shapes that danced over the desert floor. In the dim light, the entrance to the cave looked like a gaping mouth, ready to swallow anyone who drew near. Maybe in one sense it had been doing that from the very beginning.

Hartman, who'd remained with the reporters until they'd left, now joined her. He cleared his throat. "There's something I'd like to say to you. It's going to be difficult, so bear with me." He paused for several long seconds. "This is your dig. Yet tonight, when we both believed it was your first surefire opportunity for good press, you handed me the limelight. That finally opened my eyes and forced me to see that I've been hiding from the truth."

"I don't follow you," she said warily.

He looked haggard, as if an immense weight rested on his shoulders. "I know I've been hard on you, Garrett. But knowing you were alone out here with a handful of students was a constant reminder of the accident that claimed my wife's life. It's something I've been having trouble coping with. When Brianne had her accident, I wasn't around to help her, and I should have been. I felt I could redeem myself a little by watching out for you and the operations at this site. I thought my intervention would help keep things under control." He took a deep breath. "But I failed and Lena died."

"No one but her murderer is to blame for that."

He shrugged. "The memories and guilt that have come rushing back haven't been easy for me to cope with." He glanced around, studying their surroundings. "I'm beginning to believe there *is* some sort of curse on this place. I've seen many things during my career that haven't always co-

incided with what science teaches. But since you're determined to finish what you started, I won't continue to make
your job impossible by loading you down with paperwork.
All I'm going to ask is that you keep good records, and stay
in touch with me. In the meantime, I'll see if I can get some
additional funds for you out of the departmental budget.
Just don't count on that." He offered her his hand. "So
what do you say? Shall we call a truce?"

"There's nothing that would please me more," she said,
shaking his hand.

MARLA WAS UP EARLY the following morning when Sam
came to her door. She'd packed up her small laptop computer, and was zipping up the case as he stepped inside.

"What's up?"

"Hartman and I had a serious talk last night," she said,
filling Sam in. "After he left, I thought of how much my
career means to me. In that way, he and I are both alike. He
has no wife or children, and nothing else waiting at the end
of the line when he retires. More than anything, he needs
his last years at the college to be filled with challenges and
rewards. These are the memories he'll draw on in years to
come. I know he's wanted to work this site from the very
beginning. Though it's filled with problems, it also has
more promise than anything that's come our way in years.
I'm going to see if I can get a supplementary grant that
would enable him to take an active part here."

"How do you go about doing that?"

"The first step is for me to gather enough data to write
out his résumé. I need one for the grant proposal."

"That shouldn't be hard. All you have to do is ask him."

"No, I'd rather not do it that way. It might raise his
hopes, and I could get turned down, anyway. There are
going to be few sponsors who want to be associated with us
here. If I can get someone to look at my proposal, then I'll
let him know."

"But how will you get the information you need?"

"From the computer files at the college, and his sister. She lives in Durango, and I'm sure she'll help. I'm going to pay her a visit this morning."

"Would you like a ride?"

"Yes, but I'd better not this time. This is college business—something I have to do alone," she answered. "I won't be gone more than a few hours."

"Okay. That'll give me a chance to speak to the tribal leaders. I'm sure your proposal will be put to a vote soon. By the time you return I should know what their decision is."

"Good." She walked to her van, and placed the laptop inside. "I'll be back as soon as possible."

Marla drove more quickly than she should have, eager to complete the errand. For the first time since she'd arrived at the site, things promised to work out. She no longer felt at odds with the tribe, nor with Hartman. From now on, things would run smoothly. She was sure of it.

She made a brief stop at the college. Then, after looking up Louise Hartman's address in the phone book, she drove directly to the condos, which were located on a tree-lined boulevard not far from downtown Durango.

Marla parked next to the curb in front of the door marked 14, and walked up the path. She used the antique brass knocker, then waited. No one answered. She tried again, but there was no response from inside.

A woman in her early sixties came up the adjacent walkway carrying a bag of groceries, and gave her a cursory look. "She's not there. Can I help you with something?" She struggled to balance the bag as she fished out her keys.

"I'm Professor Marla Garrett and I work with Louise's brother," she said. "Do you have any idea what time she'll be home? I need to talk to her."

"Is something wrong?"

"No, not all," Marla assured.

Just then the woman's bag burst open, scattering groceries everywhere. Small cans rolled down the walkway into the flower bed. "Oh, no!" the woman wailed, hurrying after a can that was rolling toward the street.

Marla stepped over the small flower border that separated the entrances. "Here, let me give you a hand."

"Thanks. I'll go find another sack." She rushed inside her home, then returned a moment later holding two new bags. "*These* never give me trouble."

After making sure they'd collected all the groceries, Marla handed the bag back to her. "Here you go."

"Before you leave, would you like some iced tea? I really appreciate your help with this mess."

"It was no trouble, but something cold to drink would be nice," she admitted. "It's awfully hot and humid today."

The air-conditioned apartment felt wonderful, and she gratefully accepted the cold drink. "Thanks."

"I'm Claire Tilton. I've been Louise's neighbor for years. Would you like me to give her a message?"

"Sure." Marla fished out a card. "Tell her I came by. I'm trying to arrange a surprise for Dr. Hartman at work, but I'll need some information from Louise first."

"Oh, that man has had so many troubles! I'm glad you'll be doing something nice for him. He's a widower, you know. And if you ask me, he's much better off alone. His wife made his life miserable. Right to the end, all she ever did was raise his hopes just so she could break his heart."

Marla stared at the kindly old face. The hard words and vehemence seemed completely incongruous. "Well, the accident couldn't have come at a worse time," she said gently. "They'd just managed to settle their differences and get back together."

"Oh, no, that's not true. Dr. Hartman was trying to save face with that story. She was planning to leave him again, for good. She'd fallen in love with a younger man."

"I didn't know about that."

"I normally don't take such a dislike to anyone, but Brianne was trouble. Poor Louise was always trying to talk Dr. Hartman into leaving her, but he was obsessed with that woman. Then fate interceded. I've always said it was divine retribution.''

The news left her stunned. For a moment she wasn't sure what to say. Marla sipped her iced tea and feigned interest in the glass, trying to gather her thoughts.

''Well, you shouldn't listen to me. I have a tendency to gossip. But at my age, I've earned the right to say what I think.''

Marla finished her tea. ''Thanks for the drink,'' she said, standing. What she'd learned didn't mean anything in context with the dig. The knowledge, however, filled her with overwhelming sympathy for Dr. Hartman. She couldn't blame him for trying to salvage some of his pride by not letting the real story be known.

''You should try coming back to Louise's at around four-thirty or five. She's usually home by then.''

After thanking Mrs. Tilton, Marla drove back through the long river valley to the archaeological site. Dr. Hartman had been more of a victim than she'd ever imagined. Only a saint could derive any pleasure in loving someone who didn't love in return. Yet he'd stuck by his wife. She felt herself pitying and admiring Hartman at the same time. More determined than ever to do something for him, she decided to return to Louise's at around six and try again.

She arrived at the site sometime later. Everything looked peaceful, and she breathed a sign of relief. Sam was just coming out of the cave as she left the van. She waved at him, and went to join them. ''Anything new?''

''Your students found some shell ornaments, but not ones that would fall under the agreement you have with the tribe.''

''Do we have an agreement?''

He nodded. ''I heard the news about twenty minutes ago. It wasn't unanimous, but it's in effect.''

''Great!''

Hearing her, Carmen came out. ''We're ready to start going deeper into the cave, Professor. Shall we get to it?''

Marla nodded. "But there's something you should know first. There's a chamber toward the back that entombs several people. There might be dangerous coal gases there, too. Stay away for now."

"Where exactly is that chamber?" Tony asked.

"I really can't say." Marla glanced at Sam. "We found it when we were searching for the source of some unexplained lights, but neither of us has ventured that far back again. I thought that to preserve the site, we had to continue in an orderly manner, sticking to our overall plan."

"Well then, we'll worry about it when we get there. For now, we'll start on the third chamber," Hector said. "We've already got a grid laid out, and so far we've found several projectile points near the entrance."

Once the students got started, Marla walked with Sam back to the entrance. "I'm going to have to go back to Durango." She filled him in on what she'd learned about Hartman.

"I want to go with you. You've accidentally uncovered something that was meant to remain private. You may find your return visit difficult."

"I'll be okay with Louise. She's really a very nice lady."

"Maybe, but circumstances have changed. Once she learns that you spoke to her neighbor, she'll question the woman to find out exactly what you learned. She won't be pleased to discover that you now have information that puts her brother in a bad light. She could easily assume that you're trying to find someone to take the blame for all the trouble you've had here."

Marla considered it. "But once she hears that my questions have nothing to do with Dr. Hartman's wife, surely she'll relax."

"That's just it, though. Maybe you should find a way to ask about his wife. If there's a chance the professor could have been even remotely implicated in another's death, we have to follow up on it."

Chapter Twenty

They left in Sam's truck a short time later. "Maybe we shouldn't go," Marla said as they started down the highway. "I hate to leave while the students are there."

"If we stop investigating because of fear, we'll be playing into the hands of whoever's trying to stop you."

"You're right," she conceded. "But step on it, okay? I'd like to be back as soon as possible."

As twilight covered the desert in lavender and orange, Marla wondered how such a beautiful place could hide so many mysteries. Then again, perhaps that's what added to the mystique of this country. History seemed to fill every mesa and canyon, singing of times long past. She glanced at Sam, wondering if the same would be said of the feelings they'd found and shared here. As the miles stretched out before them, the prospect of her own uncertain future gnawed at her confidence.

By the time they arrived at Louise Hartman's home, she was eager to find something to distract her thoughts. "I don't want this to turn into an inquisition, okay?" Marla said as they walked up to the entrance. "I really do want to help Dr. Hartman."

"Your instincts are good. I'll put my faith in that." Sam knocked at the door.

She started to say more when Louise Hartman appeared. Marla introduced them, then saw the expression on the woman's face harden. Louise opened the screen door, and they walked into the modestly furnished living room.

"I'm glad you came back. I spoke to Mrs. Tilton, and she said you wanted some information about my brother. What's this all about?"

Marla took a seat beside Sam on the sofa, then explained about the grant. Louise's expression didn't change. "I'd like to find a sponsor who can fund his involvement in the project," Marla added. "There might be a way we can still work together."

"My brother has already seen too much death. His wife's accident almost destroyed him. Your site, from everything I've heard, is plagued with trouble. Are you looking for a scapegoat? Is that why you tricked Mrs. Tilton into talking about Brianne?"

"I didn't trick her," Marla replied. "The conversation drifted to that subject. She meant no harm."

"I'm not worried about Mrs. Tilton's motives. It's yours I question." Louise stood and began to pace around her chair. "You say you're here to help my brother, yet you bring the Navajo lawyer. Who are you trying to kid? You're looking for ammunition to save your own hide. Now that you've found out that my brother had been questioned about his wife's death, you're trying to suggest he might somehow be responsible for that student's murder."

"I resent that!" Marla protested.

"You didn't come here just to get information about Philip for a grant proposal." Her eyes glittered with triumph as she met Marla's gaze. "It's written all over your face! You should be sticking up for your boss, not trying to bury him with innuendo. And for your information, the police cleared my brother completely. Mine inspectors who checked the support beams verified when the accident occurred. The night of Brianne's death, he was at home working. Several people saw him there."

"No one's accused your brother of anything, Louise," Marla countered softly.

"Oh sure," she replied cynically. "But once you found out that the trouble between him and Brianne hadn't really ended like most people thought, you wondered. Don't deny it." Louise's eyes were filled with fury. "If my brother wasn't entirely candid about his personal life, that was his prerogative. I should never have told Mrs. Tilton. It was no one's business—" She stopped speaking abruptly. "I think you should leave." Louise walked to the door and held it open.

Marla remained silent until they were well on their way. "What now?"

"Hartman may be innocent, but he's kept something back twice now. His sister, too, seems to be protesting just a little too much on his behalf. Behavior like that always brings out the prosecuting attorney side of me."

"Well, she does have a point. Her brother is innocent."

"The evidence suggests that, but my gut tells me there's more going on here than meets the eye."

Marla was glad when they finally started back to the site. Leaving for any length of time made her uneasy, and it was getting dark. Nervously she watched each passing car, afraid one would be an ambulance or police car on an emergency call.

An hour later, they arrived at the site.

Carmen ran up to the pickup as they stopped and Marla felt her body tense. "Trouble?"

"Professor, I'm glad you're back."

"What happened?"

Dulce came up and shook her head. "It's nothing."

"It isn't nothing. It's unnerving, that's what it is."

"What happened?" Marla repeated, her voice taut.

"We decided to keep working in the cave after the guys left. There wasn't anything else to do, so we figured we'd take the lanterns in and stay busy. Well, twice we heard these really loud thumps. We came out to look, but there was nothing there."

"The guards didn't see anyone, either, and there was no evidence that anyone had approached the cave," Dulce said. "I figured that maybe some rocks were falling off the Hogback, like a natural landslide or something."

Carmen stared at her. "It didn't sound like that at all to me."

"Let's go take a look," Marla suggested.

As they walked toward the cave, one of the guards came toward her. "Professor, I've checked everything inside the fence, and nobody else is here."

"Did you hear the sound, too?" Sam asked.

The man shook his head. "I've been making my rounds, but I didn't hear or see anything unusual, except that coyote." As he stopped speaking, the coyote's distant howl rose in the air. "He's been singing to the moon all night long," he added with a chuckle.

Coyote the trickster, the master of making things seem to be what they were not. Sam glanced at the two women. "Where did the sound come from? Could you tell?"

"It wasn't too far downhill from the cave. I know because we were sitting near the entrance taking a break when it first happened," Dulce said.

Carmen nodded. "I figured it came from around the tents, but we both checked. Nothing looked like it had just rolled there."

"And the second thump occurred in the same area?" Marla asked.

Carmen shrugged. "That one's a little harder to determine. It must have been closer to the cave, because we'd gone back to work when we heard it."

They searched the area thoroughly, taking care not to overlook anything. Though it was difficult with only the moon and their lanterns for illumination, they found no unexplained tracks or equipment on the ground that might have fallen unexpectedly.

Twenty minutes later, Marla sat down near the cave entrance with the two women. Sam leaned back against a large boulder, his eyes on the area ahead. Silence stretched out between them.

"Professor," Carmen said at last, "I'm not the kind of person who scares easily. But that sound was so strange, it gave me the creeps. It just didn't belong, if you know what I mean?"

"The desert has its own voice," Sam conceded. "You learn after a very short time to spot anything that's out of place."

As silence settled over them again, they heard a strange *whoosh*, then a deep thud. Carmen jumped to her feet, but Sam had already sprinted forward. He stopped about ten yards away from the cave entrance, and looked around.

Carmen stood beside him. "Nothing. It's exactly the way it was before."

"No, there's something here," Sam said.

Marla came up with a lantern. "What?"

"This rock. Look at it. It wasn't there before." He lifted the grapefruit-size rock with the tip of his boot, and revealed crushed snakeweed beneath.

Carmen glanced at Marla, then at the others. "Flying rocks?"

"Looks that way," Sam answered. "And not meteorites," he added with an ironic smile.

"Remember the smashed windshield?" Marla asked. "I think we've got somebody with a real strong throwing arm out there."

"Or maybe someone's devised a catapult of sorts," Sam proposed.

"Possible," Marla agreed, "but unless the mechanism is huge, he's got to be close by. That rock weighs about two pounds, I'd say."

"I remember a fraternity prank we played in college a few times. We used the fork of tree branches and surgical tubing to hurl heavy snowballs right over our own roof and against the front of a rival house half a block away. They couldn't see us, but they kept hearing the thud every time one hit the door or the porch."

"Wait a minute. That gives me an idea," Marla replied. "Do **you** recall the large pair of holes we saw on the other side of the fence? Maybe what we found was the spot where he anchored the launching system for something like a big slingshot."

"Maybe the rock that smashed the windshield was his test shot. It just went off the mark," Carmen suggested.

"You mean his original intent was what he's doing now—trying to unnerve us?" Marla considered it. "I think you may have found the answer."

Carmen nodded. "That would explain why we haven't been subjected to this since that first shot of his. He wanted to give us a chance to forget about it."

Sam agreed. "Fear would save him by creating confusion, like it did with the tube noisemaker and the doll's voice box before we discovered them," he concluded.

Carmen ran a hand through her hair. "Well, whatever's going on, that's it for me tonight. I'm going to bed—in the safe confines of the camper."

Dulce sighed. "Yeah, I've had enough, too."

"I don't like it," Marla said as the two women returned to the camper. "This shouldn't be happening now."

"I told you not to overestimate this new agreement with the tribe. There are still many who oppose what you're doing."

Marla walked with Sam to the RV. "Begay, in my opinion, is still the most likely suspect. He's got motive and plenty of opportunity."

"So do the reporters, especially Saffron. It's to their benefit to keep this story alive by any means possible." He waited by the door as she stepped up inside. "Get some sleep. Tomorrow, we'll talk about it some more."

Marla went in and glanced at the empty room. She'd always known precisely what she wanted out of life and how to get it. But now, the goals she'd held and nurtured inside her for so long no longer fit. For the first time in her life, her priorities weren't clear. Her needs seemed to be changing, and she wasn't sure it was for the better.

Marla undressed and crawled beneath the covers on her cot. Unable to sleep, she stared at the nighttime shadows that dappled the metal walls.

SHORTLY AFTER TEN the next morning, Sam came to the cave where Marla was working. "I've been asked to extend an invitation to you. The tribal leaders would like you to attend a social tonight."

"A social?"

"An informal get-together with lots of food."

"I'd love to go," she said. "But I'm surprised to be asked."

"You shouldn't be," he said. "My guess is that Billy's hoping that once the others meet you, they'll view you as less of a threat. So far, you're nothing more than a nameless concept to many of them."

"What time?"

"At sunset, or thereabouts. Time's not as rigid a concept with us, remember?"

"Right."

The day passed slowly, but the excavations revealed nothing of religious significance. Sam was grateful, not wanting the dispute to become an issue at the social. Tonight, he was hoping to show Marla that it was possible for her to carve her own place among his people. Her dreams for the future didn't have to exclude him.

As the sun began its descent, Sam watched Marla leave the cave and glance around cautiously. He knew the incident with the rocks yesterday had disturbed her more than she'd admitted. He'd checked the area earlier, and had found more of the large paired holes on the rise behind the site. But any tracks that might have been left had been deliberately obliterated by scattering sand over the marks.

"I'm sure the rock-throwing incident was meant to unnerve us, nothing else. You don't have to worry about anything here tonight. The guards will be on duty to handle any problem."

"I know, but I'm still a little nervous. I asked the guys to stay here with Dulce and Carmen until eight when they leave for class. Since they're working the late shift, that wasn't a problem. But I'd like to be back by eleven."

"Fine."

Marla dressed with care, knowing that impressions would count more than usual tonight. She wore an ankle-length Santa Fe–style skirt, and a long-sleeved silk blouse tied at the waist with a silver concha belt fashioned by a Navajo silversmith.

Sam, who'd changed clothes in his tent, met her outside. His eyes held her in an appreciative gaze. Before he could comment, the boys let out a loud wolf whistle.

Marla laughed. "Thanks, guys, but I think it's because you've never seen me wearing anything but jeans."

"Well, I should whistle at you," Carmen said, looking at Sam. "You look fantastic. Don't you think so, Professor?" Her eyes twinkled mischievously.

Marla laughed and gave Sam a speculative look. "Okay, they dragged it out of me. You look great."

"What a sincere compliment," he said, smiling.

As they got ready to leave, Marla told the others where she'd be. "Remember that you'll have the cellular phone. Call me if *anything* goes wrong, or even if you think it might."

"It won't. Relax," Carmen said. "You're doing our project a world of good by going. They need to see us just as people, not the bad guys."

Sam nodded. "Precisely my point, too."

"Yeah, but this'll work only if I can carry it off. Everyone will be staring, wondering if I'm a greedy opportunist or a regular person," she added, her voice slightly higher than normal.

"You'll be fine. I have confidence in you," Sam answered gently. "So do the Todacheenes."

She closed her eyes, and then opened them again. "Great. Now if I blow it, I'll also feel guilty for letting you all down." She started toward his pickup. This was just another reason why she had to find a way to forget about Sam. She'd never be an asset to him here. All she could do was complicate his life.

As they drove south on Highway 666 toward Window Rock, Sam's thoughts drifted. "By the way, Saffron has been asked to attend."

"They asked *him*?" she said, surprised.

"Not 'they,' just one person. Your neighbor on the reservation side of the site."

"Begay, of course. Why would he invite Saffron?"

"He's an old hand at getting the press on his side. Begay knows that the leaders don't care much for that rag, but he also knows that lots of people in the Rez read it. He's playing, that's all. He wants to stay on Saffron's good side."

"I don't think the man has one," she muttered.

They arrived ninety minutes later. The social was being held in a clearing south of the natural arch itself. A large bonfire added just enough light to make shadows even more pronounced while the beautiful red sandstone cliffs glowed against the twilight. As they approached, the juniper and piñons encircled them like sentinels—or predators; Marla wasn't sure which.

When she walked into the gathering, she could feel eyes shifting toward her. Yet there was no hostility in those gazes, only curiosity. The only warmth she felt, however, was from the bonfire.

The smell of fry bread, green chili, bread puddings and mutton stew reached her nostrils. Nervousness had made her ravenous, and the tempting aromas drifting over from the large picnic tables teased her.

Sam brought her a soft drink, then suggested she try the fry bread and stew. "The lady that fixes both is an old friend, and she's the best cook around."

Marla felt a twinge of jealousy. The only thing she could cook with impunity came frozen, and with instructions to peel back to expose dessert.

A second later, Sam introduced her to a Navajo woman in her late sixties. The relief she felt annoyed her even more.

She'd already accepted that there was no future for her with Sam. She shouldn't care about the women in his life, regardless of their age.

Marla exchanged pleasantries with the woman, then she and Sam sat together at a picnic table along with other guests and began to eat. Looking up from her place, she saw Billy Todacheene approaching with a man she didn't recognize.

"That's Curtis Destea," Sam told her. "He's head of the Shiprock chapter house. He's been a tribal representative for years, and also one of those opposed to your staying at the site. You should definitely meet and talk to him." Sam rose to greet them.

She felt her stomach tie itself into knots. Forgetting all about food, she joined Sam. Destea wore a massive silver-and-turquoise belt buckle whose edges rested against his expansive stomach. As he drew near, his coal black eyes regarded her with a distrust that cut right through her.

"I've heard much about you," Destea said, after being introduced.

No doubt, but she had no idea what to say. "My work certainly has created a lot of interest," she commented.

"I don't agree with what you're doing," Destea said flatly. "My position is plain. But I will tell you that I admire your courage. Much has happened to you on that land, yet you've shown no cowardice. There's something to be said for that."

"But I have been afraid," Marla admitted honestly.

"I was a Code-Talker in the Marines during World War II. I saw how different people deal with danger. Bravery is facing your fears, and doing what you have to despite them," Destea answered.

Saffron came up to them, camera in hand. "How about a photo of all my favorite news makers together? The college professor makes peace with the tribe type of shot?" Saffron urged, raising his camera.

Destea stepped back, his face impassive. "No photos."

"You'll be on the front page. Of course you want photos," Saffron joked, raising his camera again.

Sam stepped right up to Saffron's face. He was smiling, but his words were hard. "What part of 'No photos' don't you understand, Saffron?"

"Okay, okay, no photos," Saffron laughed nervously, backing away. "I'll catch you guys later at the site, then."

As Saffron quickly disappeared, Todacheene stepped away with Destea to exchange a few private words. Alone with Sam, Marla forced a thin smile. "Good thing the tribe didn't want photos. I'm not very photogenic. Did you look at the shots Saffron took showing us coming out of the cave? You looked distinguished. I looked like a troglodyte emerging after a year of hibernation."

He was about to answer when Todacheene called out to him. "I'll be right back," he said quickly.

Marla sat down again at the picnic table beside two women who smiled at her, but seemed intent on their own animated discussion. As she moved her plate closer, she saw something had been placed beneath it. She slid out a small note and unfolded it. It was written almost in a child's scrawl and read, "Want answers? Meet me in the parking area at 9:15."

She searched around for Sam, but saw he was still busy talking to Destea and Todacheene. Considering her options, she looked at her watch. It was five minutes after nine. Surely there could be no harm in going. There were dozens of people around. All she'd have to do was scream, and help would be there instantly. As long as she didn't approach any rows of cars, and stayed out in the open, no one was going to sneak up on her.

She waited until 9:13, then walked slowly toward the cars. Cautiously, she remained on the road beside the parking area and waited. The sound of other people nearby was reassuring.

"I'm here," she called out, "but this is as far as I'm going. If you're there, come out and show yourself."

The air just beyond a cluster of piñons bordering the parking area began to shimmer, and a heartbeat later a spectral figure emerged not fifty feet away. He was wearing leggings, his bare chest crisscrossed with white clay snake markings. His face was totally white. An unearthly glow accentuated the pallor.

It had to be a trick! She'd get closer and find out. But before her legs responded, the figure suddenly shot toward her clutching an enormous glowing knife raised high in the air. Terror seized her, and she began to scream.

Chapter Twenty-One

As her scream rose above the sound of laughter and music, the apparition abruptly stopped, turned, and disappeared from view into the trees. Whatever retreat it made was soundless, perhaps obscured by the voices and footsteps of those rushing to her aid.

A dozen or more men arrived. They looked around quickly for a threat, but found nothing. As others joined them, several stared suspiciously at her while she tried to explain. No one drew near her. She heard someone murmur a warning about ghost sickness, and a few people stepped back.

A heartbeat later, Sam found his way through the crowd. "What happened?" His gaze ran over her thoroughly, searching for injuries.

"I don't know what's going on," she managed, handing him the slip of paper and explaining what she'd seen.

"A trick of the firelight maybe?" Billy Todacheene approached, overhearing her words.

Wallace Todacheene, who'd stood by his son, walked toward the spot Marla had indicated. "If it was, it left footprints," he called out. "There was a man here. He ran down toward her, then turned and headed into the trees. He weighed about 165 pounds, I'd guess, and was wearing hard-soled boots."

"He took me by surprise," Marla said. "I thought it was a trick, but when he charged toward me like that holding a knife, I had no idea what else to do. I couldn't have outrun him." Marla accompanied Sam to where Wallace stood. "Why would anyone do this?"

Billy Todacheene crouched down next to a large boulder. "Someone else was over here, taking photos." He picked up a tab from the end of a box of high-speed film. "Looks like they wanted your photo with this 'ghost,'" he observed disgustedly.

Sam glanced around quickly and saw Saffron easing into the crowd. "Hold it!"

Saffron backed away from Sam, then stopped. As Sam approached, he popped the film from his camera and exposed the entire roll. "That's so you won't have to worry," he said, dangling it from the end.

Sam glared at him. "Or maybe you didn't want to be caught with incriminating evidence?"

"I have no incriminating evidence. What you just saw was a gesture of good faith. That's the only roll I have. You're free to search me and my car."

"We'll do that," Billy answered, signaling two tribal police officers. While several people looked on, Saffron turned out the contents of his pockets and camera bag, then went to his car. The officers, Sam and Billy Todacheene went along with him. Todacheene's face was a hard mask. Marla stood to one side, curious to see what would happen as the officers searched the vehicle.

"I told you it was my only roll," Saffron said, minutes later.

"Who was your partner? You know, the ghost?" Sam demanded.

"I don't know who you're talking about. I saw Professor Garrett leave the party, and I decided to see what she was up to. That's all."

"I don't want to see you on this reservation again," Billy Todacheene said flatly.

"You can't keep me out. This is a free country!"

"Sue us. This is the Navajo Nation. We have our own laws. By the time you get a hearing, you'll be an old man,"

Sam added calmly. "These officers will escort you back to the state highway."

As they drove off, Sam stared at the fading taillights, lost in thought. Saffron had undoubtedly faked other things in an attempt to confuse them, but the reporter hadn't been around the night he'd first seen the warrior. Sam suppressed a shudder, remembering the pain that had clouded his vision, and wondered if perhaps he'd been his own trickster then.

Marla came up to stand beside him. "What I saw was similar to the figure I saw the evening Lena was killed. Do you think Saffron's been behind this all along?"

He started to answer, when a tribal officer approached, radio in hand. "I called this incident in to the New Mexico State Police since it could have some bearing on the events at the archaeological site. In turn, they shared some information with us I thought you might find interesting. Traces of thick, dark makeup were discovered on the trowel used to stab the Mendez woman. The makeup was dark enough to have made an Anglo, no matter how fair-skinned, appear to be a Navajo, at least from a distance."

"Thanks, Bobby," Sam answered, then started back toward the gathering. "Come on. I think we should say goodbye and get back to the site."

Marla and Sam thanked their hosts, then headed back to the pickup. "I noticed something as we left the social. Begay was nowhere to be seen."

"There's no way he's in it with that reporter. He's too smart for that." Sam glanced at her, studying her expression in the glow of the instrument panel lights.

"Maybe, but I don't believe Saffron could have engineered everything that happened tonight. The markings on that warrior were accurate. I've studied enough of your culture to know. My guess is that the information came from Begay, though Saffron embellished it by adding a few touches of his own. That knife, for instance, was a bowie, not ancient Navajo."

"It happened so quickly. Are you sure?"

"Yes. It's not something I'd forget or confuse." She rubbed her temples, trying to soothe her headache. "I'll bet you anything I won't be able to get any sleep tonight. I'm way too keyed up. I sure wish I had my mother's special toddy recipe. That would have put a charging bull to sleep. And the best part was you never felt groggy in the morning."

Sam said nothing for several long minutes. "Hmm. That gives me an idea."

"Do *you* have a toddy recipe?"

"No." He smiled. "But you triggered an idea. When someone drinks too much, the tendency is to fall into a very deep sleep. I wonder how much the professor's secretary had to drink the night Lena Mendez was killed."

"June doesn't drink—ever."

"So much for that." He stared at the road, lost in thought. "Does the professor take any kind of medication, like sleeping pills or sedatives?"

"I don't know."

"Would you like to try to find out?"

"How?"

"We go to his home and take a look through his garbage. Maybe we'll find a pill bottle that's been thrown out, or a pharmacy receipt."

"Tonight would be the best time to do that, then. He lives about two miles from me and trash day is tomorrow. They come by really early. Most people put out their stuff the night before."

"Let's go for it. We really shouldn't pass up this chance. We know guards are at the site, and your students won't be back until eleven or so."

She considered it. "And if we get caught?"

"Who's going to be watching over their trash at nine o'clock at night? We'll toss it into the back of the truck, and go where we can examine it carefully without him seeing. Then afterward, we'll bring it back just to make sure he doesn't get suspicious."

"I'll remember this was your idea," she muttered.

They drove to Durango, tension high between them. The idea was good, but she was worried. Experience had taught her that even simple things could get incredibly fouled up.

Some time later, they stood in the bed of Sam's borrowed truck, just around the corner from Hartman's house. They were sifting through garbage that had cured for a week in or around his house. The smell almost gagged her, and she tried to remember to breathe only through her mouth. "This was a disgusting idea," Marla said, tossing aside a piece of decayed chicken.

"Keep looking," he said, clearing his throat.

"There's nothing in mine," she said, resealing the bag. "I suggest you burn these gloves. They're probably a major health hazard."

She took a pen flashlight from his shirt pocket. "Here. Shine it inside this one. There are some papers at the bottom."

Pulling out a series of bills, he began sorting through them.

"He uses a cellular phone frequently. I've found the most recent bill. Did you know he had one in his private vehicle?"

"No." She fell silent, weighing the idea. "The day we were trapped in the shed, I called him at home as soon as we got out. I wonder if he really was there."

Sam continued reading the bill. "Here we go. From the date and times, it looks like he took your call and made several others from the cellular phone that night."

"It still doesn't prove anything. He could have been a mile from home at the time, on the way back from the grocery store," Marla said.

"Sure. Or he could have just left the site after locking us in," Sam countered.

"We know one thing—his alibi is not as sound as we thought."

"That's a fair statement. Guess where he was the night you called him after Lena's attack?"

"In his car again?" Seeing Sam slowly nod, her stomach suddenly developed butterflies.

Sam kept the bill, and they finished checking out the garbage. Eventually they realized there was no medicine bottle.

"Let's put this trash back and get out of here," she said.

Sam picked up both bags, and signaled for her to remain in the shadows. "Let me take care of this." He peered around the tall pines bordering an empty for-sale home. "Hartman's at his window, and the fire station down the block has too many lights on."

Marla watched Sam cross the street and walk down the block. After setting the bags inside the metal trash cans by Hartman's driveway, Sam started back. He was just across the front walk when Hartman shifted. Sam froze in midstep. After an eternity, he continued toward her again.

A moment later they were on their way. "What were you waiting for back there? The way you were staring at that window, I thought you'd considered serenading him!" she snapped acerbically.

"I don't know. I just had a feeling there was something wrong."

"Did he see you?"

"No, nothing like that, I'm sure. It was...something else. I can't put my finger on it."

"Well, despite what we learned tonight, I don't think Hartman is the murderer. He had no motive for wanting Lena Mendez dead. Begay wants the site closed down, Saffron wants a story, and many Navajos want us out of there. Hartman, on the other hand, doesn't need trouble at the dig. He wants good publicity for the college, the department and himself."

"That's true, but I still wish I could take a look in his medicine cabinet." Sam stared down into the path the headlights cut through the darkness. "Something occurs to me. All along we've assumed that Lena was just in the wrong place at the wrong time, so she was killed. But what if she was the intended victim? Was Lena close to anyone in particular at school? Or for that matter, did she have any enemies?''

"Not really. She kept to herself. The only thing Lena ever showed any particular interest in was her work. She'd arrive early for class, and spend much of her day at our lab. Her papers were a joy to grade, she was always very careful with details. That was what made her such a great anthro student." Marla shifted in her seat, turning so she could look at Sam more directly. "You know, Lena had a small drawer at the lab. I assigned it to her at the beginning of the year for her tools and things. I wonder if anyone's thought to check it."

"We're close to the college now. Why don't we stop and call campus security? They can meet us at the lab. We really should go take a look, but not without a witness."

Ten minutes later, Marla used her rear door key and led the way to the lab. "I hope the guard gets here quickly. I don't like the idea of staying away from the site with Saffron's and Begay's whereabouts unknown."

He sat down on top of a desk and looked across the room. Shelves of pottery sherds lined one entire wall. If anyone had told him six months ago that he'd be inside a lab of this kind, he would have thought they were crazy. His eyes strayed over to Marla. And maybe he was, but it was a good kind of crazy. He loved this woman despite her peculiarities, though admittedly she'd never see anything peculiar about herself. He smiled ruefully, glancing around.

Marla's gaze fastened on him. "What on earth are you thinking about?"

"Peculiarities," he answered, enjoying the mystified expression on her face.

The guard came in a moment later, and Marla quickly walked over to the drawer at the end of the room. Curiosity was making her impatient. She pulled it out and turned over the contents onto the worktable. There were the usual things, like brushes, a small trowel, some pens and a caliper, but nothing out of the ordinary. "It looks like we wasted our time."

Sam looked beneath the drawer itself, and inside the opening in the cabinet. "Well, it was a good try." He continued to examine the room. "Is there any other place in here she might have used for storage?"

Marla shook her head. "We're always scrambling for space. If I hadn't taken my manuals out of that bookcase, she would have had to lug those two heavy reference books back and forth every day."

"The ones on the top shelf?" Sam glanced at the guard. "Stick around for a few minutes, okay?"

"No problem," he answered with a bored look, sipping at a cup of coffee.

She walked to the shelf and brought them down. "Nothing too awe inspiring about them, I'm afraid."

Sam picked one up and leafed through it, holding it upside down. He repeated the process with the second volume. "Nothing inside."

She took one of the books back, and pressing her palm against the spine, pushed the volume back into its place. It took some effort because of the tight spacing, and as she forced it all the way in, she felt a slight bulge beneath the binding. Puzzled, Marla pulled it out again.

"What is it?" Sam asked.

"I don't know yet." She balanced the book on its side, and ran her fingers over the binding. "I was right. There *is* something stuck in here."

Sam felt through the binding, trying to make out what lay below. "It's metal, or hard like metal."

Marla walked to her desk and retrieved a long pair of forceps. While Sam held the book, she forced the prongs into the binding itself. A second later she extracted a key.

The guard stared at it, then at them. "Nice work." He noted the three digit number stamped on the key, but refrained from touching it. "We sometimes find those around campus right around a holiday. It's probably from a storage compartment at the bus station."

They made the necessary arrangements, surprised by how fast the authorities could move when sufficiently motivated. Even the New Mexico State Police reacted more quickly than anyone expected making a request for a search. Lena's murder investigation had come to a standstill, and they were eager to uncover new leads.

Forty minutes later, they walked inside the bus station accompanied by a Durango city police sergeant and the fax copy of a judge's order. Marla felt distinctly uncomfortable about the prospect of opening Lena's locker. For all she knew, they were about to uncover a part of Lena's life that had nothing to do with her murder and deserved to have remained private. Still, they had to see this through.

The officer placed the key in the lock and turned it. A second later it clicked open and he stepped aside, giving Marla an unobstructed view. "Can you identify what's in here, Professor?"

Potsherds, several projectile points and portions of a spear were stacked inside. She leaned forward, getting a closer look, but made no move to touch them. "Those came from my archaeological site, I'm sure. You'll find they cross-reference against the list of stolen objects the New Mexico police have on file."

Marla saw the notebook lying at the bottom of the locker at the same time the officer did. She stood beside him as he retrieved it and leafed through the pages, holding the folder by the edges. "This is a diary, of sorts. Your student made a lucrative deal with your department chairman. Together they stole your records, looted the site, and even conspired to discredit you by seeding the cave with phony artifacts."

"Hartman," Sam said softly. "You always remained a threat to him. You were an up-and-coming faculty member, someone who could take away the prestige and recognition he wanted to be solely his."

"But even if he wanted to destroy me professionally, why on earth would he kill Lena?"

The sergeant looked up from where he was reading. "The young lady demanded more money in payment for her silence. She had enough to ruin him, too." He flipped to the back of the journal and pointed to an instant photo glued to the last page. "She'd taken this at the professor's house."

Marla studied the photo showing a warrior's costume and a long black-haired wig laid out on a bed. A small photo on the nightstand revealed Hartman and Brianne. "Yes, I can see why he was running scared."

"His work was all he had," Sam observed ruefully. "In essence he was fighting for his life."

"According to this—" the officer glanced at Marla and continued "—the plan was to make you believe that you were seeing ghosts and have the others think you were crazy." He paused, scanning the last of the page. "The last entry indicated she was going to meet with Dr. Hartman at the site while you were away at some kind of college seminar."

"That's when he killed her," she said in a whisper.

"From his point of view, it made all the sense in the world," Sam observed. "He'd protect himself, and in the process, his attempt to destroy you would become even more effective."

Marla's hand went up to her throat. "Where's Hartman now? He doesn't know that the game's up—he could return to the site. Everyone trusts him. There's no end to the trouble he could cause."

"Who's there now?" the officer asked.

"Our two guards. The students are at work or attending evening classes. They won't be back until about eleven-thirty or so."

"Hartman might still be at home, you know," Sam suggested. "He was there earlier." He explained what they'd found, and turned over the phone bill.

"We'll have an arrest warrant issued, and pick him up. Don't worry."

"In that case, if you don't need us anymore, we'll return to the site," Marla said. "I won't breathe easy until I know he's in custody."

As the police sped away, she climbed into the passenger side of Sam's truck. "I changed my mind. Why don't you drive past Hartman's house and verify that he's been arrested? If he's not there, then I want you to break the speed limit and get me to the site as fast as possible. I don't want my students returning before I'm there."

Sam hurried to Hartman's where a lot of activity appeared ready to take place. Parking down the block, they edged in closer on foot. From their vantage point, they could see Hartman at his desk near the window. He seemed oblivious to the world outside.

When the police knocked loudly on the door, Hartman turned his head to one side, but otherwise remained seated. "What's wrong with him?" she asked. "If we can hear the knocking from here, why can't he?"

"I don't know."

Seconds later, police, weapons drawn, broke down the door. Marla saw three officers rush into the room, and then, abruptly, Hartman disappeared from view. Marla's knees almost buckled and she reached for Sam's arm. Before she could figure out what had happened, one of the officers came rushing back outside.

"It's a trick," he yelled to the others. "Fan out. He might still be in the neighborhood."

Sam tried to hurry Marla back to the truck. "We've got to get you out of here."

"Not until I know what happened!" She jogged over to the police sergeant, who was standing near Hartman's garage door.

Recognizing her, he quickly pulled Marla into the shadows. "You shouldn't be here. The guy's still at large. All they found inside was a dummy with a painted latex face that looks like Hartman."

"But it moved, I saw it!" Marla insisted.

"The figure was attached to a hidden electric motor and a timer that shifted the head at irregular intervals."

"Call the New Mexico State Police, please. They've got to send officers over to my site! I'm afraid that's where he'll go."

"Don't worry, ma'am. We're already in contact with New Mexico law enforcement officers. They're going to call your site and instruct the guards to report in immediately if they spot Hartman. In the meantime, we'll be checking around here and at the college. We've put an APB out on his vehicle, so it's just a matter of time before we catch him."

She strode back to Sam's truck. "We gave our word to the tribe that those artifacts would be safe. Let's get back there. That's where we both belong now."

"Let's go."

Sam wasted no time. They made the trip in less time that they ever had. When Sam saw the guard keeping watch at the end of the road, and no sign of trouble, he relaxed. "Good. Looks like it's business as usual here."

Sam went up the dirt track and parked his vehicle. Moments later, they went up to the cave together. Marla entered first, shining the flashlight around the gloomy interior. "I just need to reassure myself that everything's okay."

Marla aimed the flashlight into the first and second chamber. Nothing seemed to have been disturbed.

"Okay. Things are in order. What do you say we get out of here?" Sam's tone was rigidly controlled.

"Sure. There's no sense in hanging around. Let's go have some coffee."

As they neared the entrance, they heard movement behind them. Marla spun around, illuminating the area with her flashlight. The unearthly image of a warrior shimmered into view, passing into the third chamber. Confusion, anger and a heavy dose of fear combined, sharpening all her instincts. She knew it was Hartman, but he looked like the real thing. The body makeup had been perfectly applied, and the long dark-haired wig completed an extremely effective disguise.

"He's wearing the Slayer armor," Sam said angrily. He grabbed the flashlight from her hand and sprinted after Hartman.

Marla followed, using the glow of the flashlight reflected off the cave walls ahead as a guide. Just as she reached the tunnel, she tripped over something soft on the cave floor.

Muttering a curse, she rose slowly to her knees. Marla narrowed her eyes, trying to adjust to the tomblike darkness. Shapes slowly became defined, and she saw that the lump she'd fallen over was the body of the second guard.

She knelt beside him, recovered his flashlight, and used it to determine the man's condition. He was alive, but judging from a bloody bump on the back of his head, he'd been struck from behind. Unwilling to leave him there, now that Hartman was also in the cave, she quickly dragged the unconscious man outside.

A quick search of his gear revealed that the guard's radio was missing. She'd have to go for help. Marla turned off the light and stared at the cave wondering what was happening between Sam and Hartman. As she looked pensively into the pocket of blackness, the interior exploded into a cluster of small lights. They hovered in one place. Then, in a breath, they shot across the darkness, leaving a thin glowing line that dissipated in the blink of an eye.

There was no time to run for help now. Both men were in grave danger. A strange odor, like the reek of decay, was coming from within, but there was nothing around that could account for it. She turned on her light and ran inside. A rhythmic drumming reverberated through the entire cavern. The sound went through her like an icy January wind. If it was a trick, it was a good one. The rock walls seemed to vibrate, absorbing and releasing the deep baritone sound.

Marla ran through the tunnels as quickly as her flashlight could show the way, heading into the heart of the cave. She hadn't gone far when she heard men's voices. Sam was there and he was okay. Marla stopped in her tracks, but she'd already gone too far.

"Hello, Garrett." Hartman's voice, cold and deadly, came from a dark opening behind her. "Move over there by your friend."

She turned her head and saw the barrel of a shotgun aimed at her. "Why should I do what you want? You're not going to get away with this."

"Refuse, and I'll shoot you right now."

"Let her walk away." Sam's voice echoed through the cavern. "I'll be your bargaining chip. With me as a hostage, you'll have the leverage you need to make your escape."

"Escape to what?" He motioned for Marla to join Sam, who was cornered in a dead end. "I'm not after escape. I want revenge. Get over there, Garrett. I'm running out of patience."

"I've never done anything to you!" Marla protested. "Why are you doing this?" As she reached Sam, he quickly pulled her into the shadows with him.

"You really don't know? The way you've been digging into my past, I thought you'd figured it out by now." Hartman positioned himself so that he blocked Sam and Marla's only escape route. "My wife was my entire world once. But she used my love to control me. Brianne thought she could do anything she wanted and I'd always welcome her back with open arms. Finally she got tired of using me, and decided to leave forever. She didn't care about ruining my life. That's when I saw her for what she really was. I couldn't let her win after what she'd done. In a way, she did get what she wanted. She left me, but she did it in a hearse.

"Then you came along. You wanted to take the only thing I had left—my career. You didn't care, either. You never gave a thought to what you'd be doing to me. You used your looks and your youth, everything that gave you the advantage. You had the dean eating out of your hand, too. I overheard him the day you got this grant. He'd already decided to recommend that you succeed me as chairman. What's worse, I knew it wouldn't have stopped there. You would have continued chipping away at everything I'd worked for, taking charge of all the important work. I would have ended up teaching Anthro 101 to English majors!''

''You're wrong, but none of that matters now,'' Marla answered. ''The police know you murdered Lena and why. She left a diary and a photo of the warrior's disguise, just in case you turned on her, too. That costume won't protect you anymore. Give yourself up. That's your only chance.''

''You think you've won,'' he observed in a weary voice. ''But I won't let that happen. I may be finished, but so are you.''

''You can't shoot us where we're at now,'' Sam reasoned. ''You'd have to risk coming right up to us. Why jeopardize your own life? You've got nothing to gain by pressing this.''

''I don't intend to get any closer to you. I'm going to do what I need from right here. Brianne, like you, Marla, valued her work more than she ever did me. It was fitting that it should play a part in her death. It'll be the same for you now.''

''You can't engineer a cave-in here. These walls are too solid,'' Sam objected.

''True. That's why I'm going to use a propane torch and set fire to a small vein of coal I found in here. You'll die of asphyxiation. I'll be near the cave entrance. Try to rush past me, and I'll shoot you.''

''The uninjured guard would hear the shot,'' Marla countered.

''If he comes, then so be it. I'll be arrested, but you'll still be dead.'' He lit the burner and the smell quickly permeated the cave. ''You both valued this place very highly. It seems right that you should die here. Maybe you'll become the cave's new guardians.''

As he completed the last word, low, unearthly wails, like the agonized cries of the damned, began to infiltrate the cave. They came from everywhere, reverberating against the walls, rising in pitch and intensity with every passing second. Marla fell to her knees, her hands over her ears. Her head throbbed with the deafening sound.

She wasn't sure how long it lasted, but the sounds eventually tapered off and stopped. The silence that followed was as profound as it was unnerving. As she began once again to focus on the cave, she realized she'd been nestled against Sam, held protectively against his chest.

She straightened slowly and looked at him, the question in her eyes never reaching her lips. Hartman was gone.

Sam brushed her face with his palm, then held a finger to his lips. "I'll be back," he mouthed.

He started to move away, but she was right behind him. She gave him an infuriating little smile that told him she had no intention of letting him go alone. With a quiet sigh, he crept forward again.

They kept their backs pressed against the wall. Marla half expected a volley of shots or flames to stop them, but only more of the sound-absorbing silence encircled them. Then Sam stopped in midstride, and muttered something under his breath.

Marla leaned over slightly, following his line of vision. Hartman was splayed out on the cave floor, his neck nearly severed by the flint knife that was part of Slayer's weaponry. It was imbedded to the hilt within the jagged folds of skin at his neck, now stained a deep crimson. Blood spilled onto the cave floor, running in a wide stream that turned the ground into a sea of red. Her stomach lurched, and for a moment she was afraid she was going to be sick.

"Who killed him?" Marla asked, her voice barely a whisper. "Local Navajos?"

Sam held her back, studying the ground with Marla's flashlight. "They would have left footprints. Look for yourself. There are none."

Marla stared down at the body. "Suicide? Those screams were horrible. Maybe the sound drove him over the edge. He must have thought that he'd opened the gates of Hell." She paused. "I'm not sure he didn't."

His gaze swept the area in a methodical search. "Where's the propane torch he said he had?" Sam glanced up as a strange smell filled his nostrils.

Marla gasped, seeing the string of pinpoint lights across the cave emerging from another chamber. "That's what drove me in here," she whispered. "I saw the lights and then smelled something odd, like decaying leaves."

"That's not what I smell now. It's burning coal!" Sam yelled.

Death at their heels, Sam grasped her hand and ran through the tunnel with her as fast as he could.

Chapter Twenty-Two

Seeing the entrance less than thirty feet ahead, Sam increased his pace. "We're almost there!"

A sudden explosion rocked the cave, knocking them off their feet in a hot blast. As rocks broke loose from the roof, debris and dust showered over them.

Marla scrambled to her feet first and tugged at Sam's arm, pulling him forward. "Come on! The propane bottle must have exploded. There are gasoline lanterns back there, too. They won't last long now."

Sam got up as another rumble shook the cave and thick smoke began filling the air. "The passageways are collapsing."

They could no longer see any of the chambers behind them. Chaos looming at their backs, they ran for the entrance. As a violent tremor shuddered through the cave, Sam gripped her hand, and dived through the cave entrance. They fell hard, rolling down a slope several yards before stopping.

Bright tongues of orange flame spit out from the entrance for one brief moment, followed by dense black smoke. As they stared in horror at the nightmarish scene they'd left behind, the uninjured guard ran up.

He helped Marla to her feet, then glanced at Sam, making sure they were both okay. "I know you dragged Charley out, but you should have called me. What happened? I found Hartman's car in an arroyo, but no sign of him. Where is he?"

"In there," she answered wearily, gesturing toward the cave. The other guard approached, still holding a handkerchief on his head wound. Marla gave him a thin smile. "Are you okay?"

"Yeah, thanks to you."

She was glad to see that he seemed steady on his feet. "Have the police been notified?"

"They should be here any minute."

Before she could say anything else, she saw the flashing red lights coming up the highway, then heard the wail of distant sirens.

TWO HOURS LATER, while firemen pumped water onto the coal fire, Marla tried patiently to relate what had happened to the state police detective. She told him about the lights and the screams, but was careful not to offer any explanations.

"The screams were probably Hartman's, and the lights must have come from the coal or the propane burner," the detective said with a shrug. "Of course, you were frightened at the time, and that affected your perceptions."

She remained silent. She wouldn't bother to tell him that he was wasting his time trying to find answers based solely on physical evidence. Some things went beyond science. She knew that now.

As they stood near the entrance, paramedics wearing breathing apparatus brought out Hartman's unburned body. "The explosion must have blown him clear of the flames," one of the medics said, moving away.

Marla glanced at Sam. "They wanted us to find him," she said quietly, knowing she wouldn't have to explain whom she'd meant by "they."

"It's a warning to others—an effective one, too," he conceded.

They watched the coroner as he studied the corpse, then finally helped the others place it inside a black plastic body bag.

"What's your call?" the detective asked.

The coroner stood up. "From the pressure necessary to bury that wide flint blade to the hilt, he must have fallen on the knife and forced it completely through his neck. Tentatively, I'd say he accidentally killed himself."

Marla stood beside Sam, but said nothing as the men gathered their equipment. A moment later, the investigator approached. "I thought you'd like to know, the Durango police found your notes and videotape buried in waterproof containers in Hartman's backyard. Your records are intact, and eventually will be returned to you."

She looked back at the cave, which had been consumed in smoke and debris. "Good, because that site's destroyed. Coal fires can smolder for years. Even if it becomes safe to go in, it's doubtful there'll be anything left to salvage."

As the emergency workers left the site, Sam led Marla away from the place that had seen so much death. Guided by the glow of the moon, he walked with her down along the reservation fence line to a spot overlooking the river. Water was life in the desert, and it was here he wanted to speak to her.

"Dreams always carry a price, *sawe*. And if it's the wrong dream, a piece of us dies with it. But the right one demands all the love you can give it for as long as you live. When you first came, you were searching for things that you weren't even sure existed. Much has happened since that time." He stepped closer to her and cupped her face until she looked directly at him. "Have you found what you need?"

As the desert sang its night song, she settled into his arms. "More. I found my heart," she whispered, "and a new home."

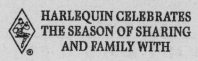

**HARLEQUIN CELEBRATES
THE SEASON OF SHARING
AND FAMILY WITH**

*Friends, Families,
Lovers*

Harlequin introduces the latest member in its family of
seasonal collections. Following in the footsteps of the popular
My Valentine, Just Married and *Harlequin Historical Christmas
Stories,* we are proud to present FRIENDS, FAMILIES,
LOVERS. A collection of three new contemporary romance
stories about America at its best, about welcoming others into
the circle of love.... Stories to warm your heart...

By three leading romance authors:

> **KATHLEEN EAGLE
> SANDRA KITT
> RUTH JEAN DALE**

Available in October, wherever
Harlequin books are sold.

THANKS

CHRISTMAS STALKINGS

All wrapped up in
spine-tingling packages,
here are two books
sure to keep you on
edge this holiday season!

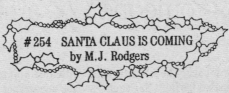

#254 SANTA CLAUS IS COMING
by M.J. Rodgers

On the first day of Christmas, newscaster Belle Breeze was
sung a bad rendition of "The Twelve Days of Christmas."
Then, one by one, the gifts started to arrive, and Belle knew
the twelfth gift would play havoc with her very life....

#255 SCARLET SEASON
by Laura Gordon

The night was *too* silent when, on a snowy Denver street,
Cassie Craig found herself the lone witness to a crime that no
one believed happened. Her search for the truth would make
this Christmas season chilling....

**DON'T MISS THESE SPECIAL HOLIDAY INTRIGUES
IN DECEMBER 1993!**

1993 Keepsake

CHRISTMAS

Stories

Capture the spirit and romance of Christmas with KEEPSAKE CHRISTMAS STORIES, a collection of three stories by favorite historical authors. The perfect Christmas gift!

Don't miss these heartwarming stories, available in November wherever Harlequin books are sold:

ONCE UPON A CHRISTMAS by Curtiss Ann Matlock
A FAIRYTALE SEASON by Marianne Willman
TIDINGS OF JOY by Victoria Pade

ADD A TOUCH OF ROMANCE TO YOUR HOLIDAY SEASON WITH KEEPSAKE CHRISTMAS STORIES!

HX93

Are you looking for more titles by

AIMÉE THURLO

Don't miss these fabulous stories by one of
Harlequin's great authors:

Harlequin Intrigue®

#22141	SUITABLE FOR FRAMING	$2.50	☐
#22162	STRANGERS WHO LINGER	$2.75	☐
#22175	NIGHT WIND	$2.79	☐
#22217	SHADOW OF THE WOLF	$2.89	☐

(limited quantities available on certain titles)

TOTAL AMOUNT	$
POSTAGE & HANDLING	$
($1.00 for one book, 50¢ for each additional)	
APPLICABLE TAXES*	$_____
TOTAL PAYABLE	$_____
(check or money order—please do not send cash)	

To order, complete this form and send it, along with a check or money order for the total above, payable to Harlequin Books, to: *In the U.S.:* 3010 Walden Avenue, P.O. Box 9047, Buffalo, NY 14269-9047; *In Canada:* P.O. Box 613, Fort Erie, Ontario, L2A 5X3.

Name: _____

Address: _____ City: _____

State/Prov.: _____ Zip/Postal Code: _____

*New York residents remit applicable sales taxes.
Canadian residents remit applicable GST and provincial taxes.

HATBACK1

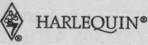
HARLEQUIN®